MINECRAFT™

WITHER WITHOUT YOU

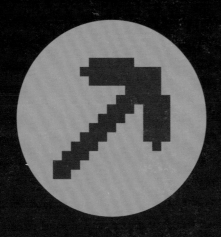

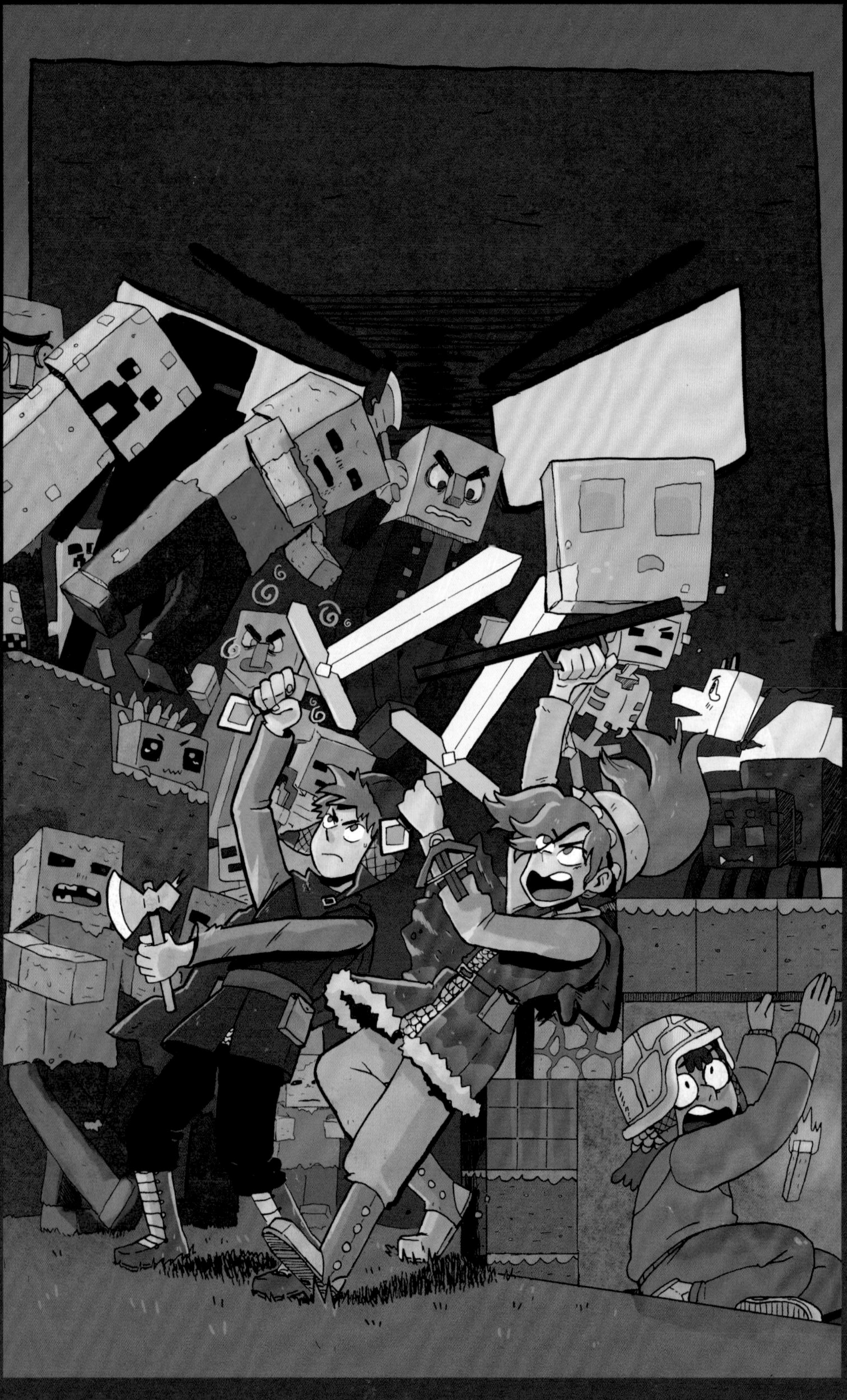

◻ MOJANG

MINECRAFT ™

WITHER WITHOUT YOU

BY

KRISTEN GUDSNUK

DARK HORSE BOOKS

EDITOR
SHANTEL LAROCQUE

ASSISTANT EDITOR
BRETT ISRAEL

DESIGNER
KEITH WOOD

DIGITAL ART TECHNICIAN
JOSIE CHRISTENSEN

SPECIAL THANKS TO
JENNIFER HAMMERVALD, AND
ALEX WILTSHIRE.

Published by Dark Horse Books
A division of Dark Horse Comics LLC
10956 SE Main Street
Milwaukie, OR 97222

MINECRAFT.NET
DARKHORSE.COM

To find a comics shop in your area, visit ComicShopLocator.com.

First edition: May 2020
ISBN 978-1-50670-835-5

10 9 8 7 6 5 4 3 2 1

Printed in Italy

Library of Congress Cataloging-in-Publication Data

Names: Gudsnuk, Kristen, artist, author.
Title: Minecraft : wither without you / by Kristen Gudsnuk.
Other titles: Wither without you
Description: First edition. | Milwaukie, OR : Dark Horse Books, 2020. |
Series: Minecraft ; v. 1 | Audience: Ages 8+ | Summary: Cahira and Orion
are twin monster hunters who go on a mission to get their mentor back,
and meet Atria, a girl cursed as a monster lure, whom they convince to
join their rescue mission to use her monster-attracting abilities to
find the enchanted wither.
Identifiers: LCCN 2019053733 | ISBN 9781506708355 (trade paperback) |
ISBN
9781506708645 (epub)
Subjects: LCSH: Graphic novels.
Classification: LCC PZ7.7.G83 Min 2020 | DDC 741.5/973--dc23
LC record available at https://lccn.loc.gov/2019053733

MINECRAFT™

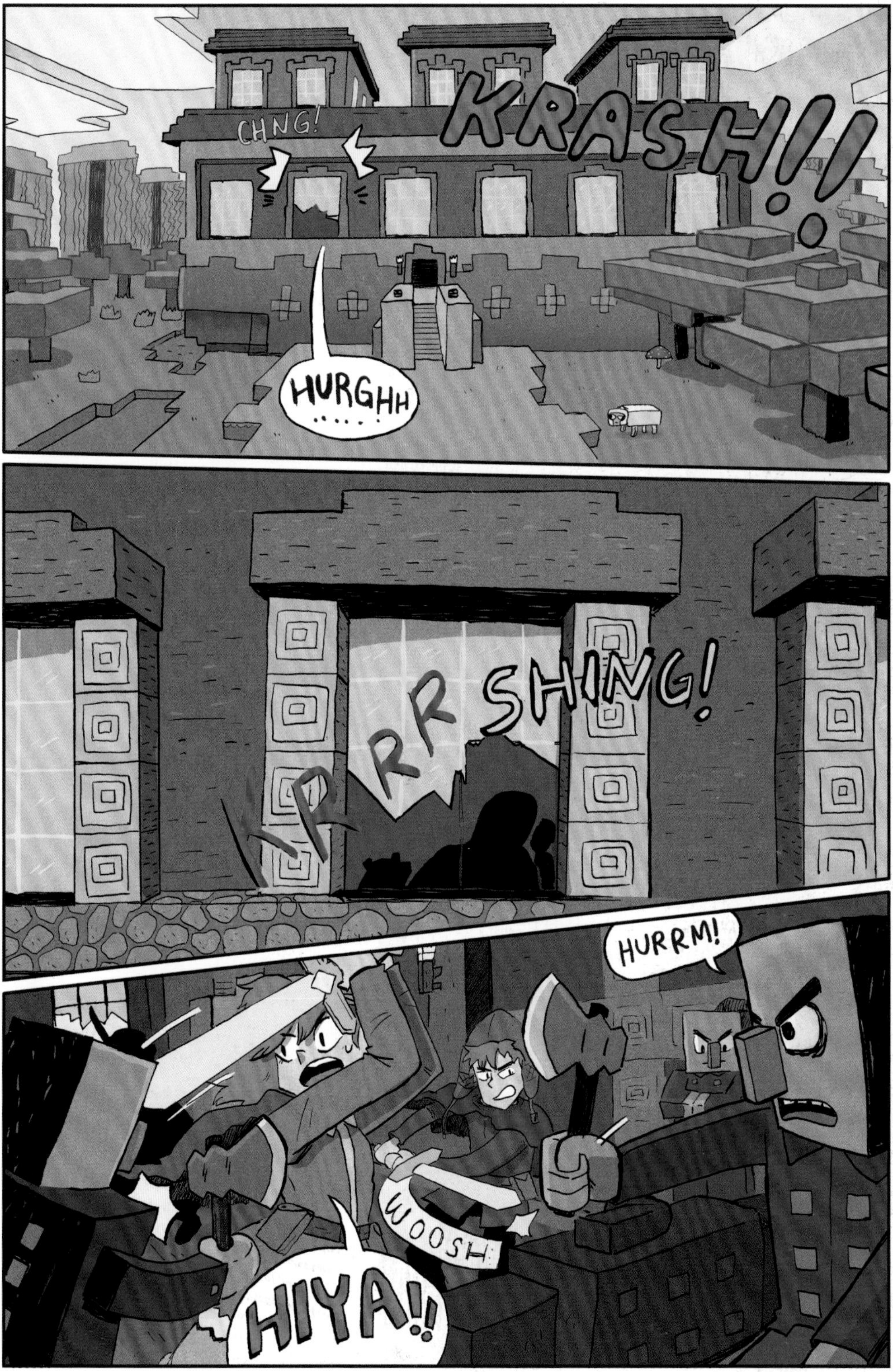
CHNG!
KRASH!!
HURGHH.....
KRRR SHING!
HURRM!
WOOSH
HIYA!!

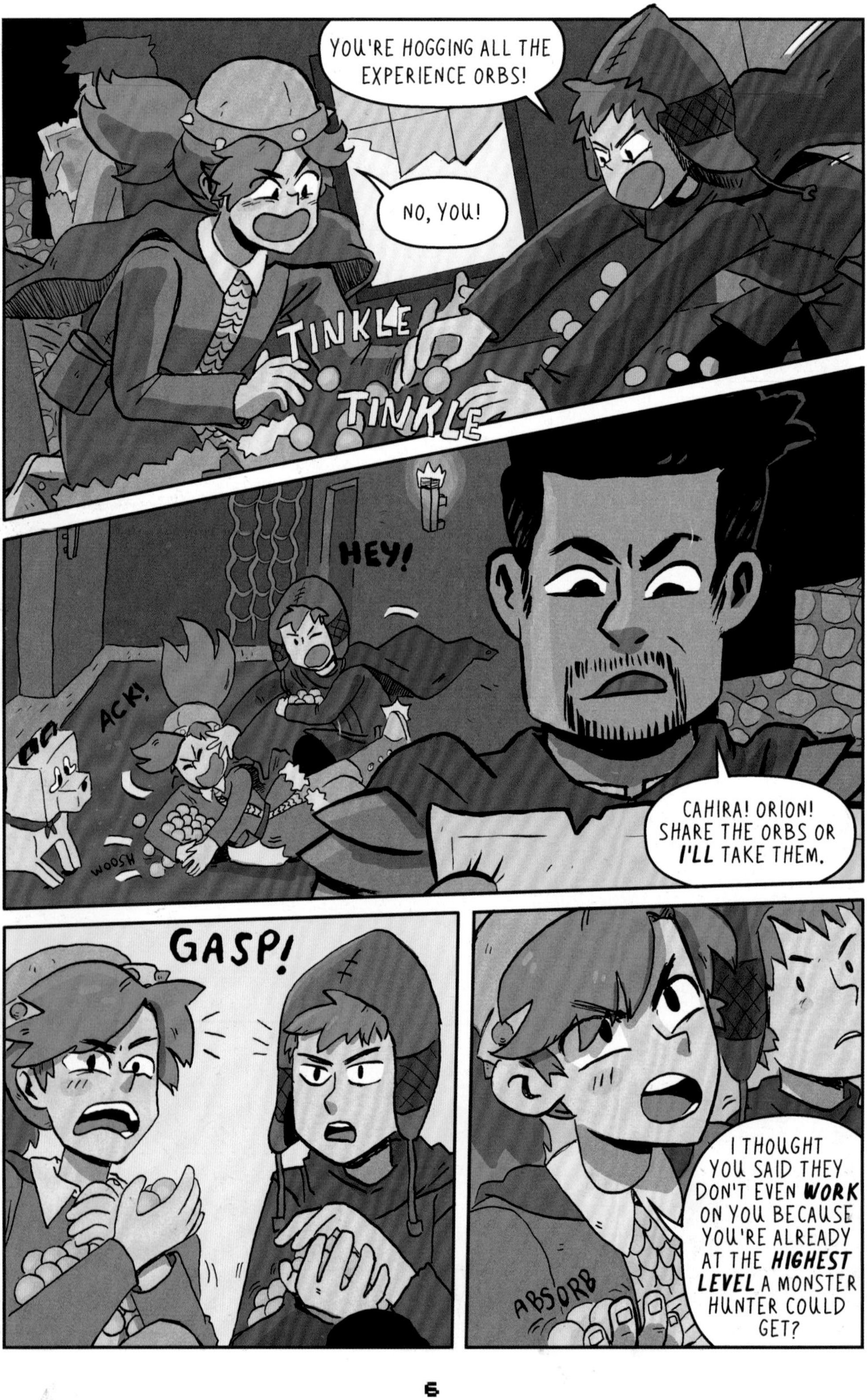
YOU'RE HOGGING ALL THE EXPERIENCE ORBS!
NO, YOU!
TINKLE
TINKLE
HEY!
ACK!
WOOSH
CAHIRA! ORION! SHARE THE ORBS OR I'LL TAKE THEM.
GASP!
ABSORB
I THOUGHT YOU SAID THEY DON'T EVEN WORK ON YOU BECAUSE YOU'RE ALREADY AT THE HIGHEST LEVEL A MONSTER HUNTER COULD GET?

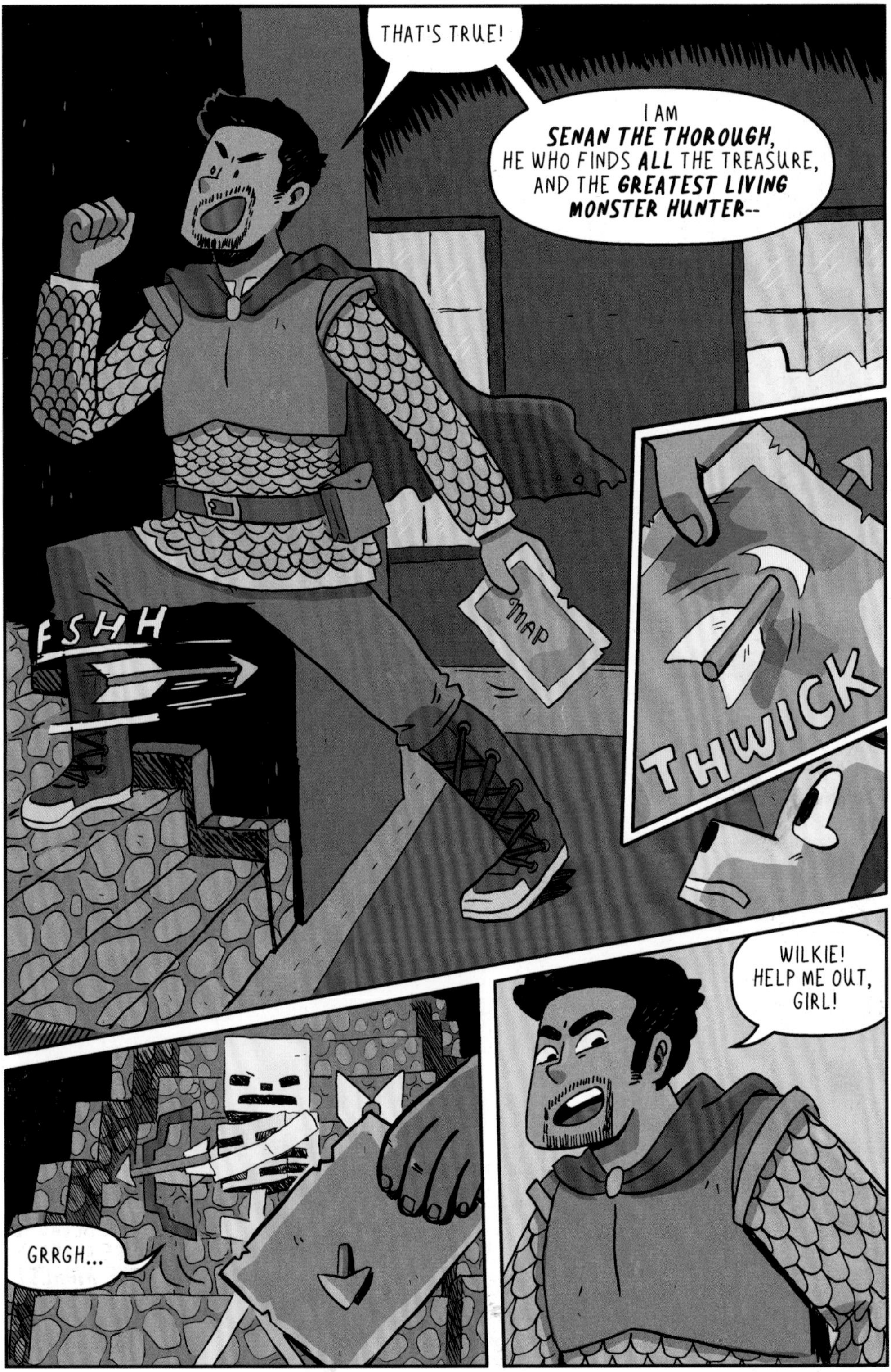
THAT'S TRUE!
I AM SENAN THE THOROUGH, HE WHO FINDS ALL THE TREASURE, AND THE GREATEST LIVING MONSTER HUNTER--
MAP
FSHH
THWICK
WILKIE! HELP ME OUT, GIRL!
GRRGH...

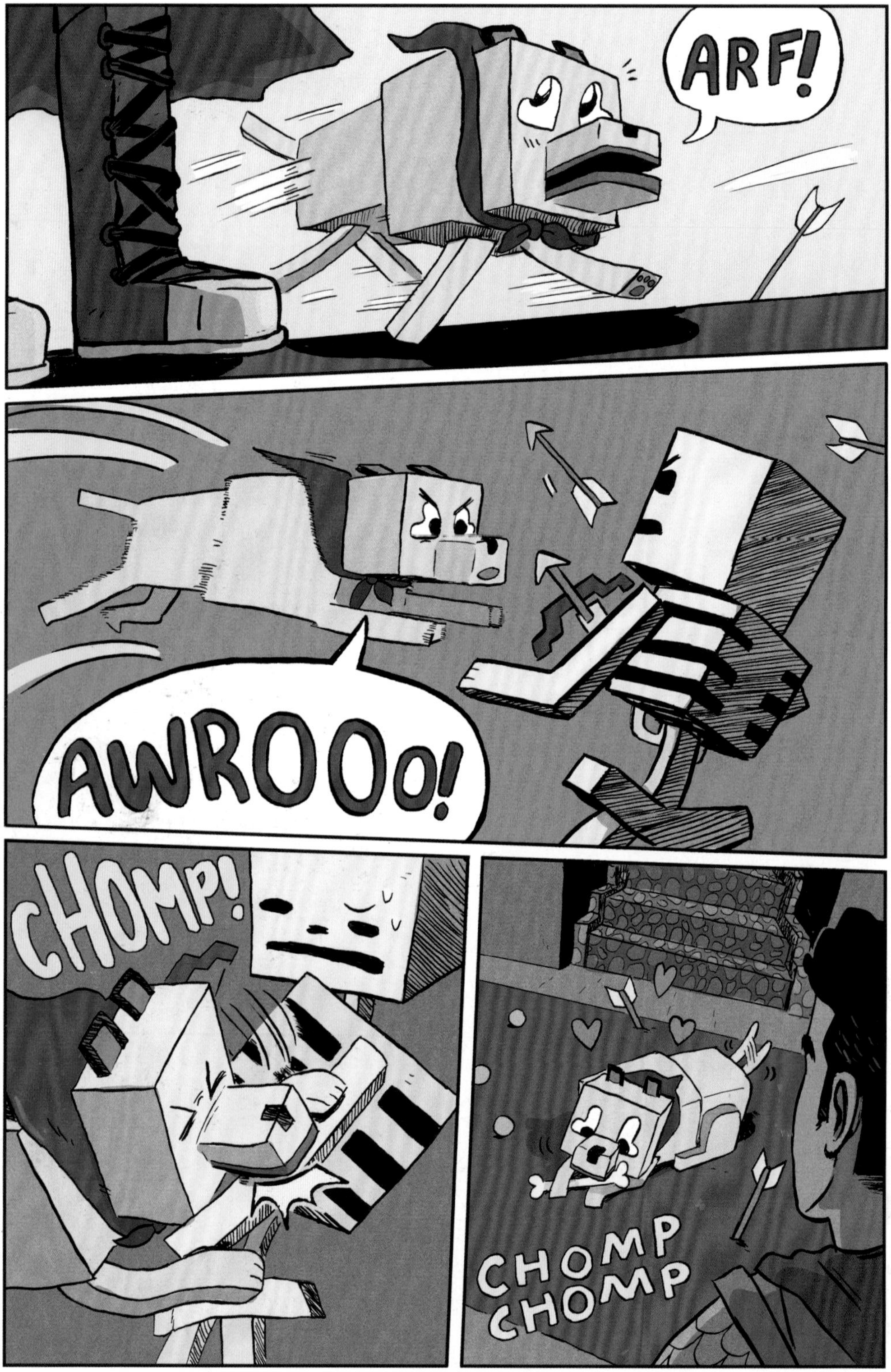
ARF!
AWROOo!
CHOMP!
CHOMP
CHOMP

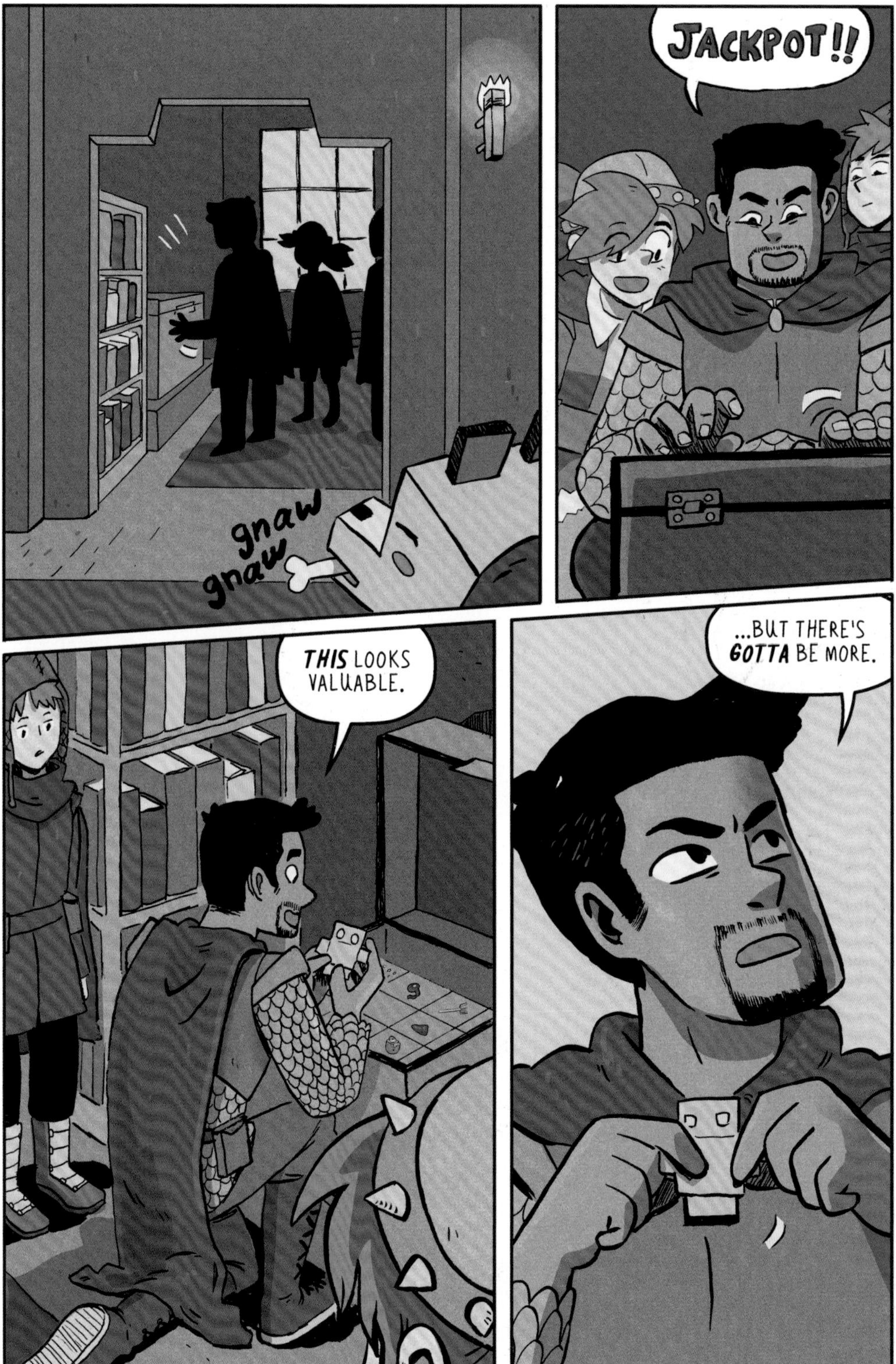
gnaw gnaw
JACKPOT!!
THIS LOOKS VALUABLE.
...BUT THERE'S GOTTA BE MORE.

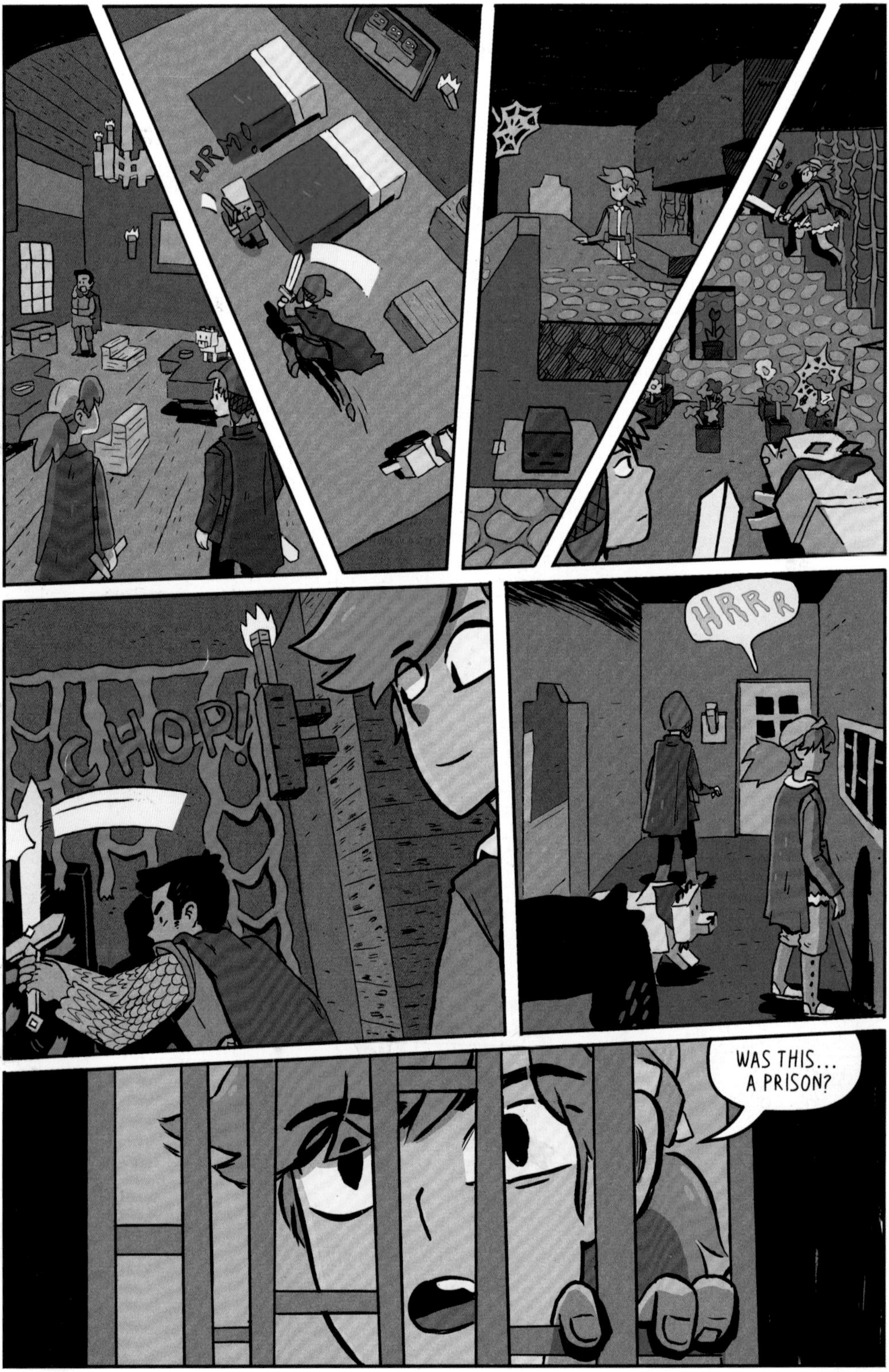
HRM!
CHOP!
HRRR
WAS THIS... A PRISON?

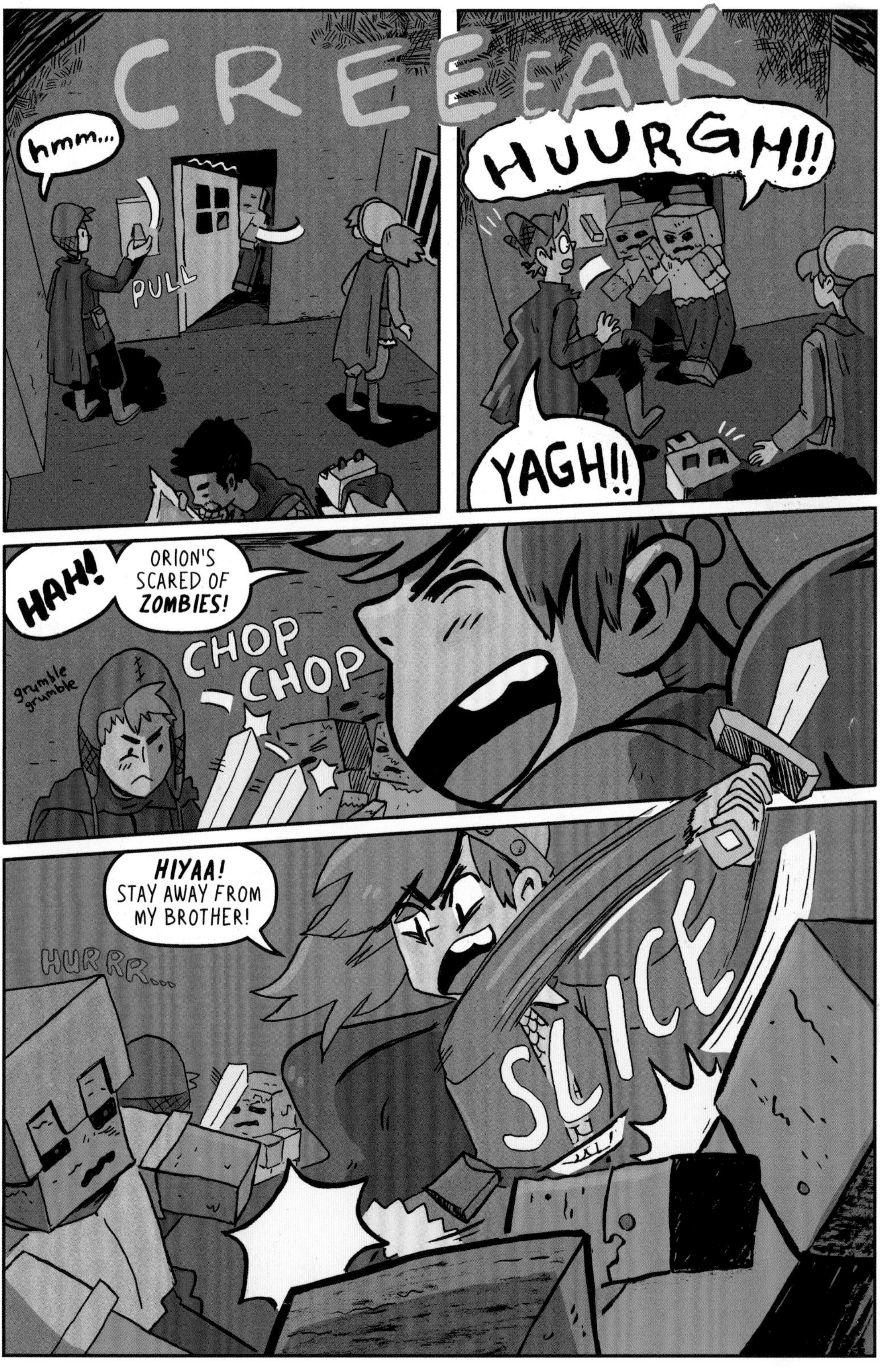
CREEEAK
hmm...
PULL
HUURGH!!
YAGH!!
HAH!
ORION'S SCARED OF ZOMBIES!
CHOP CHOP
grumble grumble
HIYAA! STAY AWAY FROM MY BROTHER!
HURRR...
SLICE

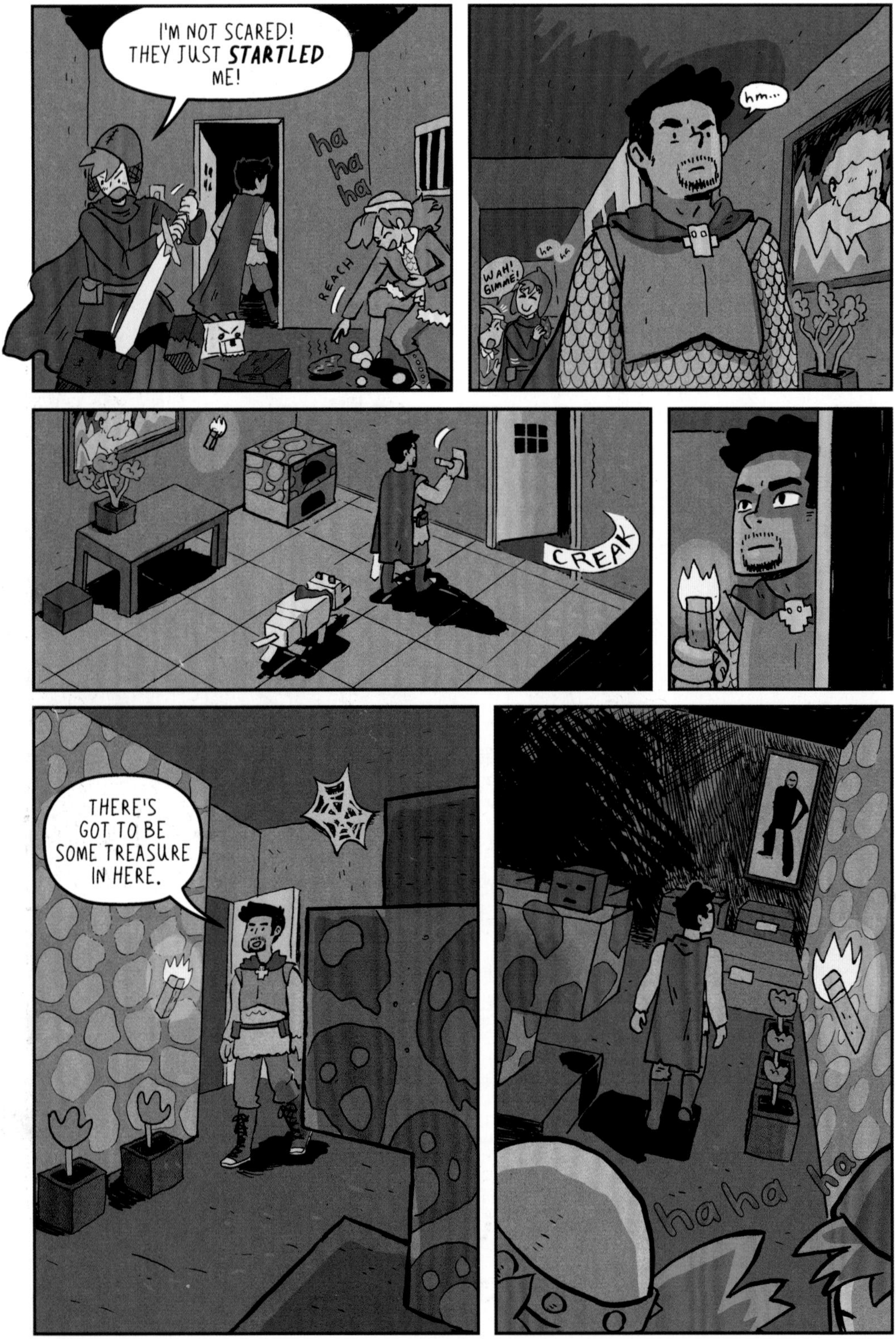
I'M NOT SCARED! THEY JUST STARTLED ME!
ha ha ha
REACH
hm...
WAH! GIMME!
ha ha
CREAK
THERE'S GOT TO BE SOME TREASURE IN HERE.
ha ha ha

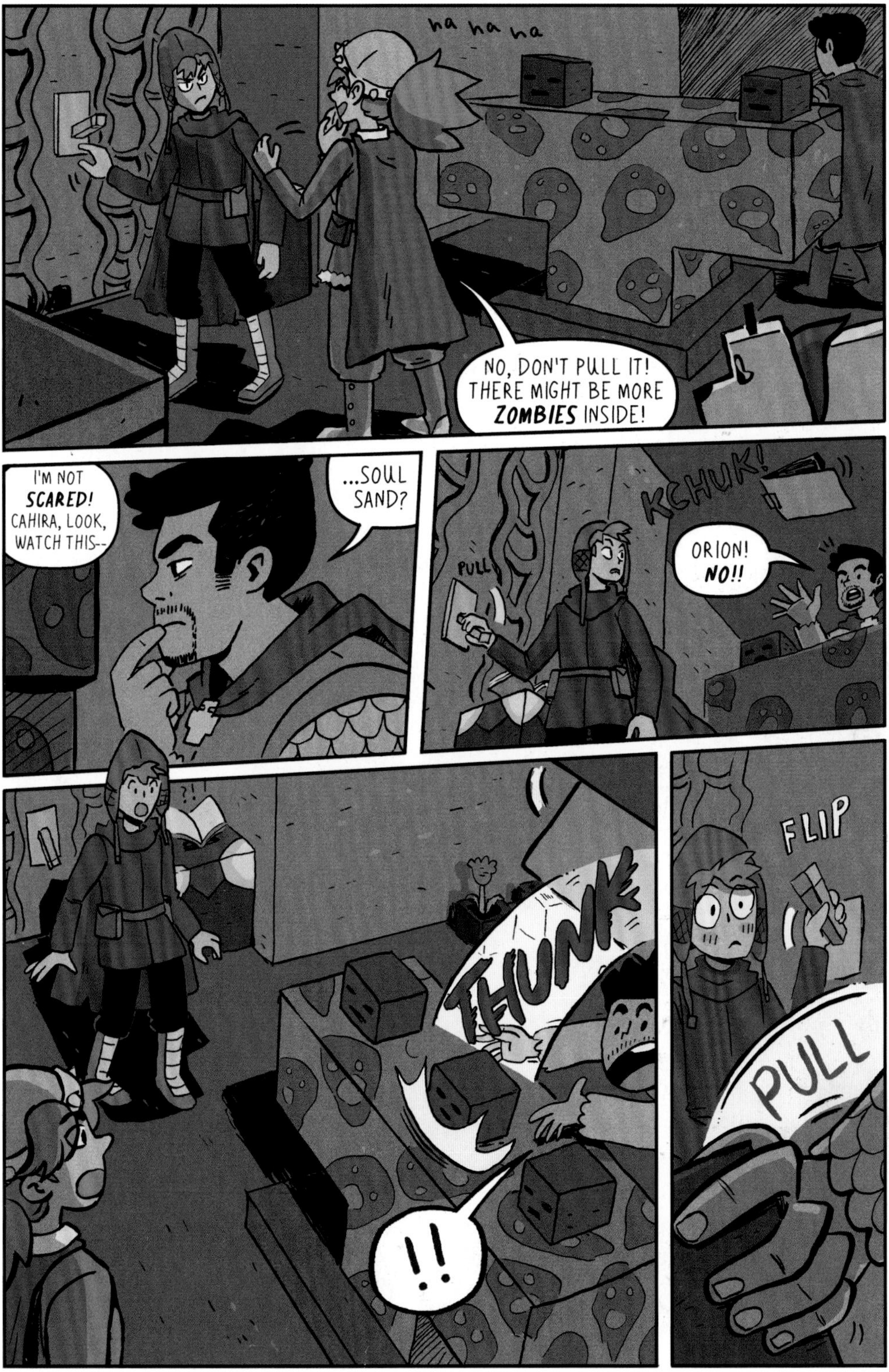
ha ha ha
NO, DON'T PULL IT! THERE MIGHT BE MORE ZOMBIES INSIDE!
I'M NOT SCARED! CAHIRA, LOOK, WATCH THIS--
...SOUL SAND?
KCHUK!
PULL
ORION! NO!!
THUNK
!!
FLIP
PULL

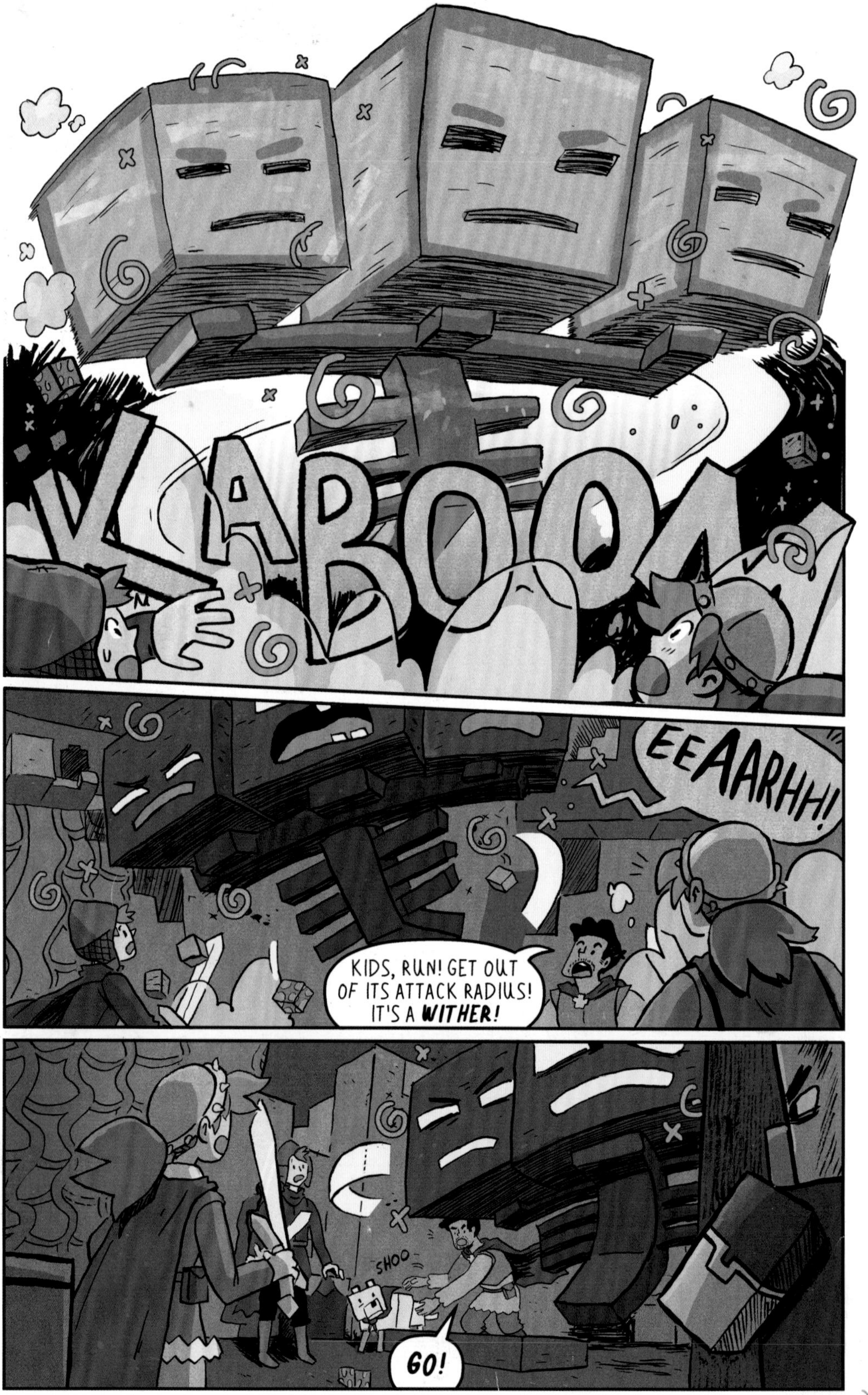
KABOOM
EEAARHH!
KIDS, RUN! GET OUT OF ITS ATTACK RADIUS! IT'S A **WITHER!**
SHOO
GO!

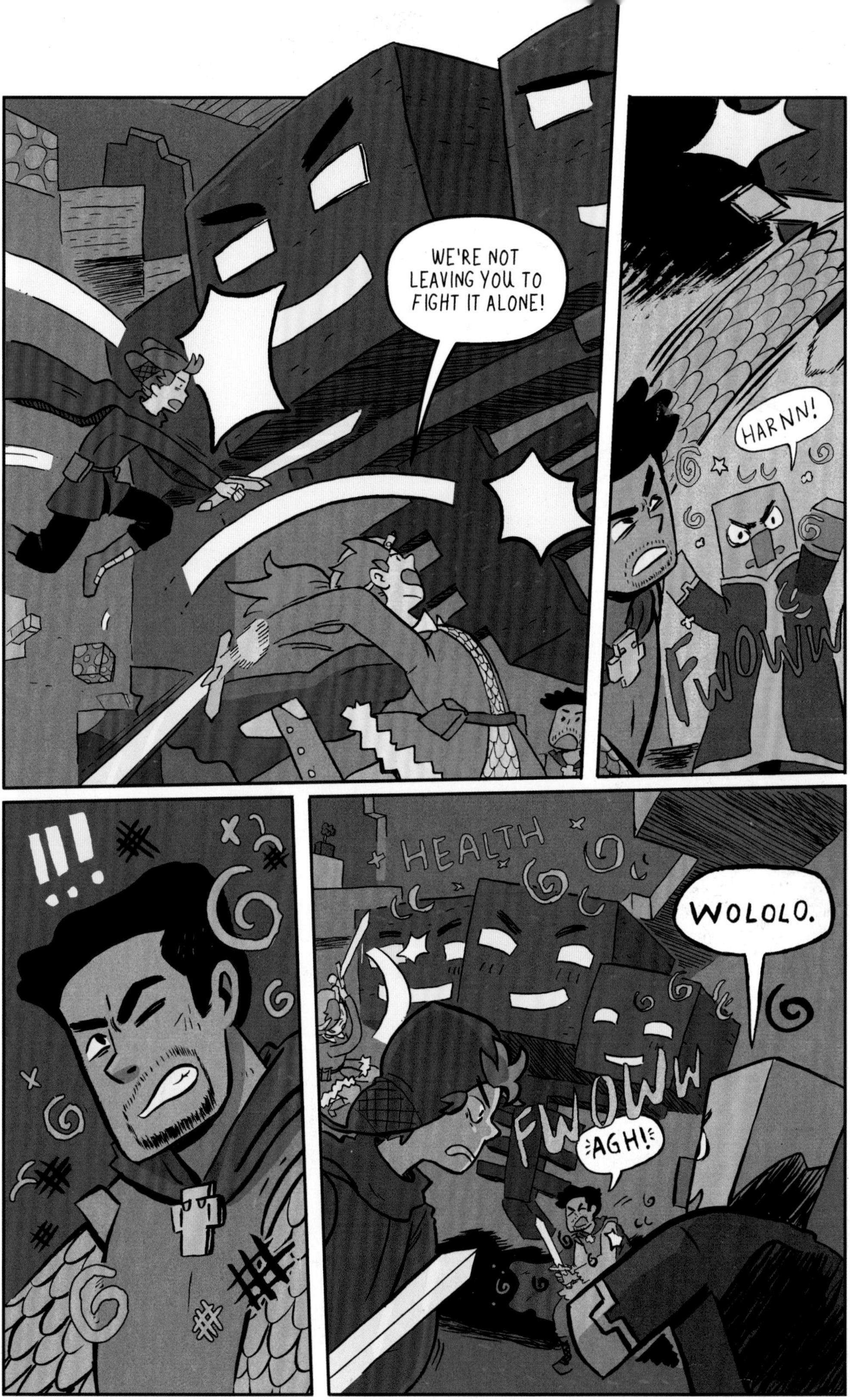
WE'RE NOT LEAVING YOU TO FIGHT IT ALONE!
HARNN!
FWOWW
!!!
HEALTH
WOLOLO.
FWOWW
AGH!

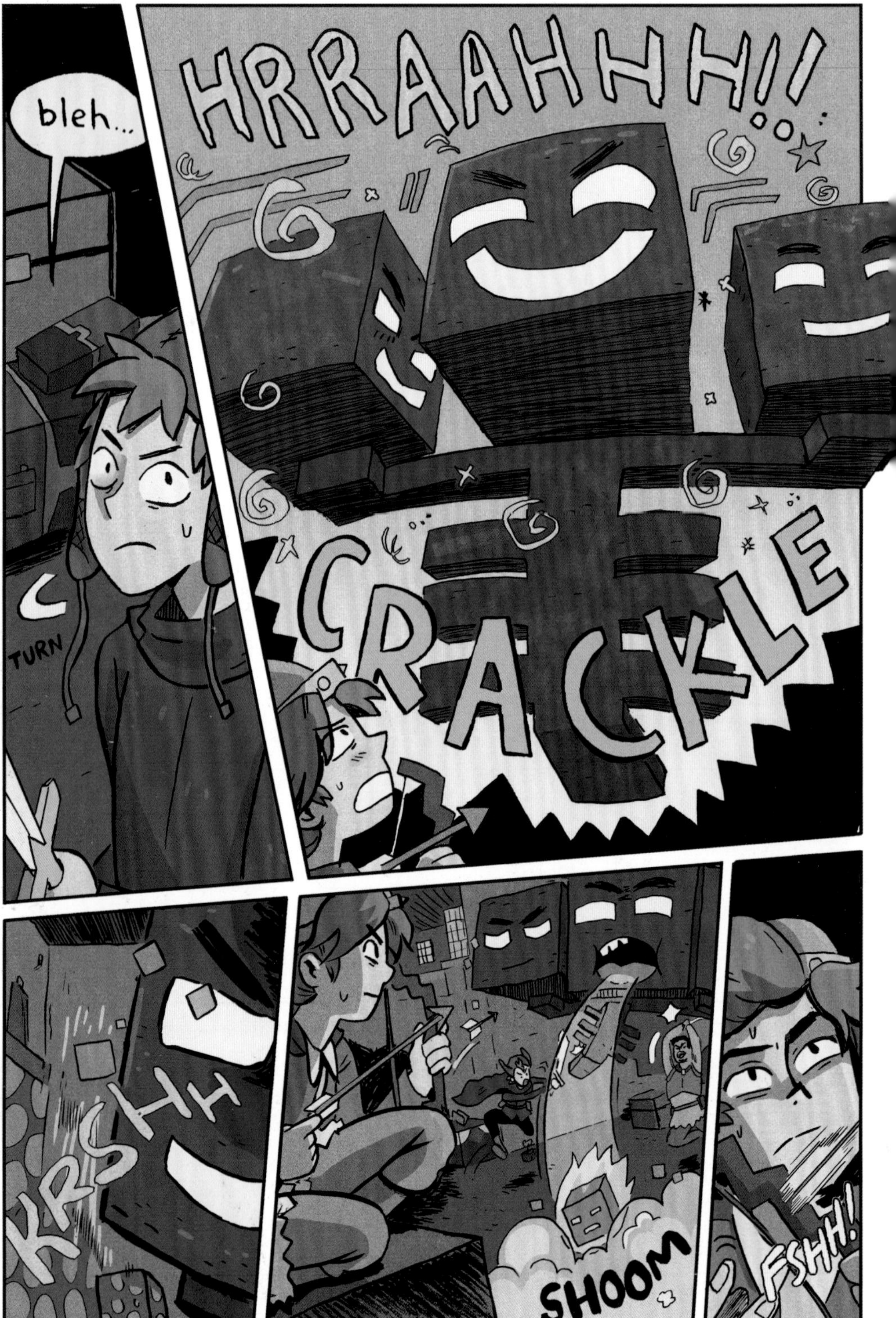
bleh...
TURN
HRRAAHHH!!
CRACKLE
KRSHH
SHOOM
FSHH!

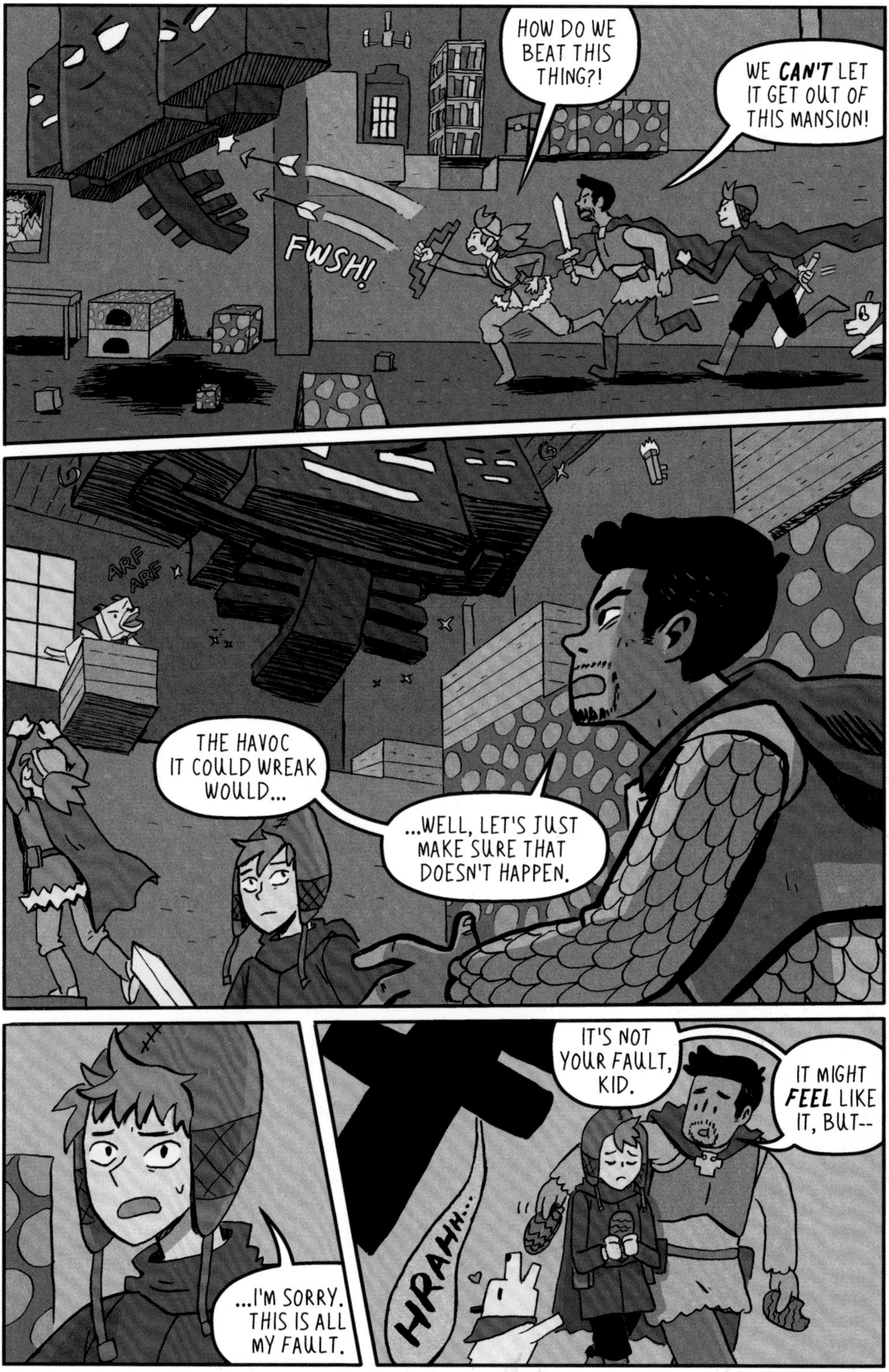
HOW DO WE BEAT THIS THING?!
WE **CAN'T** LET IT GET OUT OF THIS MANSION!
FWSH!
ARF ARF
THE HAVOC IT COULD WREAK WOULD...
...WELL, LET'S JUST MAKE SURE THAT DOESN'T HAPPEN.
...I'M SORRY. THIS IS ALL MY FAULT.
HRAHH...
IT'S NOT YOUR FAULT, KID.
IT MIGHT **FEEL** LIKE IT, BUT--

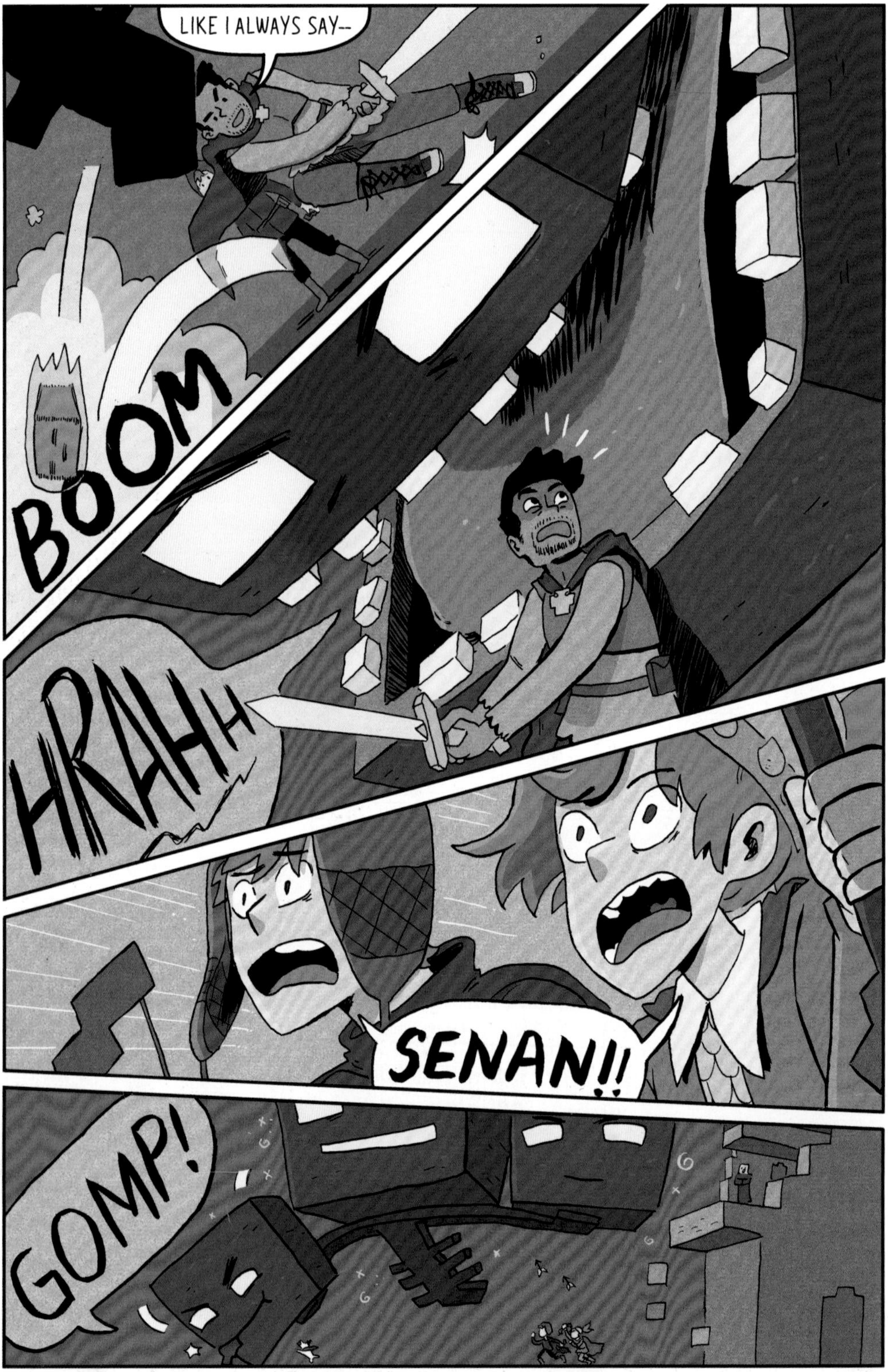
LIKE I ALWAYS SAY--
BOOM
HRAHH
SENAN!!
GOMP!

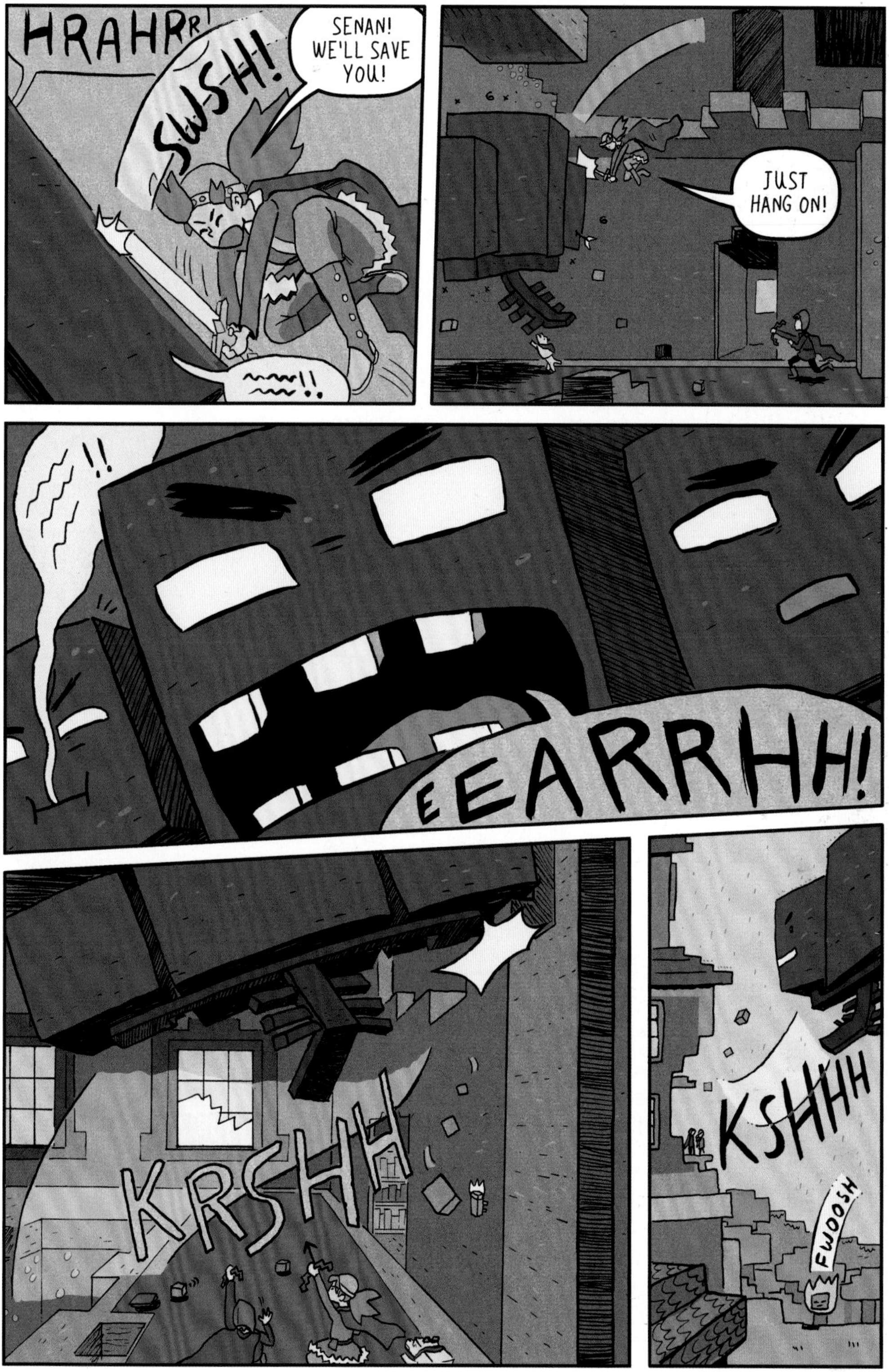
HRAHRR!
SWSH!
SENAN! WE'LL SAVE YOU!
~~~!!
JUST HANG ON!
!!
EEARRHH!
KRSHH
KSHHH
FWOOSH
~~~

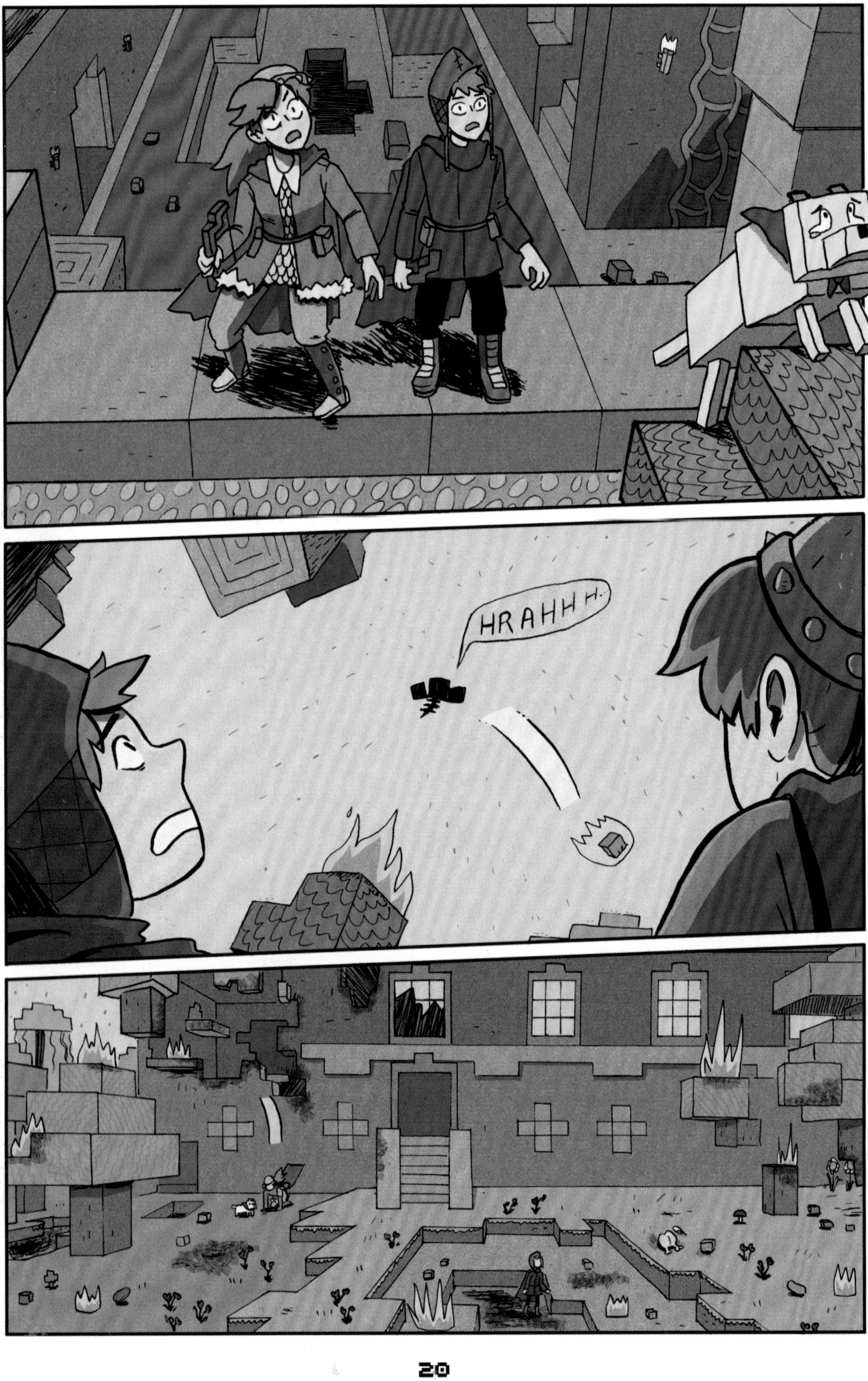
HRAHHH..

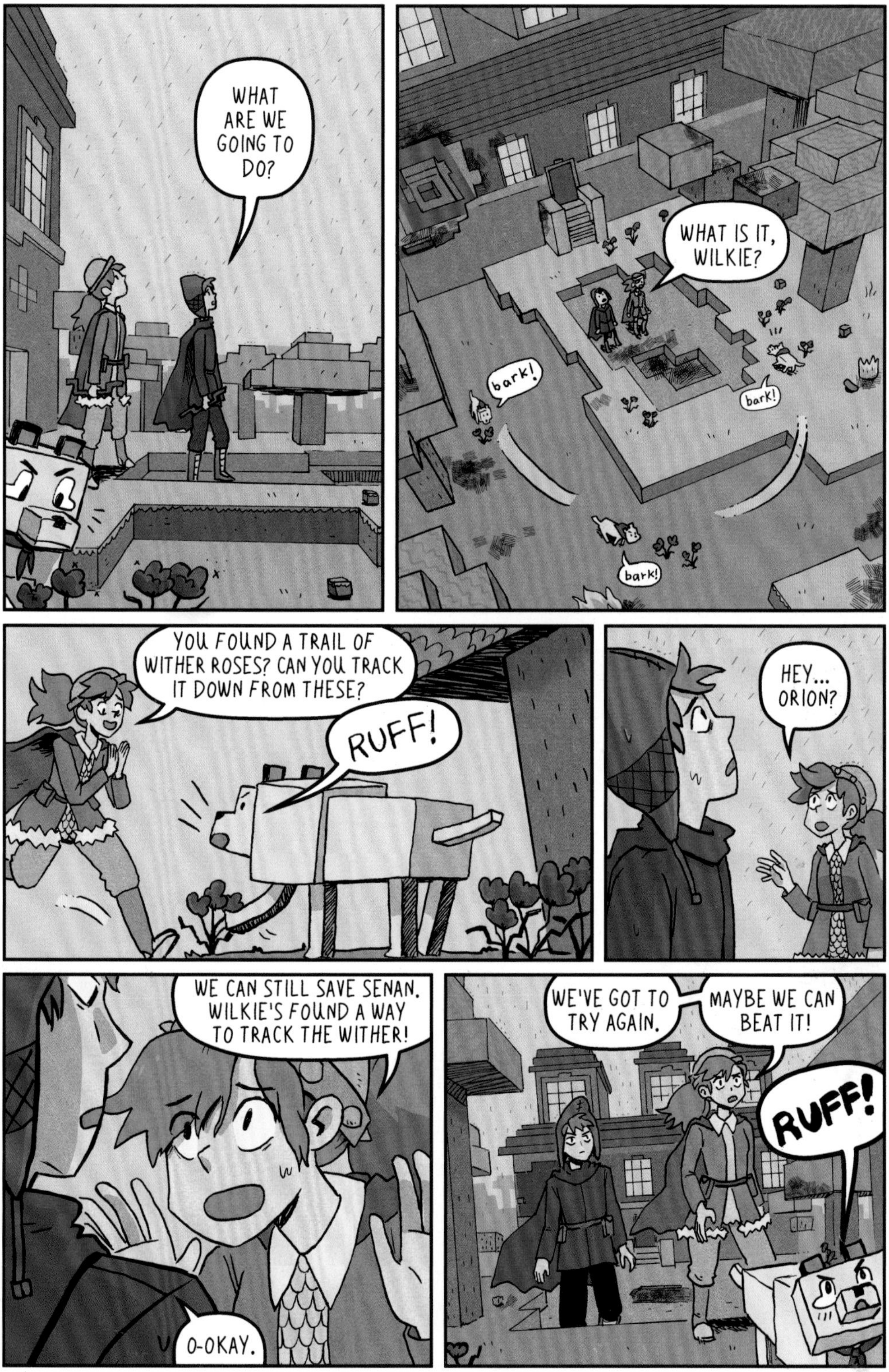
WHAT ARE WE GOING TO DO?
WHAT IS IT, WILKIE?
bark!
bark!
bark!
YOU FOUND A TRAIL OF WITHER ROSES? CAN YOU TRACK IT DOWN FROM THESE?
RUFF!
HEY... ORION?
WE CAN STILL SAVE SENAN. WILKIE'S FOUND A WAY TO TRACK THE WITHER!
O-OKAY.
WE'VE GOT TO TRY AGAIN.
MAYBE WE CAN BEAT IT!
RUFF!

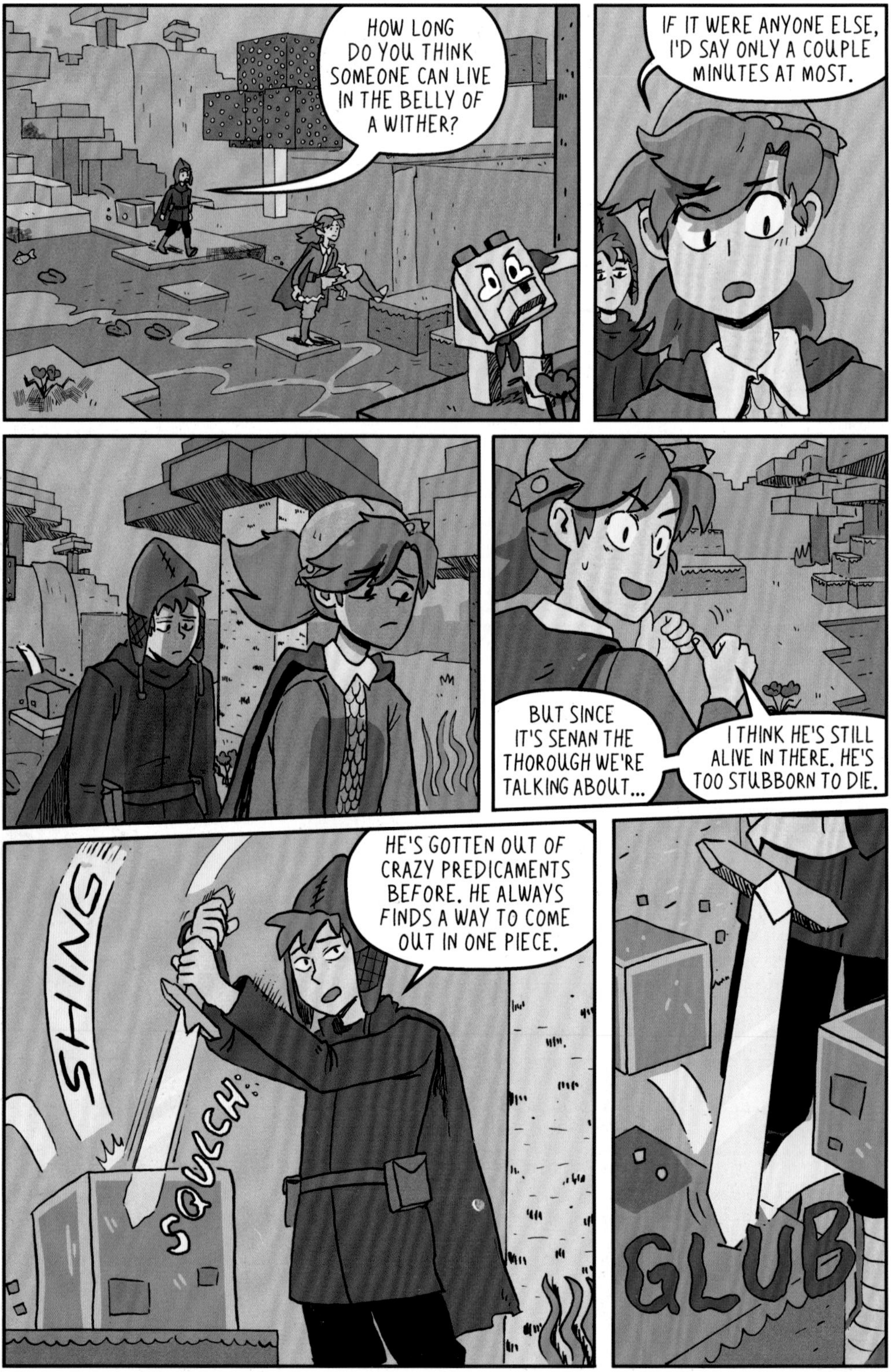

HOW LONG DO YOU THINK SOMEONE CAN LIVE IN THE BELLY OF A WITHER?
IF IT WERE ANYONE ELSE, I'D SAY ONLY A COUPLE MINUTES AT MOST.
BUT SINCE IT'S SENAN THE THOROUGH WE'RE TALKING ABOUT...
I THINK HE'S STILL ALIVE IN THERE. HE'S TOO STUBBORN TO DIE.
HE'S GOTTEN OUT OF CRAZY PREDICAMENTS BEFORE. HE ALWAYS FINDS A WAY TO COME OUT IN ONE PIECE.
SHING
SQUCH
GLUB

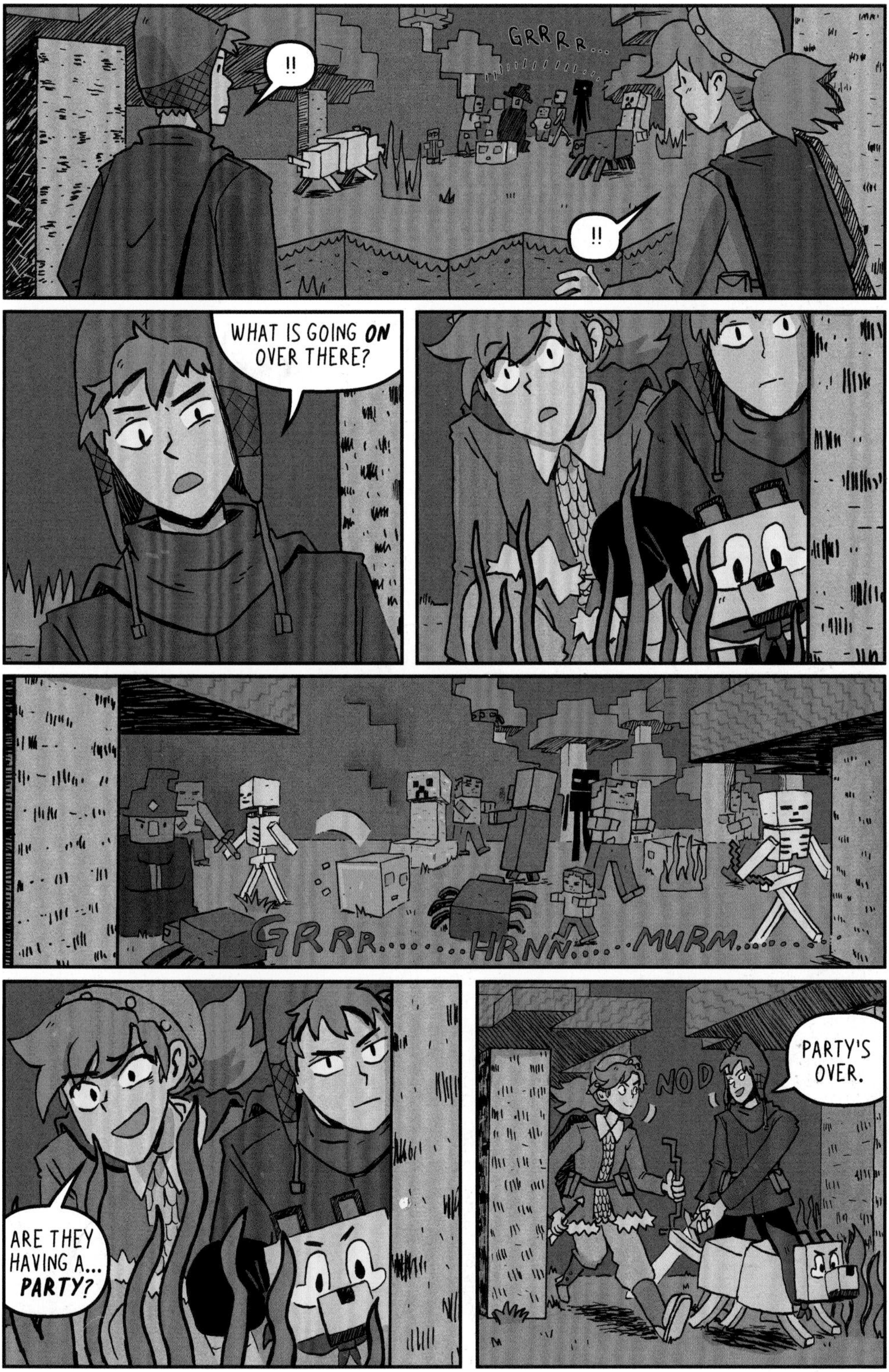
!!
GRRRR...
!!
WHAT IS GOING *ON* OVER THERE?
GRRRR.......HRNN......MURM.......
ARE THEY HAVING A... *PARTY*?
NOD
PARTY'S OVER.

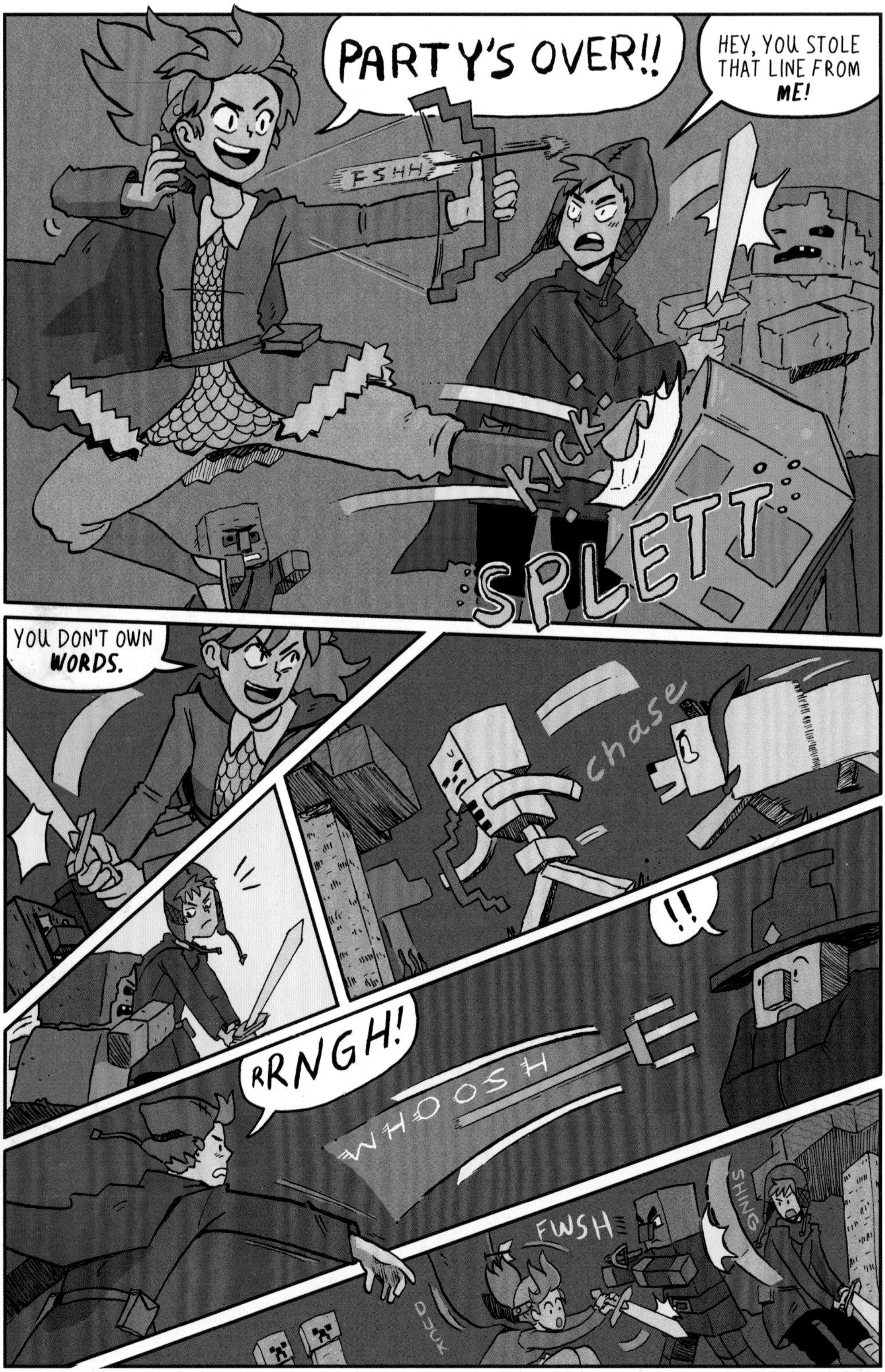
PARTY'S OVER!!
FSHH
HEY, YOU STOLE THAT LINE FROM **ME!**
KICK
SPLETT
YOU DON'T OWN **WORDS.**
chase
!!
RRNGH!
WHOOSH
FWSH
SHING
DUCK

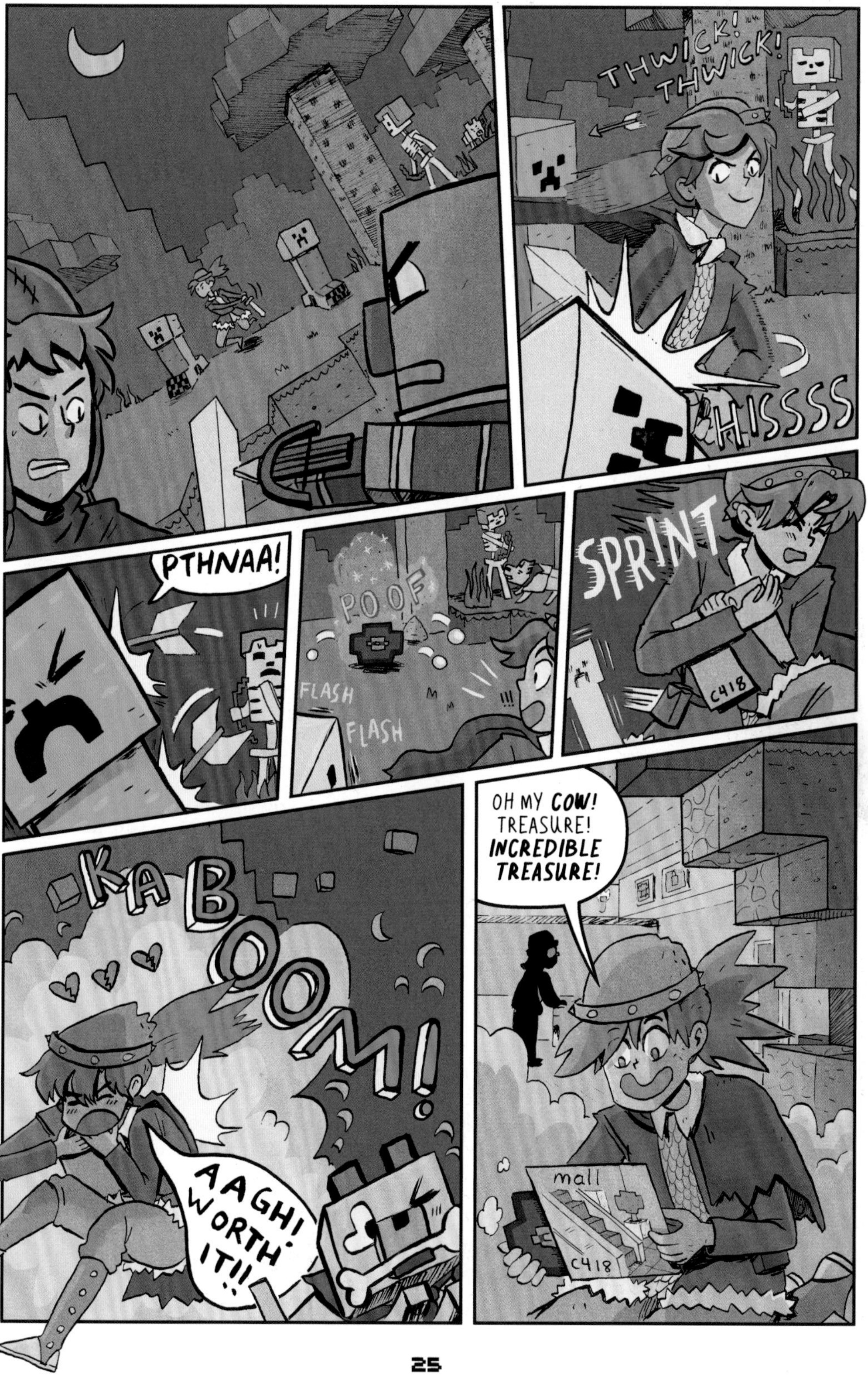
THWICK! THWICK!
HISSSS
PTHNAA!
POOF
FLASH
FLASH
SPRINT
C418
KABOOM!
AAGH! WORTH IT!!
OH MY **COW**! TREASURE! **INCREDIBLE TREASURE!**
mall
C418

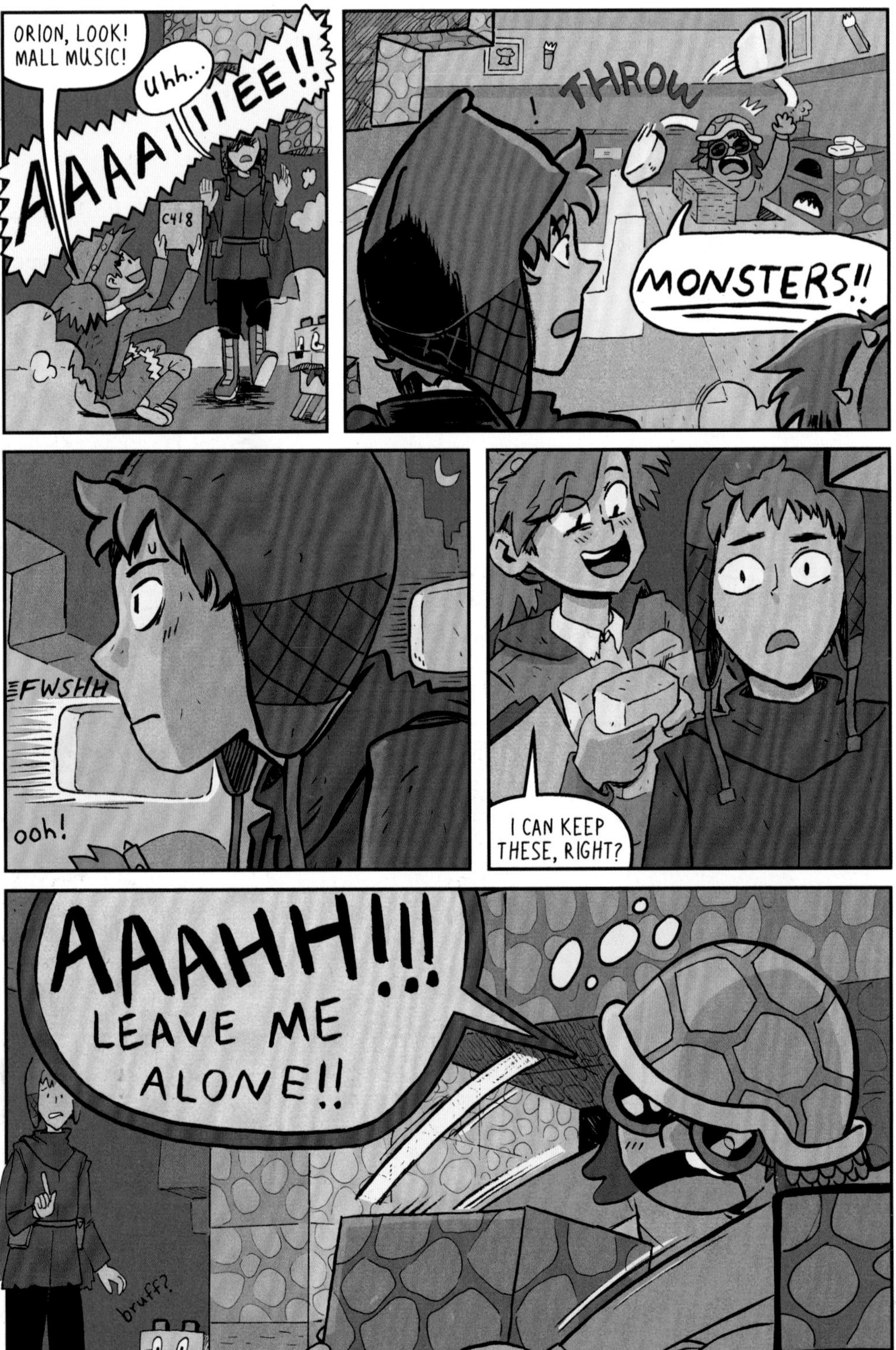
ORION, LOOK! MALL MUSIC!
Uhh...
AAAAIIIIEE!!
C418
THROW
!
MONSTERS!!
FWSHH
ooh!
I CAN KEEP THESE, RIGHT?
AAAHH!!! LEAVE ME ALONE!!
bruff?

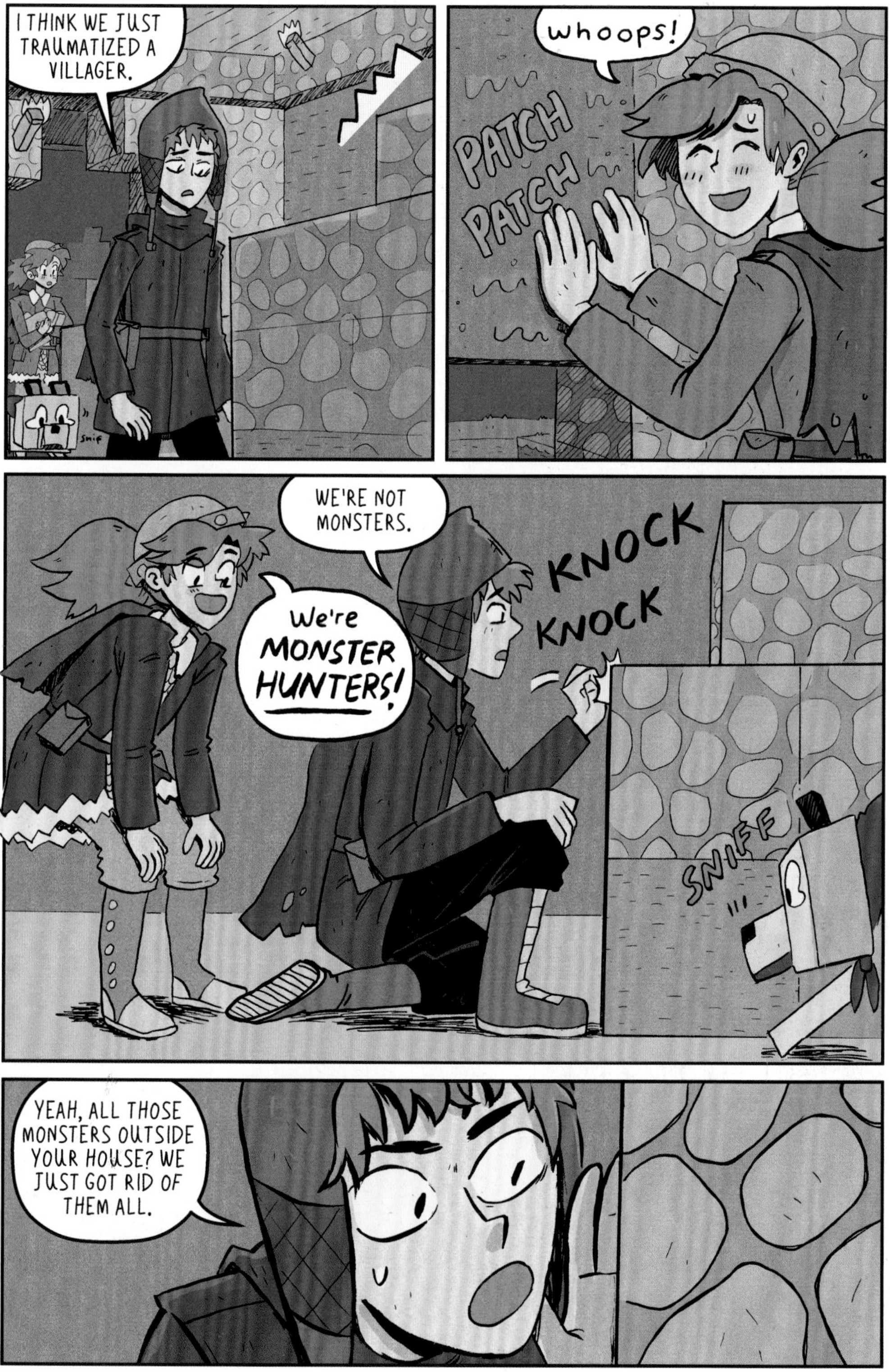
I THINK WE JUST TRAUMATIZED A VILLAGER.
SNIF
WHOOPS!
PATCH
PATCH
WE'RE NOT MONSTERS.
We're MONSTER HUNTERS!
KNOCK
KNOCK
SNIFF
YEAH, ALL THOSE MONSTERS OUTSIDE YOUR HOUSE? WE JUST GOT RID OF THEM ALL.

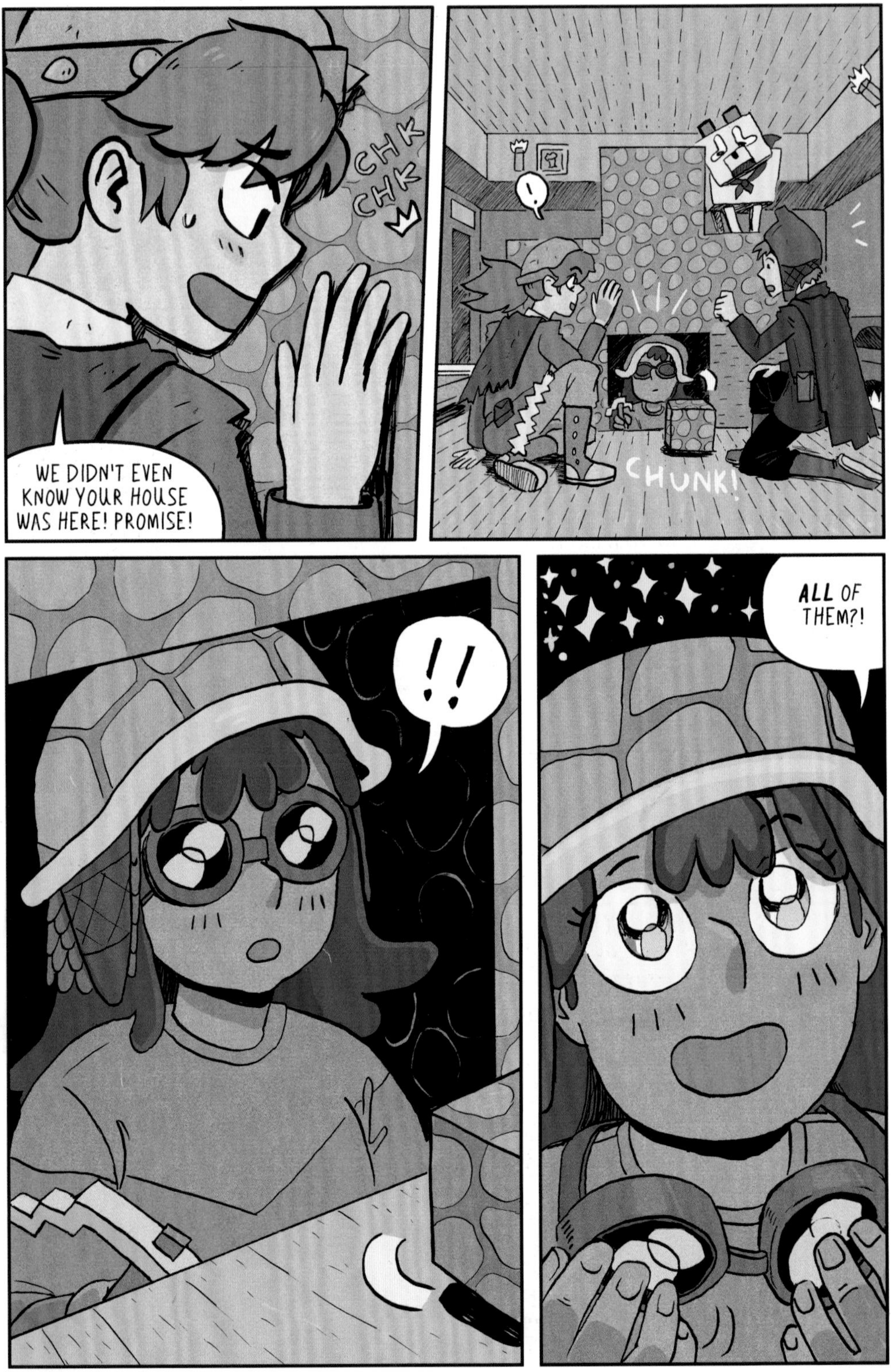
CHK
CHK
WE DIDN'T EVEN KNOW YOUR HOUSE WAS HERE! PROMISE!
!
CHUNK!
!!
ALL OF THEM?!

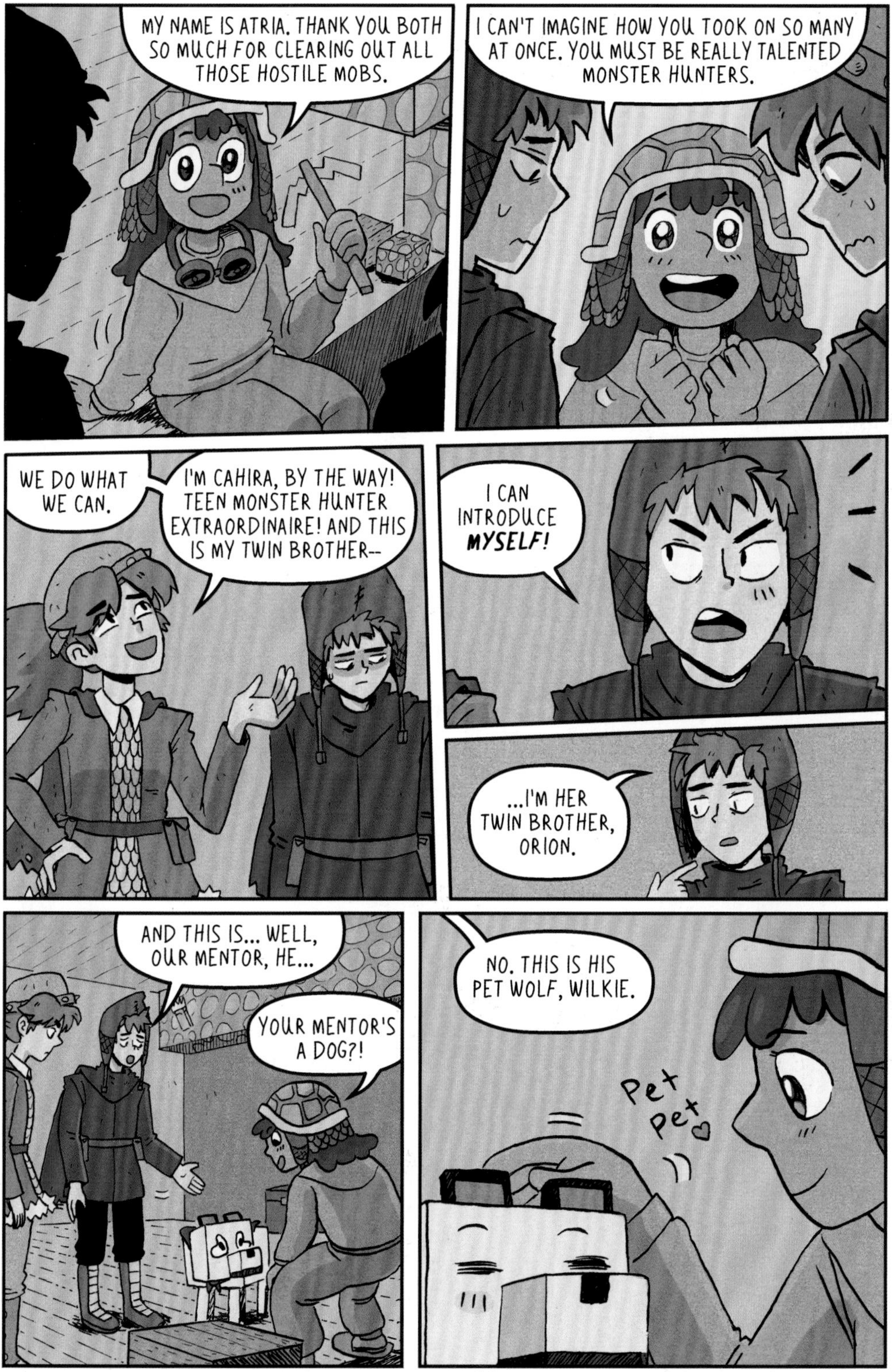
MY NAME IS ATRIA. THANK YOU BOTH SO MUCH FOR CLEARING OUT ALL THOSE HOSTILE MOBS.
I CAN'T IMAGINE HOW YOU TOOK ON SO MANY AT ONCE. YOU MUST BE REALLY TALENTED MONSTER HUNTERS.
WE DO WHAT WE CAN.
I'M CAHIRA, BY THE WAY! TEEN MONSTER HUNTER EXTRAORDINAIRE! AND THIS IS MY TWIN BROTHER--
I CAN INTRODUCE ***MYSELF!***
...I'M HER TWIN BROTHER, ORION.
AND THIS IS... WELL, OUR MENTOR, HE...
YOUR MENTOR'S A DOG?!
NO. THIS IS HIS PET WOLF, WILKIE.
Pet Pet ♡

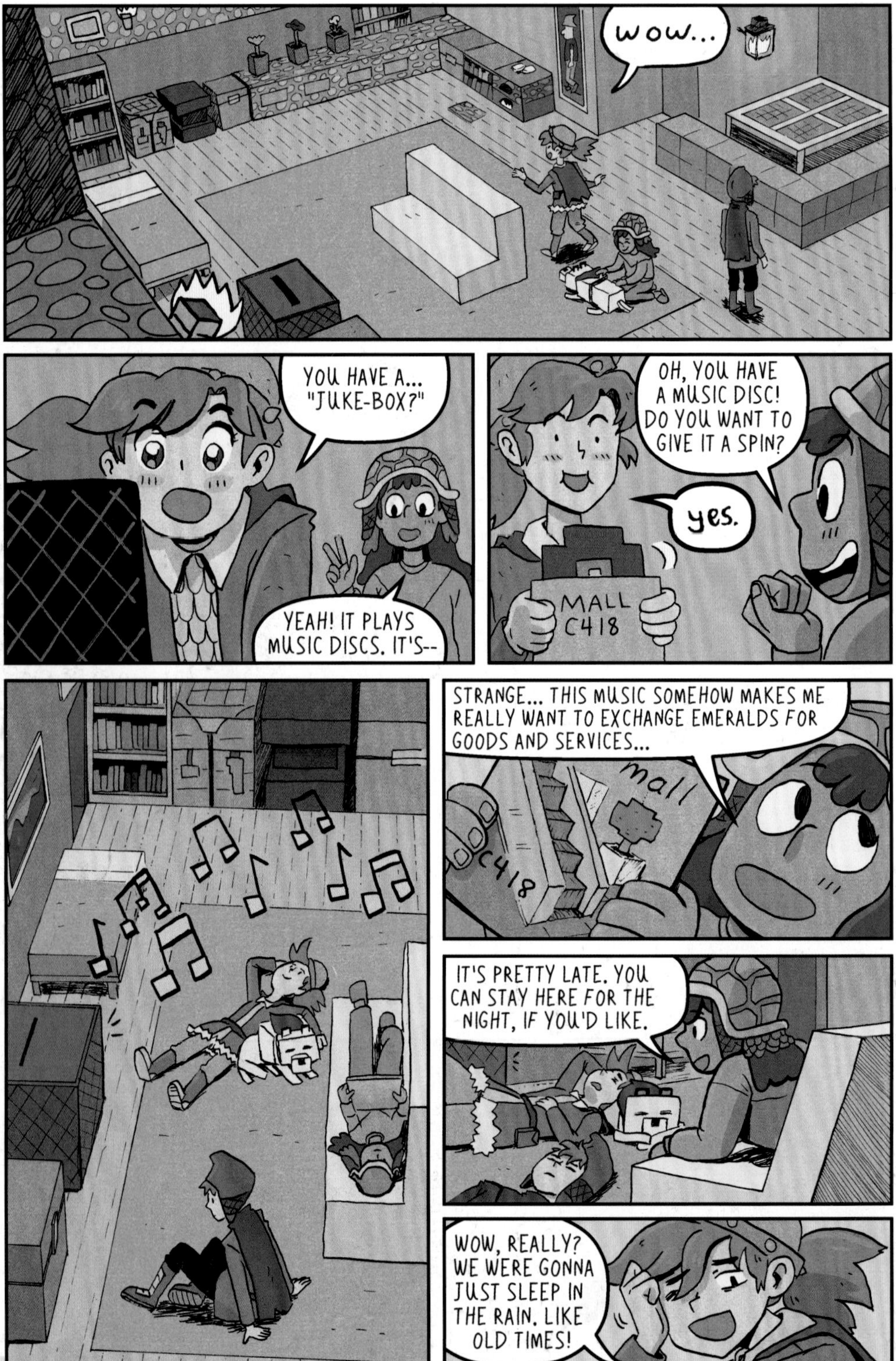
WOW...
YOU HAVE A... "JUKE-BOX?"
YEAH! IT PLAYS MUSIC DISCS. IT'S--
OH, YOU HAVE A MUSIC DISC! DO YOU WANT TO GIVE IT A SPIN?
yes.
MALL C418
STRANGE... THIS MUSIC SOMEHOW MAKES ME REALLY WANT TO EXCHANGE EMERALDS FOR GOODS AND SERVICES...
mall C418
IT'S PRETTY LATE. YOU CAN STAY HERE FOR THE NIGHT, IF YOU'D LIKE.
WOW, REALLY? WE WERE GONNA JUST SLEEP IN THE RAIN. LIKE OLD TIMES!

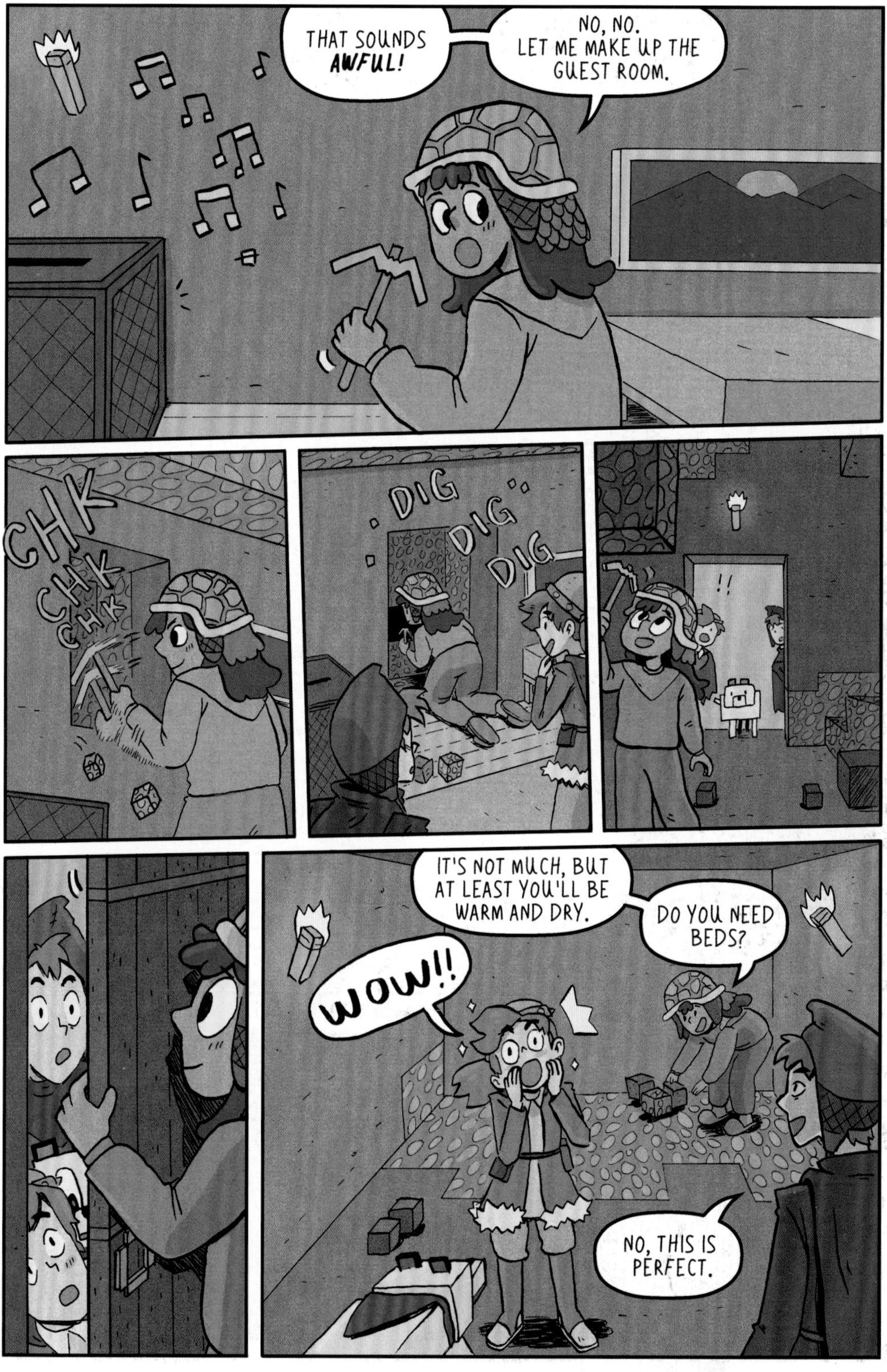
THAT SOUNDS **AWFUL!**
NO, NO.
LET ME MAKE UP THE GUEST ROOM.
CHK
CHK
CHK
DIG
DIG
DIG
!!
IT'S NOT MUCH, BUT AT LEAST YOU'LL BE WARM AND DRY.
DO YOU NEED BEDS?
WOW!!
NO, THIS IS PERFECT.

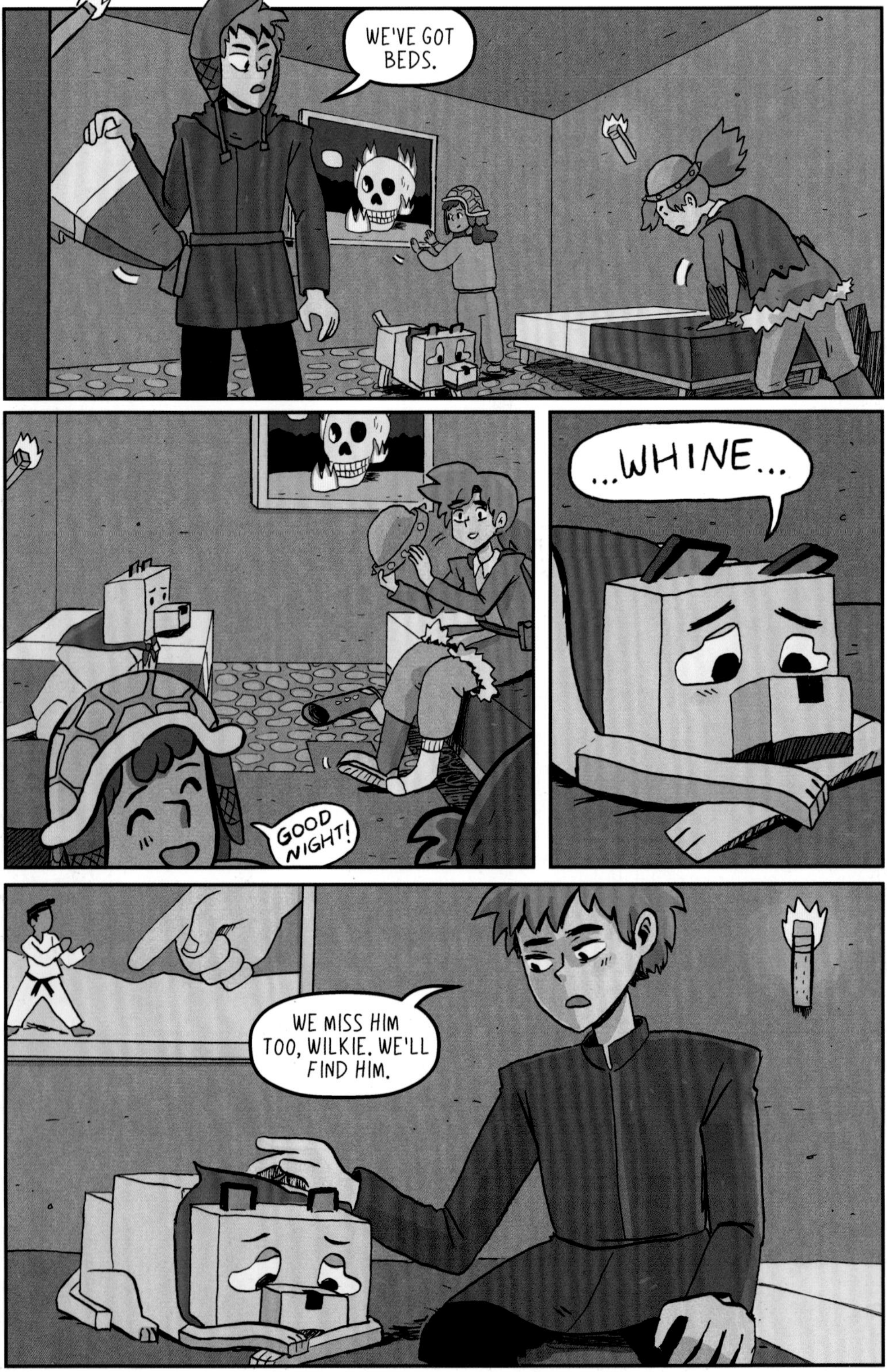
WE'VE GOT BEDS.
...WHINE...
GOOD NIGHT!
WE MISS HIM TOO, WILKIE. WE'LL FIND HIM.

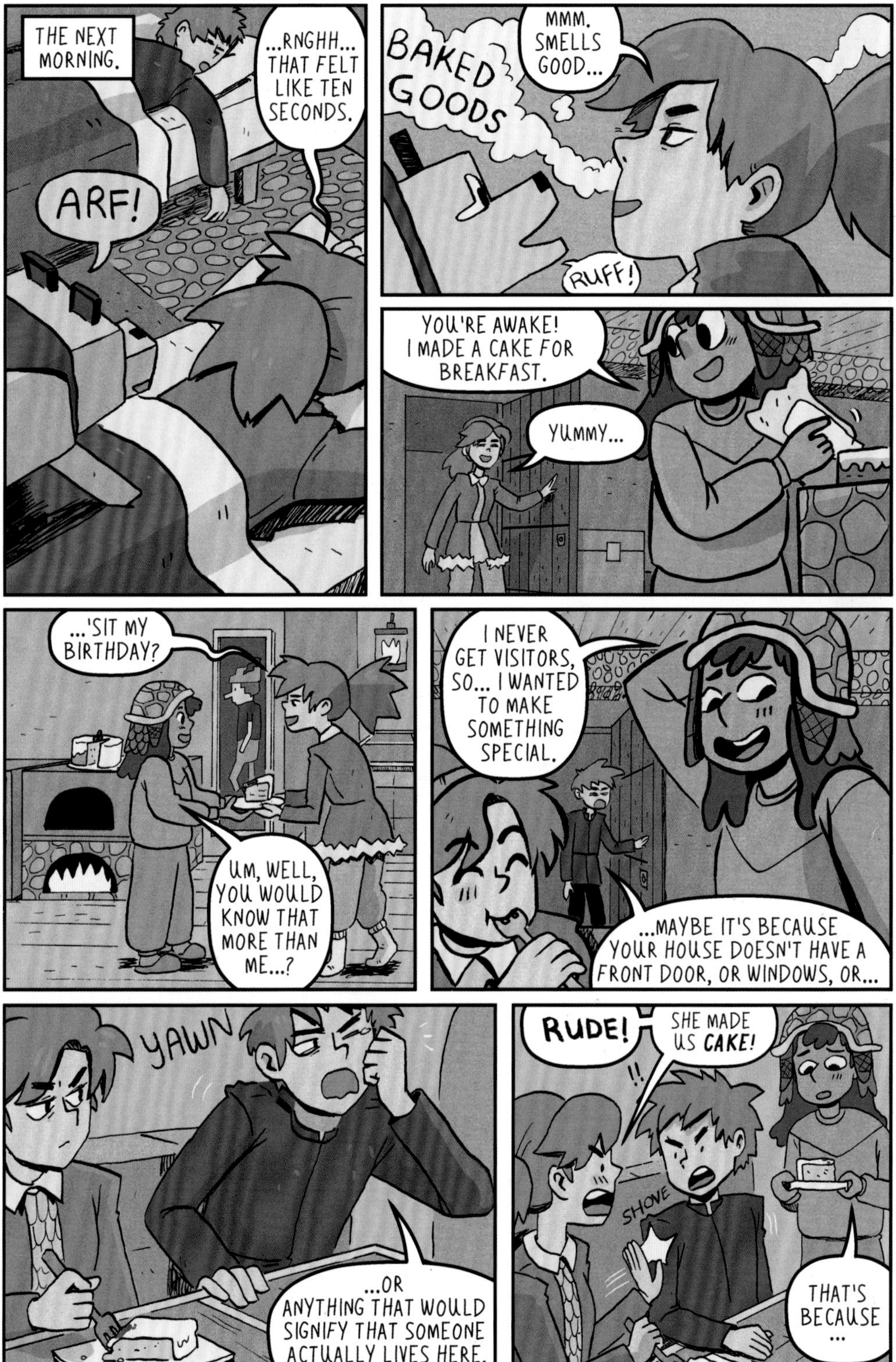
THE NEXT MORNING.
...RNGHH... THAT FELT LIKE TEN SECONDS.
ARF!
BAKED GOODS
MMM. SMELLS GOOD...
RUFF!
YOU'RE AWAKE! I MADE A CAKE FOR BREAKFAST.
YUMMY...
...'SIT MY BIRTHDAY?
UM, WELL, YOU WOULD KNOW THAT MORE THAN ME...?
I NEVER GET VISITORS, SO... I WANTED TO MAKE SOMETHING SPECIAL.
...MAYBE IT'S BECAUSE YOUR HOUSE DOESN'T HAVE A FRONT DOOR, OR WINDOWS, OR...
YAWN
...OR ANYTHING THAT WOULD SIGNIFY THAT SOMEONE ACTUALLY LIVES HERE.
RUDE!
SHE MADE US CAKE!
!!
SHOVE
THAT'S BECAUSE ...

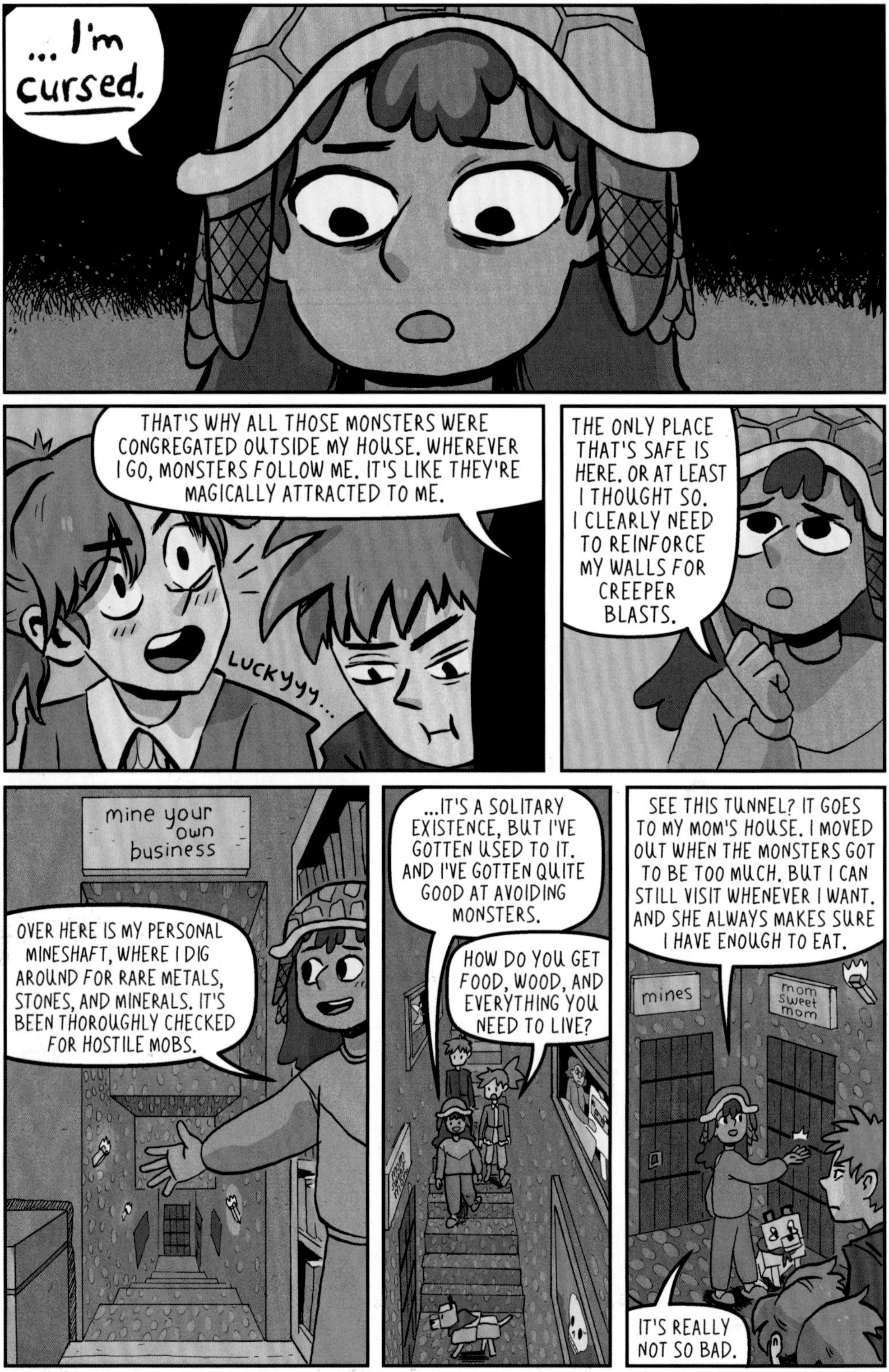
... I'm cursed.
THAT'S WHY ALL THOSE MONSTERS WERE CONGREGATED OUTSIDE MY HOUSE. WHEREVER I GO, MONSTERS FOLLOW ME. IT'S LIKE THEY'RE MAGICALLY ATTRACTED TO ME.
LUCKYYY...
THE ONLY PLACE THAT'S SAFE IS HERE. OR AT LEAST I THOUGHT SO. I CLEARLY NEED TO REINFORCE MY WALLS FOR CREEPER BLASTS.
mine your own business
OVER HERE IS MY PERSONAL MINESHAFT, WHERE I DIG AROUND FOR RARE METALS, STONES, AND MINERALS. IT'S BEEN THOROUGHLY CHECKED FOR HOSTILE MOBS.
...IT'S A SOLITARY EXISTENCE, BUT I'VE GOTTEN USED TO IT. AND I'VE GOTTEN QUITE GOOD AT AVOIDING MONSTERS.
HOW DO YOU GET FOOD, WOOD, AND EVERYTHING YOU NEED TO LIVE?
SEE THIS TUNNEL? IT GOES TO MY MOM'S HOUSE. I MOVED OUT WHEN THE MONSTERS GOT TO BE TOO MUCH. BUT I CAN STILL VISIT WHENEVER I WANT. AND SHE ALWAYS MAKES SURE I HAVE ENOUGH TO EAT.
mines
mom sweet mom
IT'S REALLY NOT SO BAD.

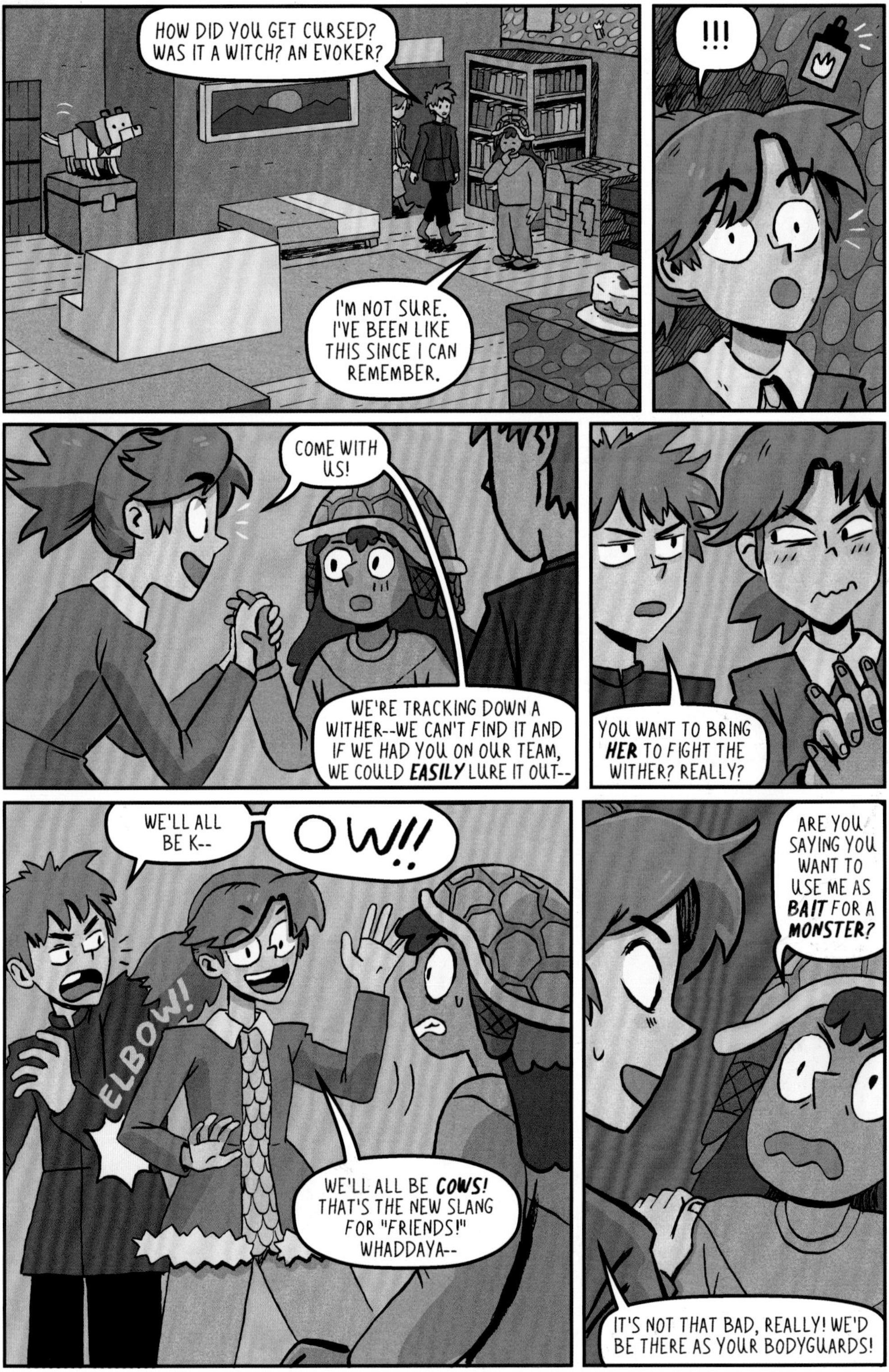
HOW DID YOU GET CURSED? WAS IT A WITCH? AN EVOKER?
I'M NOT SURE. I'VE BEEN LIKE THIS SINCE I CAN REMEMBER.
!!!
COME WITH US!
WE'RE TRACKING DOWN A WITHER--WE CAN'T FIND IT AND IF WE HAD YOU ON OUR TEAM, WE COULD **EASILY** LURE IT OUT--
YOU WANT TO BRING **HER** TO FIGHT THE WITHER? REALLY?
WE'LL ALL BE K--
OW!!
ELBOW!
WE'LL ALL BE **COWS!** THAT'S THE NEW SLANG FOR "FRIENDS!" WHADDAYA--
ARE YOU SAYING YOU WANT TO USE ME AS **BAIT** FOR A **MONSTER?**
IT'S NOT THAT BAD, REALLY! WE'D BE THERE AS YOUR BODYGUARDS!

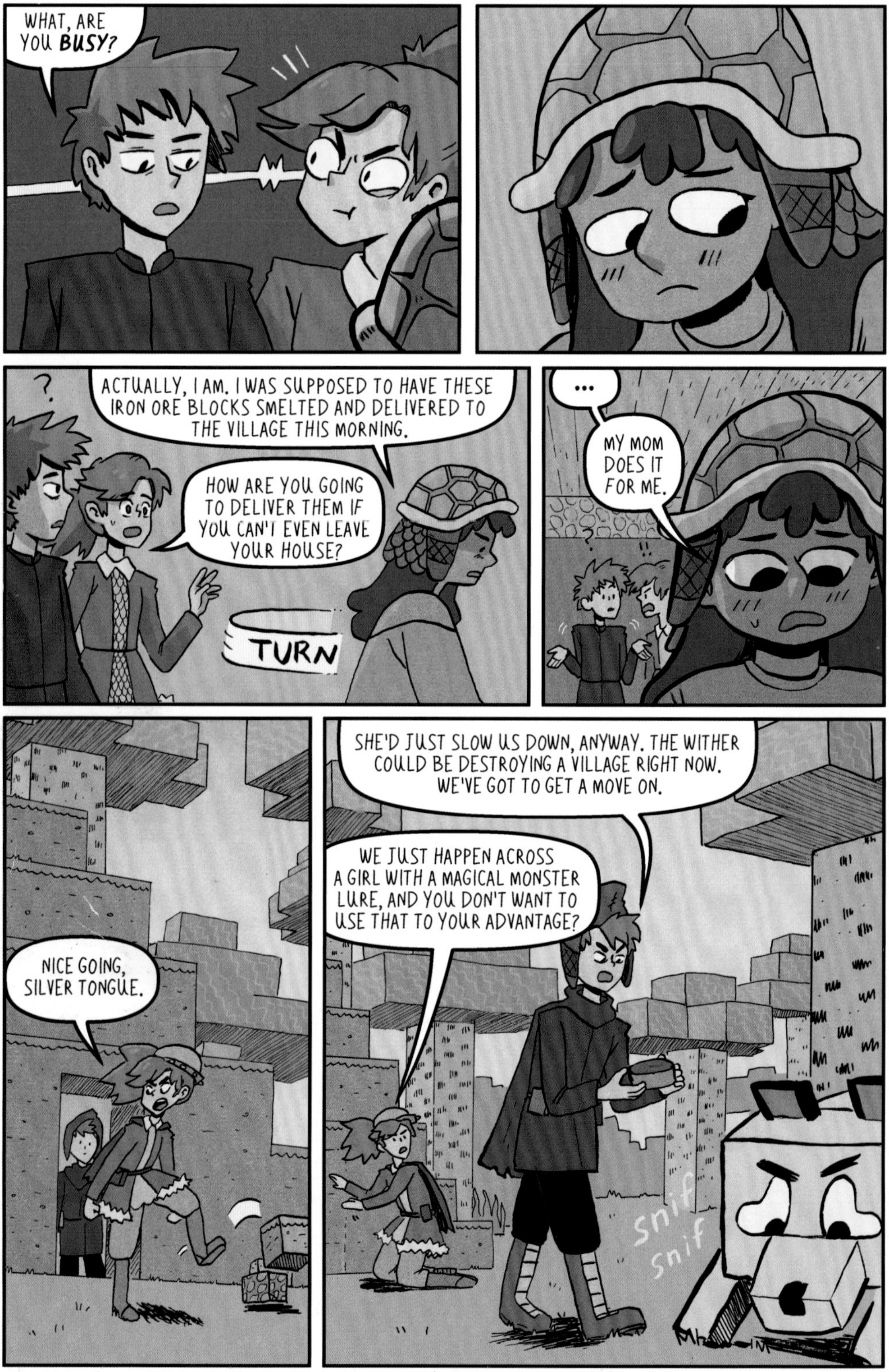
WHAT, ARE YOU **BUSY**?
ACTUALLY, I AM. I WAS SUPPOSED TO HAVE THESE IRON ORE BLOCKS SMELTED AND DELIVERED TO THE VILLAGE THIS MORNING.
HOW ARE YOU GOING TO DELIVER THEM IF YOU CAN'T EVEN LEAVE YOUR HOUSE?
TURN
...
MY MOM DOES IT FOR ME.
NICE GOING, SILVER TONGUE.
SHE'D JUST SLOW US DOWN, ANYWAY. THE WITHER COULD BE DESTROYING A VILLAGE RIGHT NOW. WE'VE GOT TO GET A MOVE ON.
WE JUST HAPPEN ACROSS A GIRL WITH A MAGICAL MONSTER LURE, AND YOU DON'T WANT TO USE THAT TO YOUR ADVANTAGE?
Snif Snif

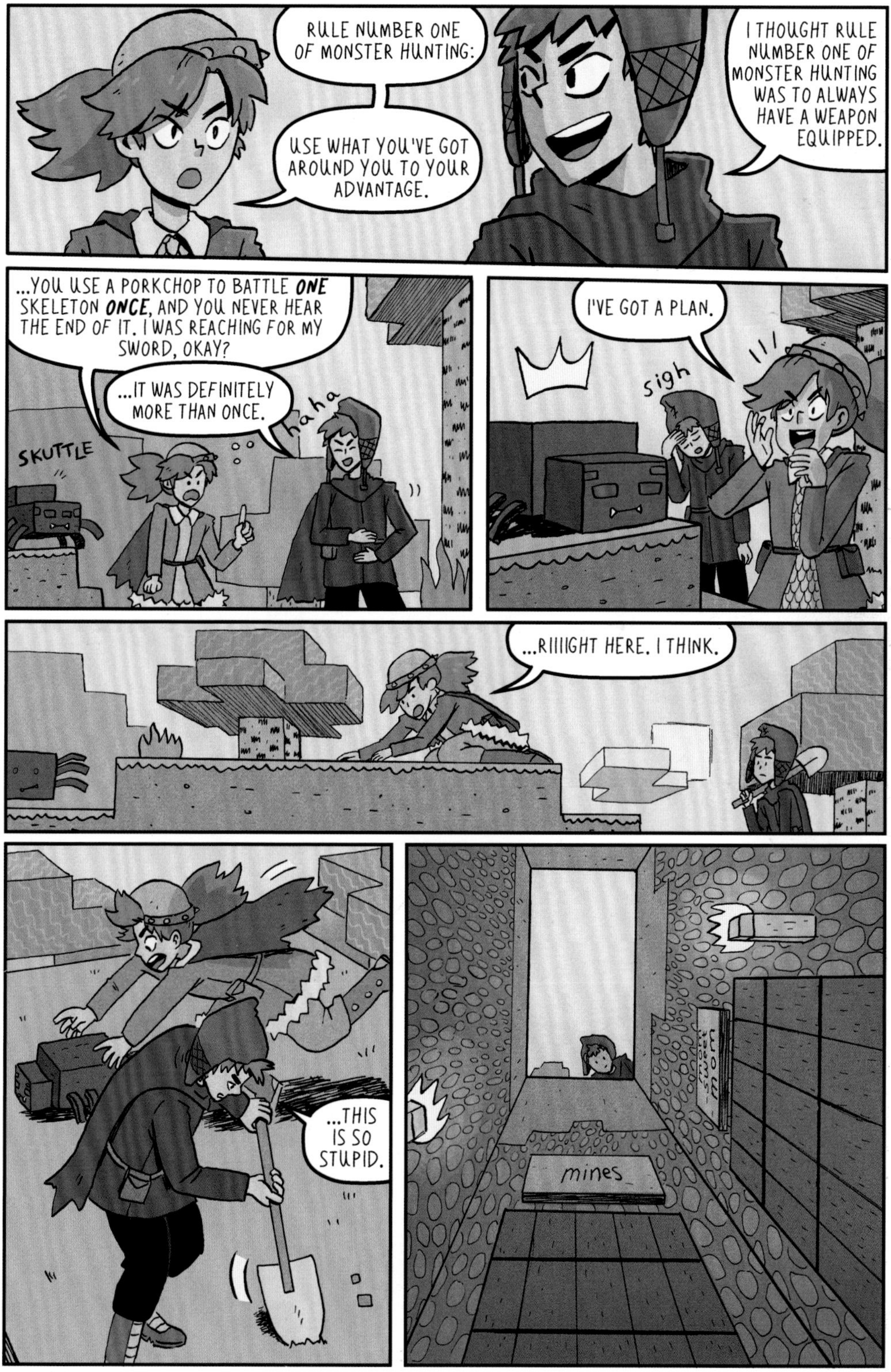

RULE NUMBER ONE OF MONSTER HUNTING:
USE WHAT YOU'VE GOT AROUND YOU TO YOUR ADVANTAGE.
I THOUGHT RULE NUMBER ONE OF MONSTER HUNTING WAS TO ALWAYS HAVE A WEAPON EQUIPPED.
...YOU USE A PORKCHOP TO BATTLE ONE SKELETON ONCE, AND YOU NEVER HEAR THE END OF IT. I WAS REACHING FOR MY SWORD, OKAY?
...IT WAS DEFINITELY MORE THAN ONCE.
haha
SKUTTLE
I'VE GOT A PLAN.
sigh
...RIIIIGHT HERE. I THINK.
...THIS IS SO STUPID.
mines

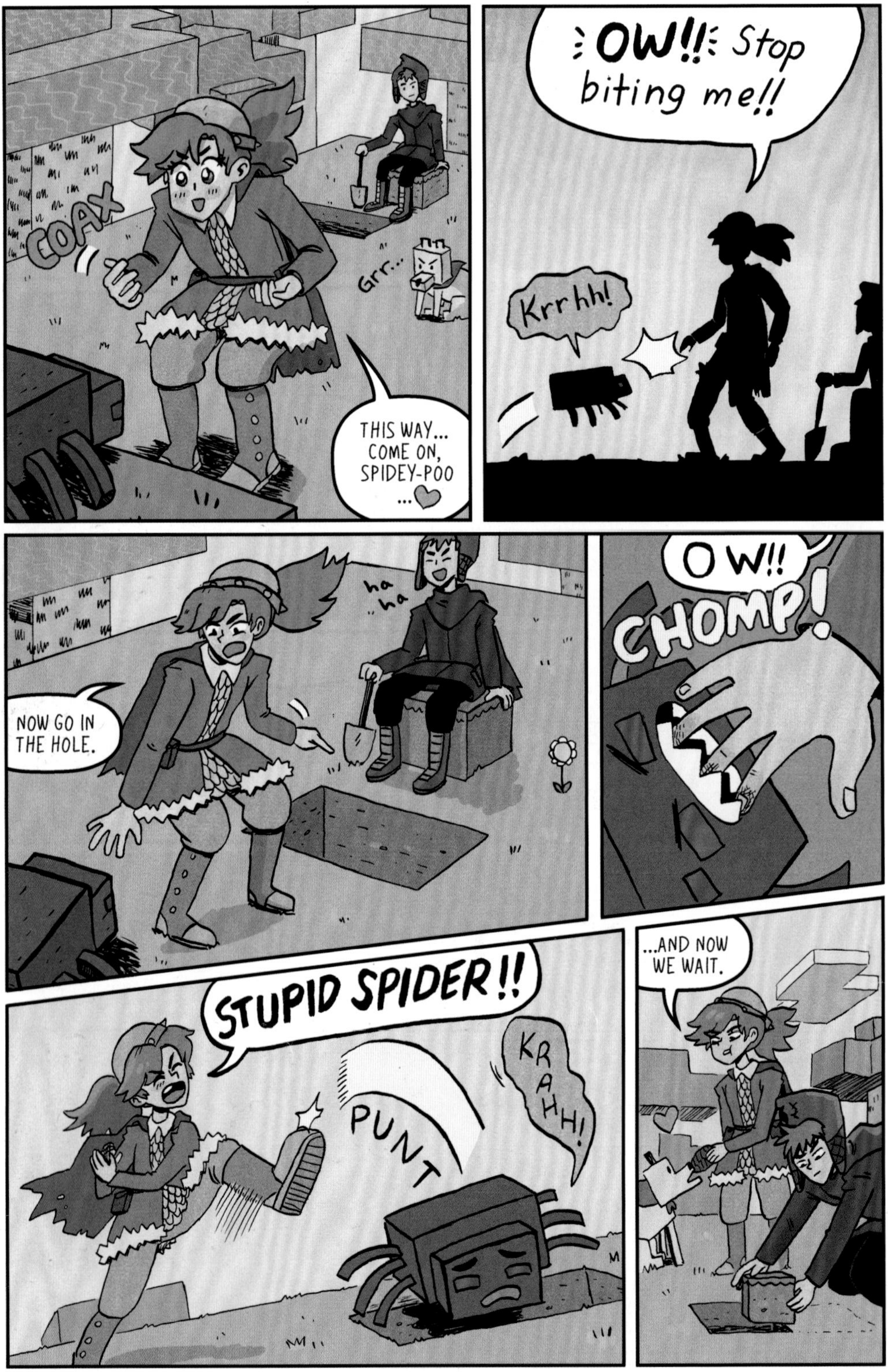

COAX
Grr..
THIS WAY... COME ON, SPIDEY-POO ...♡
OW!! Stop biting me!!
Krr hh!
NOW GO IN THE HOLE.
ha ha
OW!!
CHOMP!
STUPID SPIDER!!
PUNT
KRAHH!
...AND NOW WE WAIT.

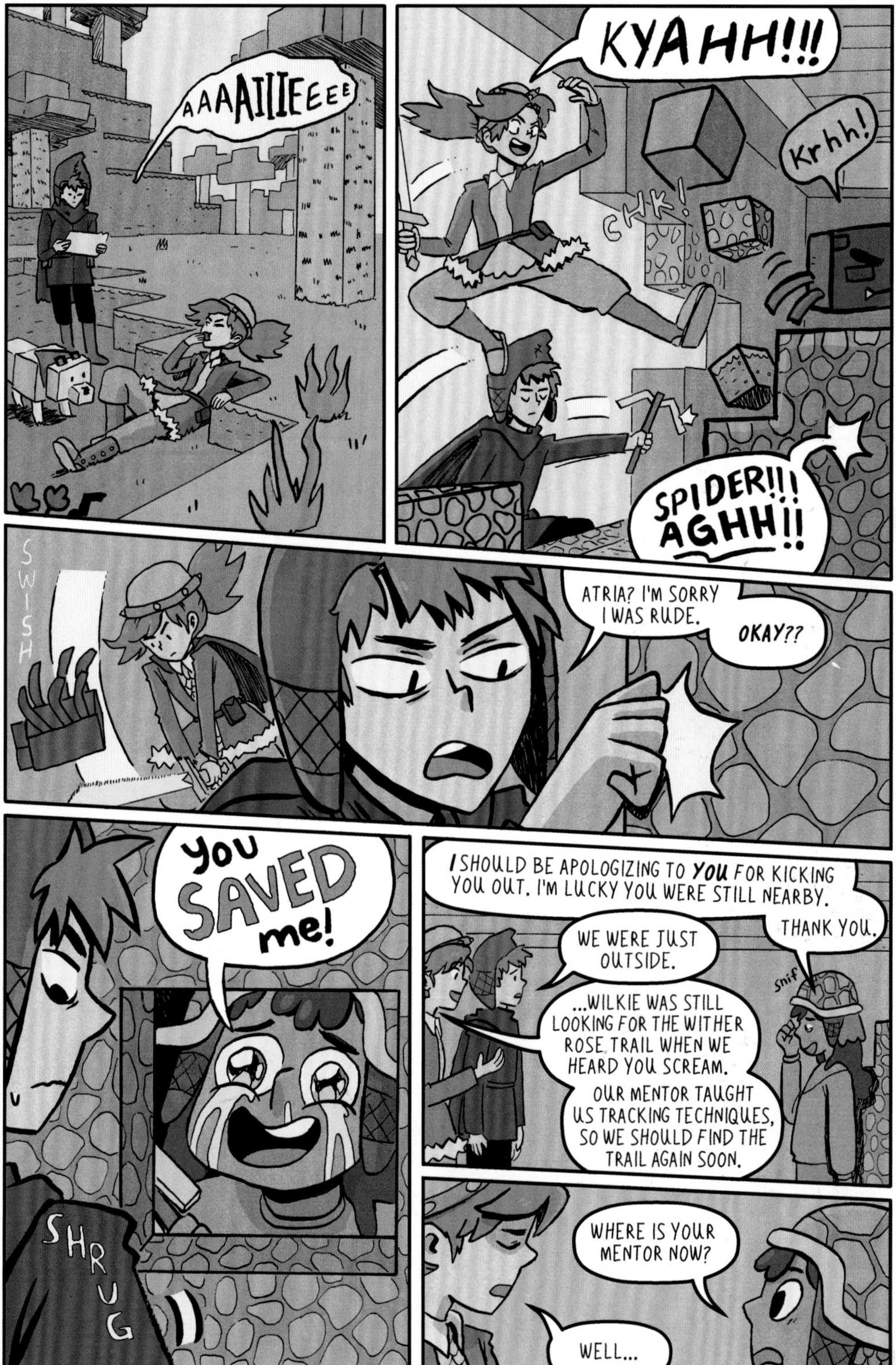
AAAAIIIEEEE
KYAHH!!!
CHK!
Krhh!
SPIDER!!!
AGHH!!
SWISH
ATRIA? I'M SORRY I WAS RUDE.
OKAY??
You SAVED me!
SHRUG
I SHOULD BE APOLOGIZING TO YOU FOR KICKING YOU OUT. I'M LUCKY YOU WERE STILL NEARBY.
THANK YOU.
WE WERE JUST OUTSIDE.
Snif
...WILKIE WAS STILL LOOKING FOR THE WITHER ROSE TRAIL WHEN WE HEARD YOU SCREAM.
OUR MENTOR TAUGHT US TRACKING TECHNIQUES, SO WE SHOULD FIND THE TRAIL AGAIN SOON.
WHERE IS YOUR MENTOR NOW?
WELL...

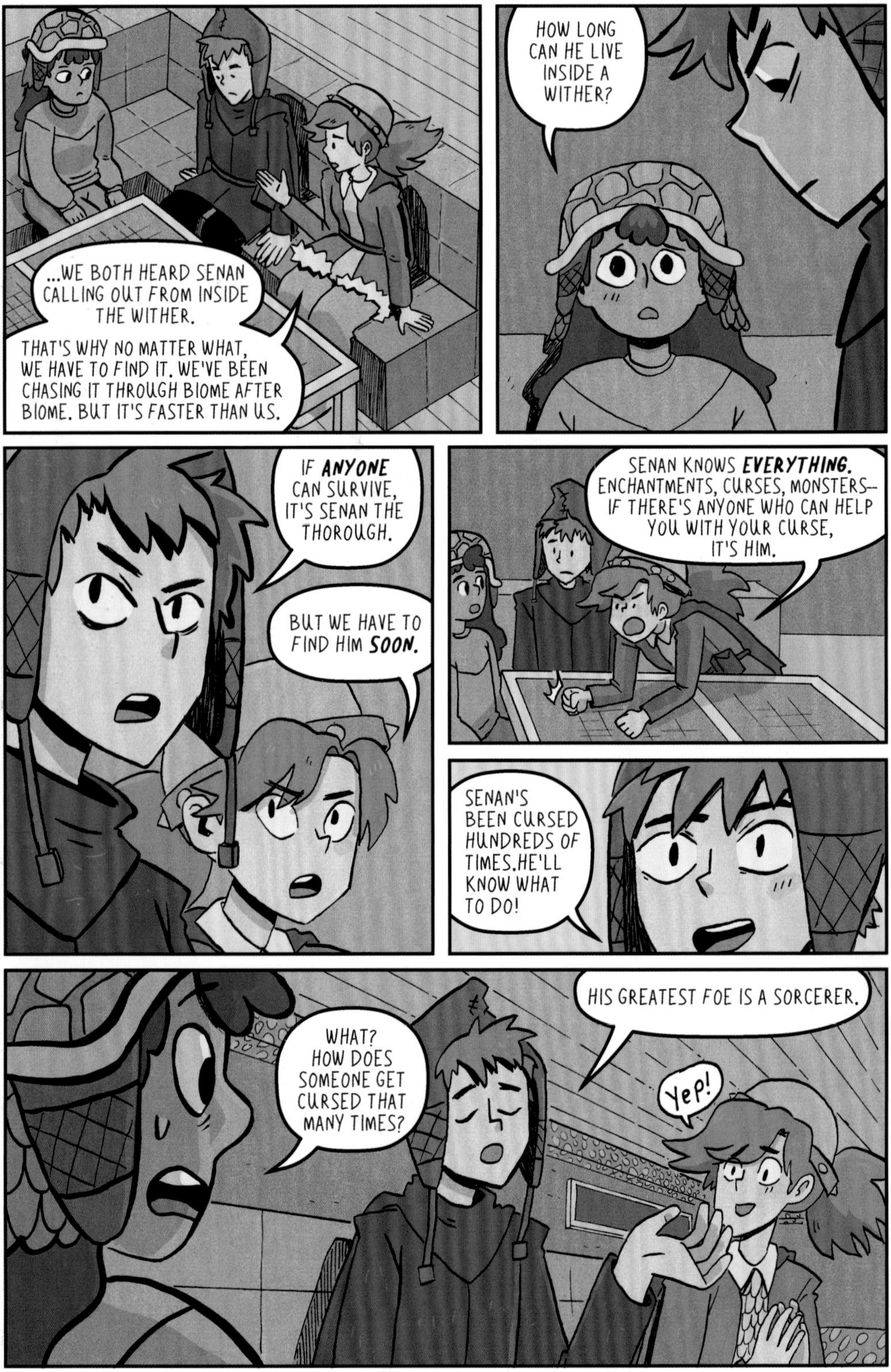
...WE BOTH HEARD SENAN CALLING OUT FROM INSIDE THE WITHER.
THAT'S WHY NO MATTER WHAT, WE HAVE TO FIND IT. WE'VE BEEN CHASING IT THROUGH BIOME AFTER BIOME. BUT IT'S FASTER THAN US.
HOW LONG CAN HE LIVE INSIDE A WITHER?
IF ANYONE CAN SURVIVE, IT'S SENAN THE THOROUGH.
BUT WE HAVE TO FIND HIM SOON.
SENAN KNOWS EVERYTHING. ENCHANTMENTS, CURSES, MONSTERS-- IF THERE'S ANYONE WHO CAN HELP YOU WITH YOUR CURSE, IT'S HIM.
SENAN'S BEEN CURSED HUNDREDS OF TIMES. HE'LL KNOW WHAT TO DO!
WHAT? HOW DOES SOMEONE GET CURSED THAT MANY TIMES?
HIS GREATEST FOE IS A SORCERER.
Yep!

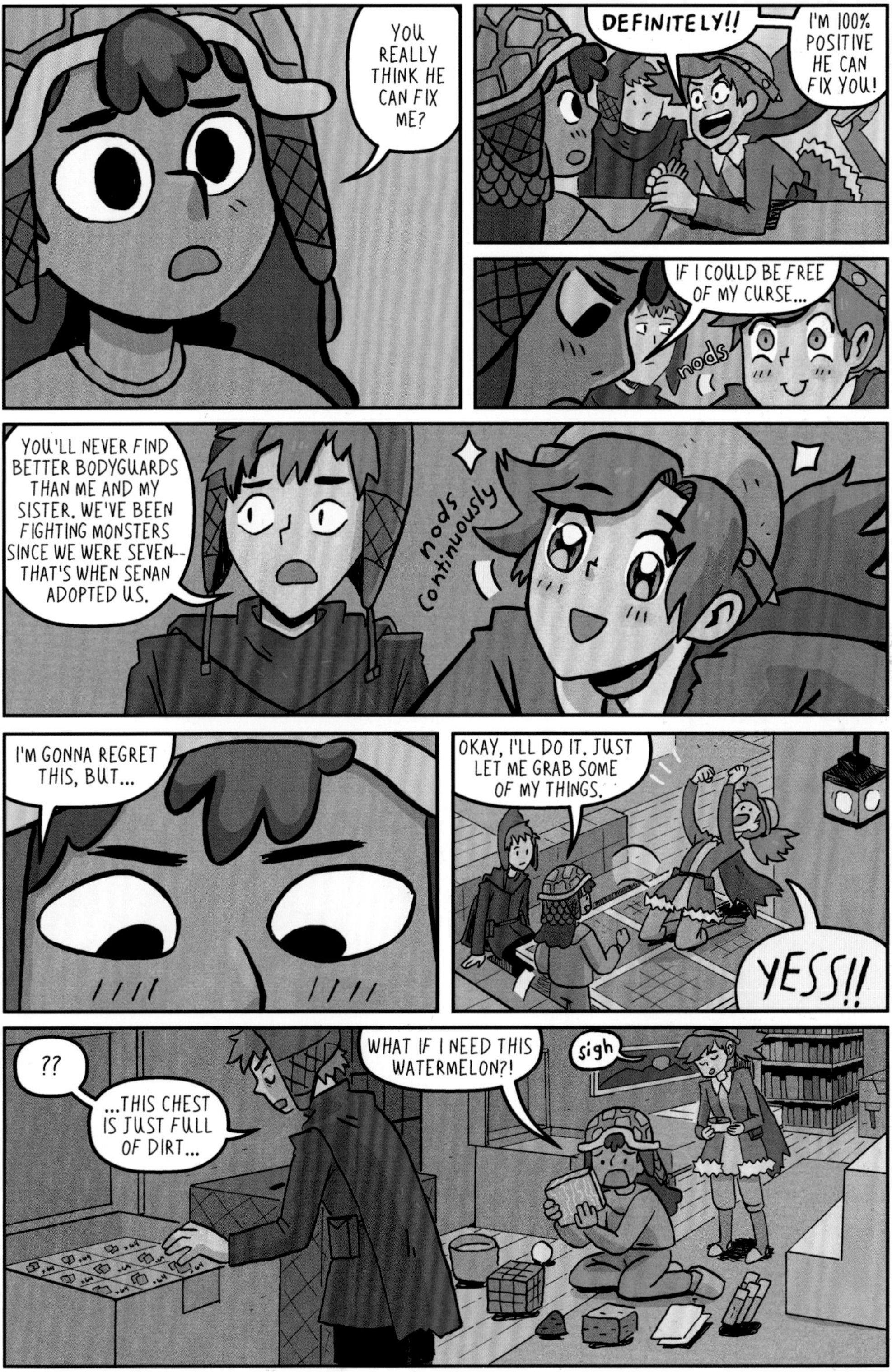
YOU REALLY THINK HE CAN FIX ME?
DEFINITELY!!
I'M 100% POSITIVE HE CAN FIX YOU!
IF I COULD BE FREE OF MY CURSE...
nods
YOU'LL NEVER FIND BETTER BODYGUARDS THAN ME AND MY SISTER. WE'VE BEEN FIGHTING MONSTERS SINCE WE WERE SEVEN-- THAT'S WHEN SENAN ADOPTED US.
nods continuously
I'M GONNA REGRET THIS, BUT...
OKAY, I'LL DO IT. JUST LET ME GRAB SOME OF MY THINGS.
YESS!!
??
...THIS CHEST IS JUST FULL OF DIRT...
WHAT IF I NEED THIS WATERMELON?!
sigh

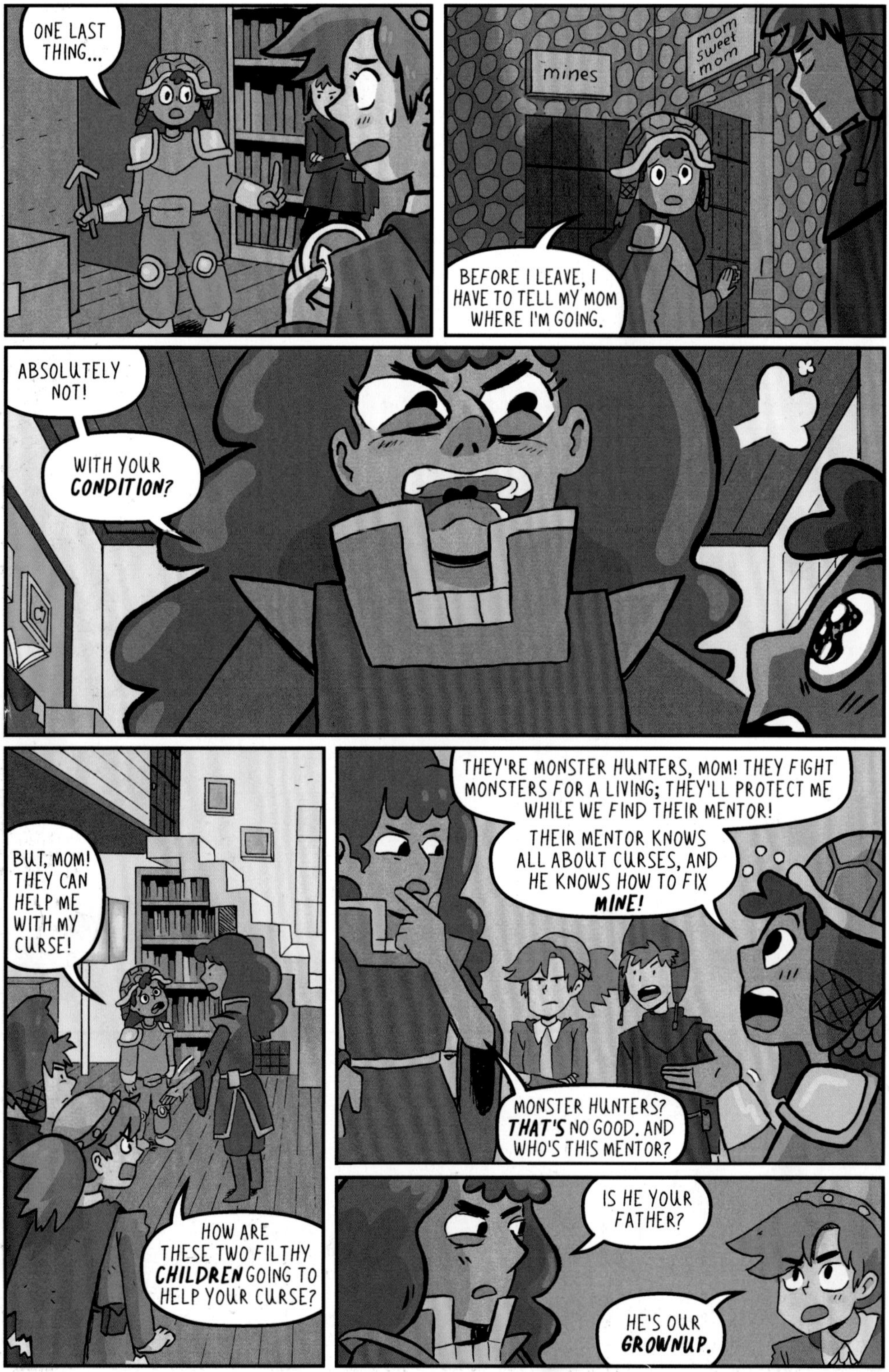
ONE LAST THING...
mines
mom sweet mom
BEFORE I LEAVE, I HAVE TO TELL MY MOM WHERE I'M GOING.
ABSOLUTELY NOT!
WITH YOUR **CONDITION?**
BUT, MOM! THEY CAN HELP ME WITH MY CURSE!
HOW ARE THESE TWO FILTHY **CHILDREN** GOING TO HELP YOUR CURSE?
THEY'RE MONSTER HUNTERS, MOM! THEY FIGHT MONSTERS FOR A LIVING; THEY'LL PROTECT ME WHILE WE FIND THEIR MENTOR!
THEIR MENTOR KNOWS ALL ABOUT CURSES, AND HE KNOWS HOW TO FIX **MINE!**
MONSTER HUNTERS? **THAT'S** NO GOOD. AND WHO'S THIS MENTOR?
IS HE YOUR FATHER?
HE'S OUR **GROWNUP.**

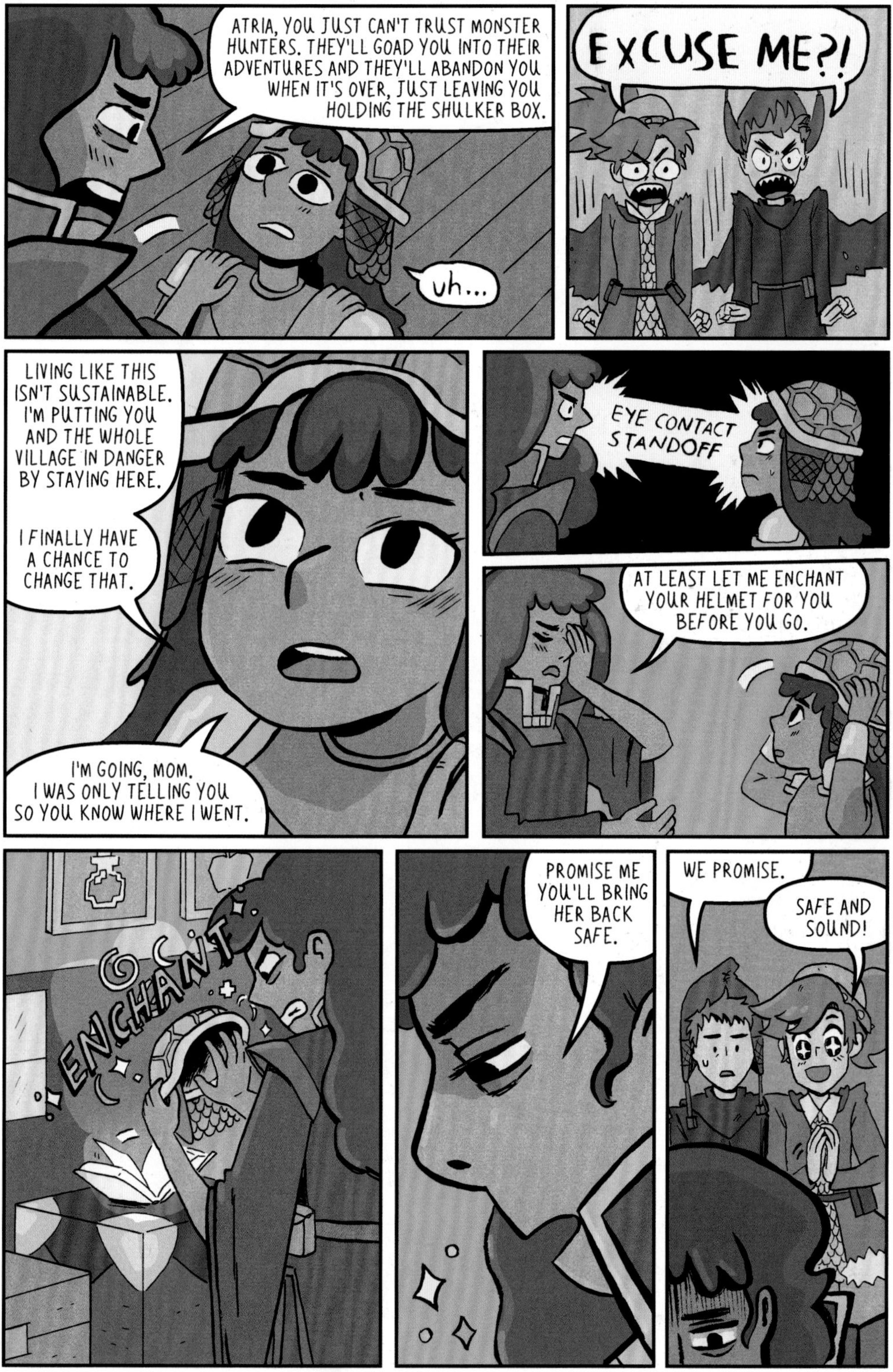
ATRIA, YOU JUST CAN'T TRUST MONSTER HUNTERS. THEY'LL GOAD YOU INTO THEIR ADVENTURES AND THEY'LL ABANDON YOU WHEN IT'S OVER, JUST LEAVING YOU HOLDING THE SHULKER BOX.
uh...
EXCUSE ME?!
LIVING LIKE THIS ISN'T SUSTAINABLE. I'M PUTTING YOU AND THE WHOLE VILLAGE IN DANGER BY STAYING HERE.
I FINALLY HAVE A CHANCE TO CHANGE THAT.
I'M GOING, MOM. I WAS ONLY TELLING YOU SO YOU KNOW WHERE I WENT.
EYE CONTACT STANDOFF
AT LEAST LET ME ENCHANT YOUR HELMET FOR YOU BEFORE YOU GO.
ENCHANT
PROMISE ME YOU'LL BRING HER BACK SAFE.
WE PROMISE.
SAFE AND SOUND!

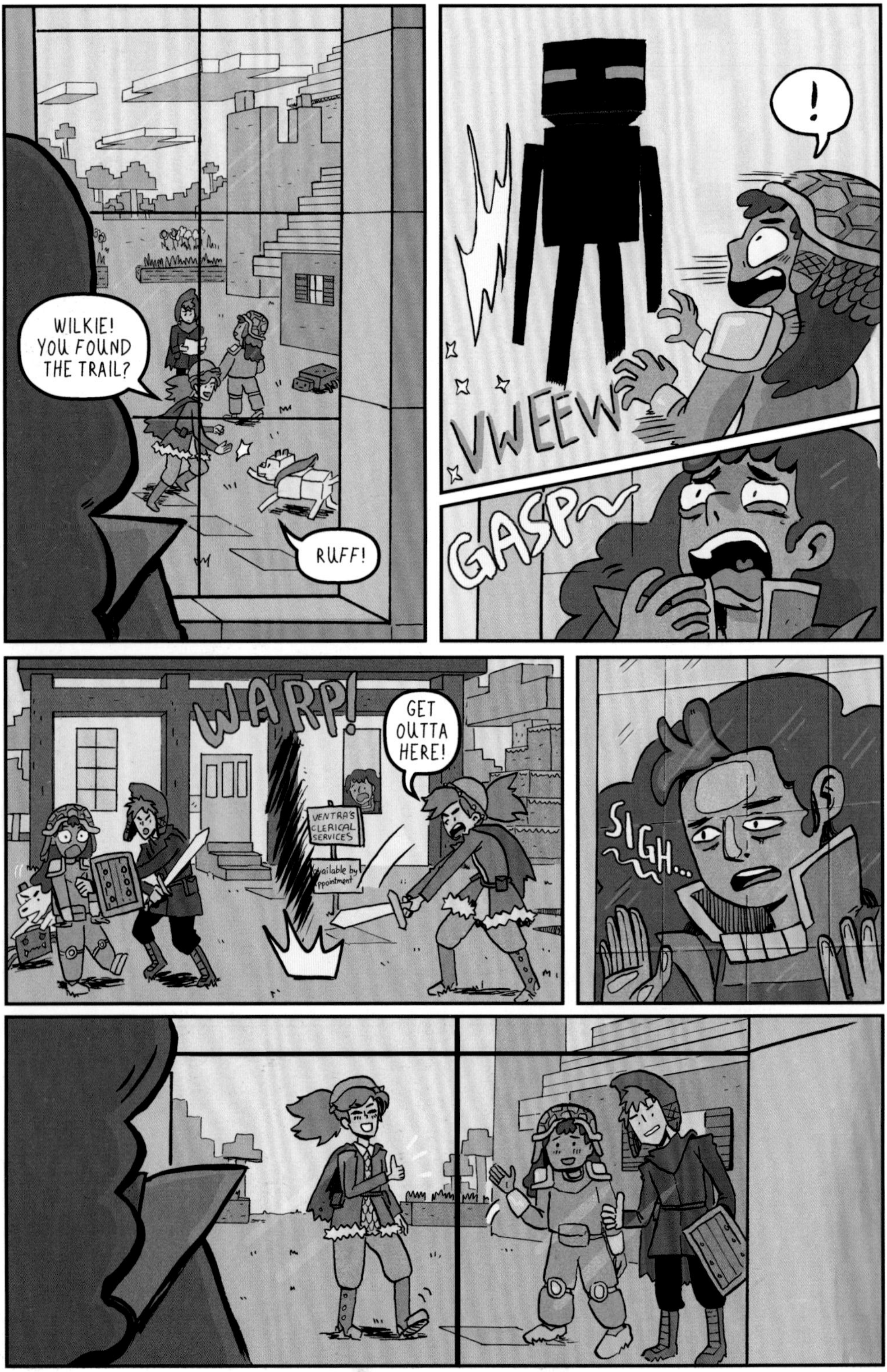
WILKIE! YOU FOUND THE TRAIL?
RUFF!
!
VWEEW
GASP~
WARP!
GET OUTTA HERE!
VENTRA'S CLERICAL SERVICES
available by appointment
SIGH...

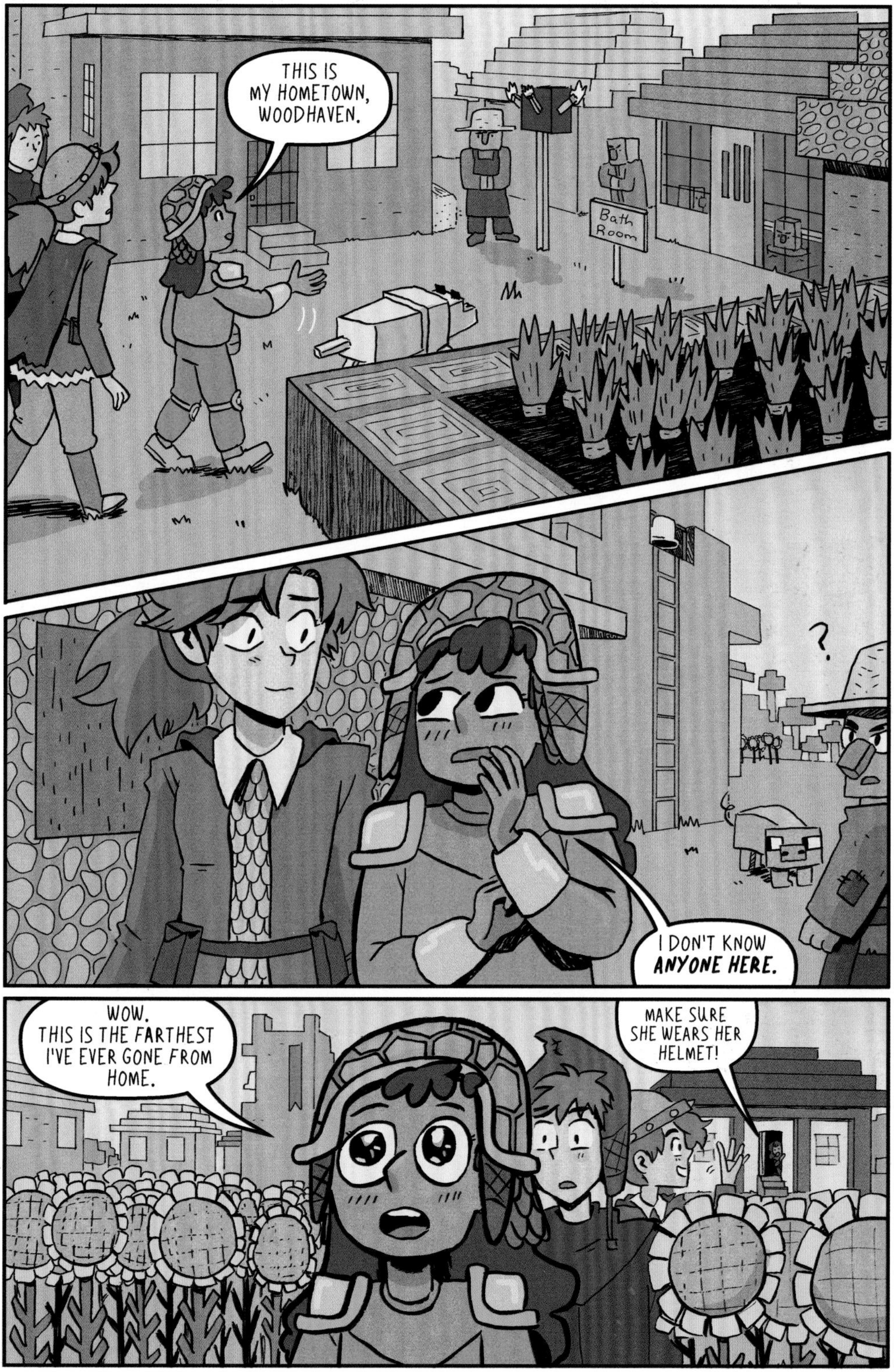
THIS IS MY HOMETOWN, WOODHAVEN.
Bath Room
I DON'T KNOW ANYONE HERE.
WOW. THIS IS THE FARTHEST I'VE EVER GONE FROM HOME.
MAKE SURE SHE WEARS HER HELMET!

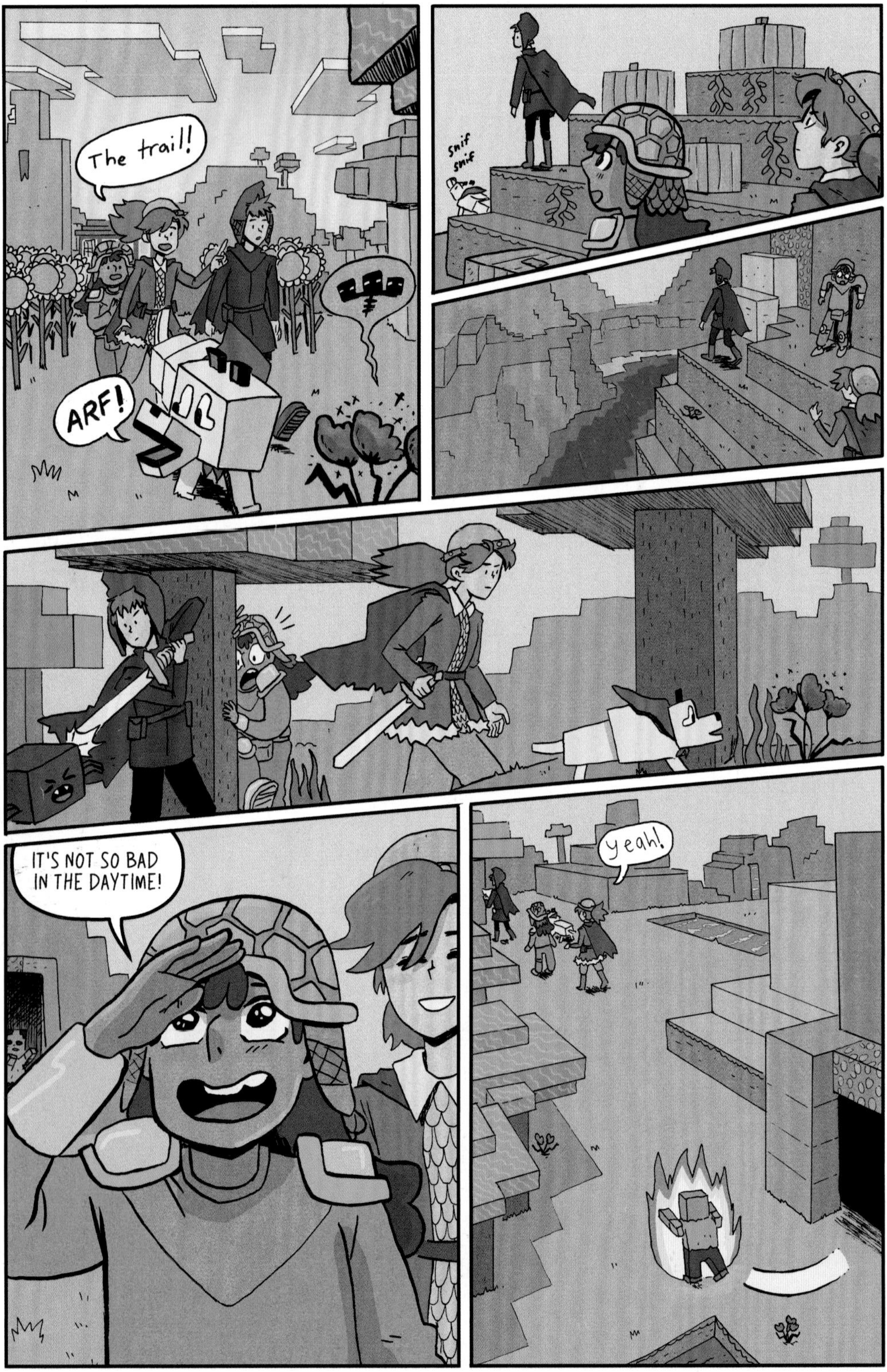
The trail!
ARF!
snif
snif
IT'S NOT SO BAD IN THE DAYTIME!
yeah!

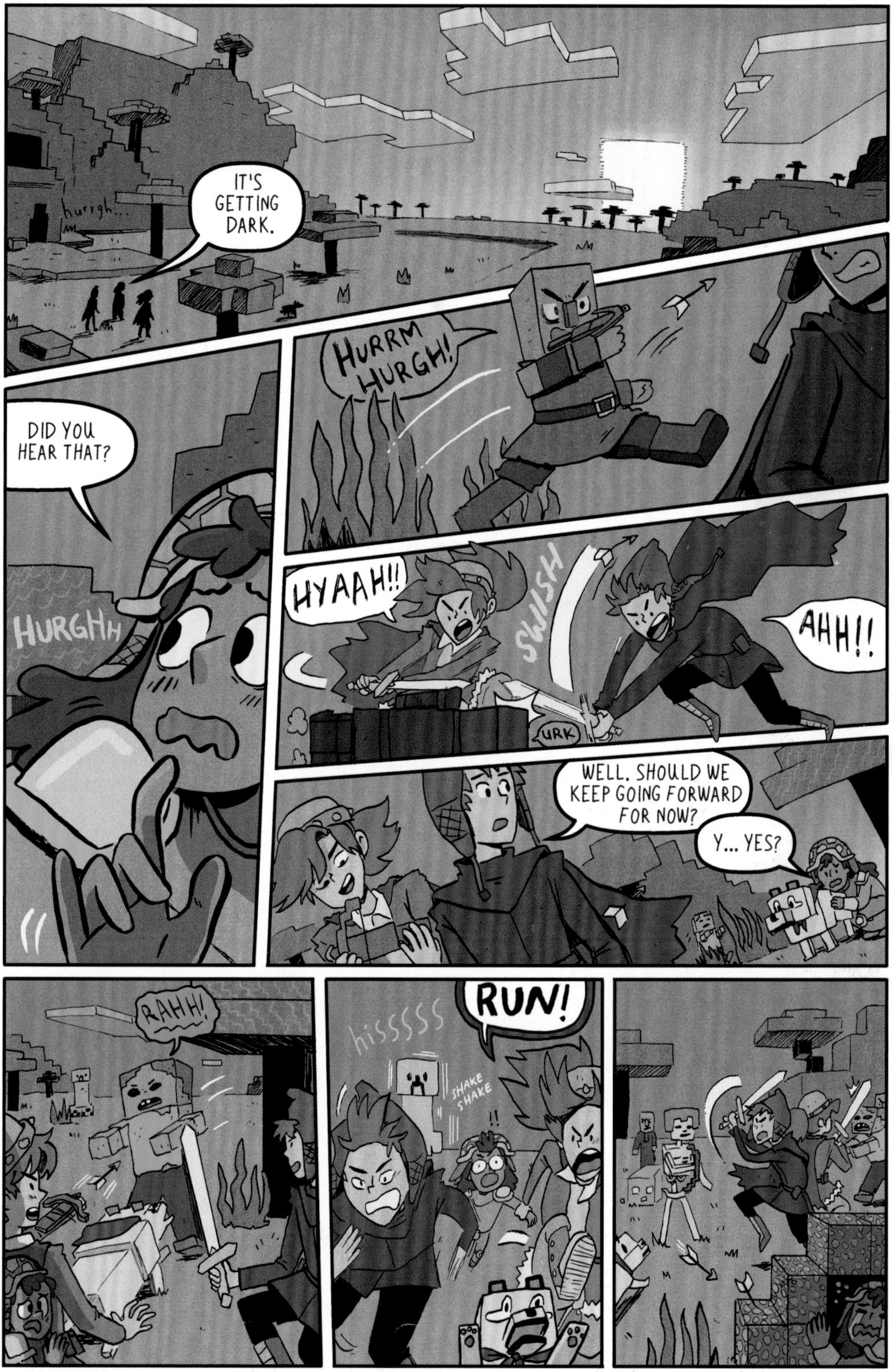
hurrgh...
IT'S GETTING DARK.
HURRM HURGH!
DID YOU HEAR THAT?
HURGHH
HYAAH!!
SWISH
AHH!!
URK
WELL. SHOULD WE KEEP GOING FORWARD FOR NOW?
Y... YES?
RAHH!
hisssss
RUN!
SHAKE SHAKE
!!

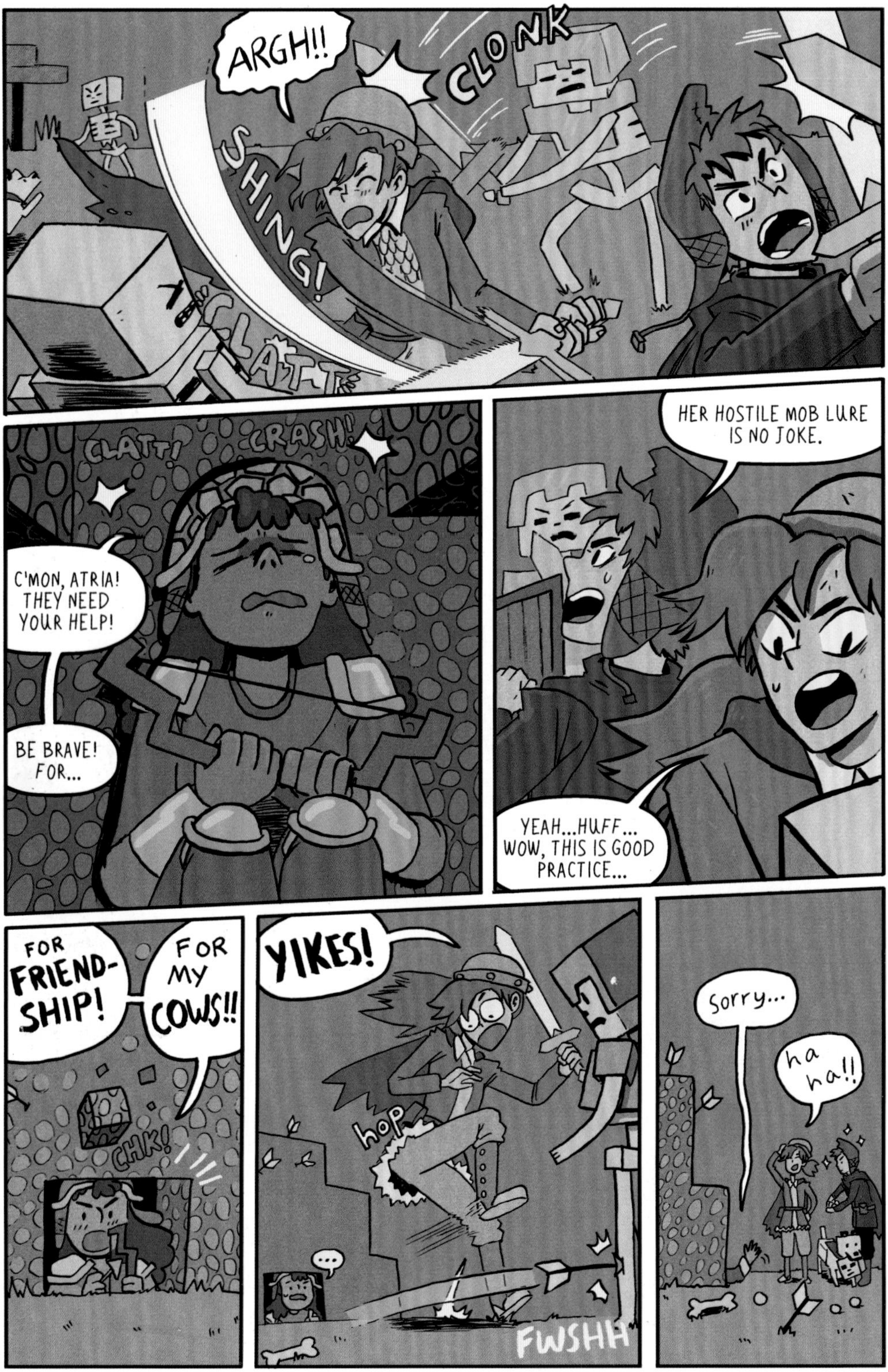
ARGH!!
CLONK
SHING!
CLATT
CLATT!
CRASH!
C'MON, ATRIA! THEY NEED YOUR HELP!
BE BRAVE! FOR...
HER HOSTILE MOB LURE IS NO JOKE.
YEAH...HUFF... WOW, THIS IS GOOD PRACTICE...
FOR FRIENDSHIP!
FOR MY COWS!!
CHK!
YIKES!
hop
...
FWSHH
Sorry...
ha ha!!

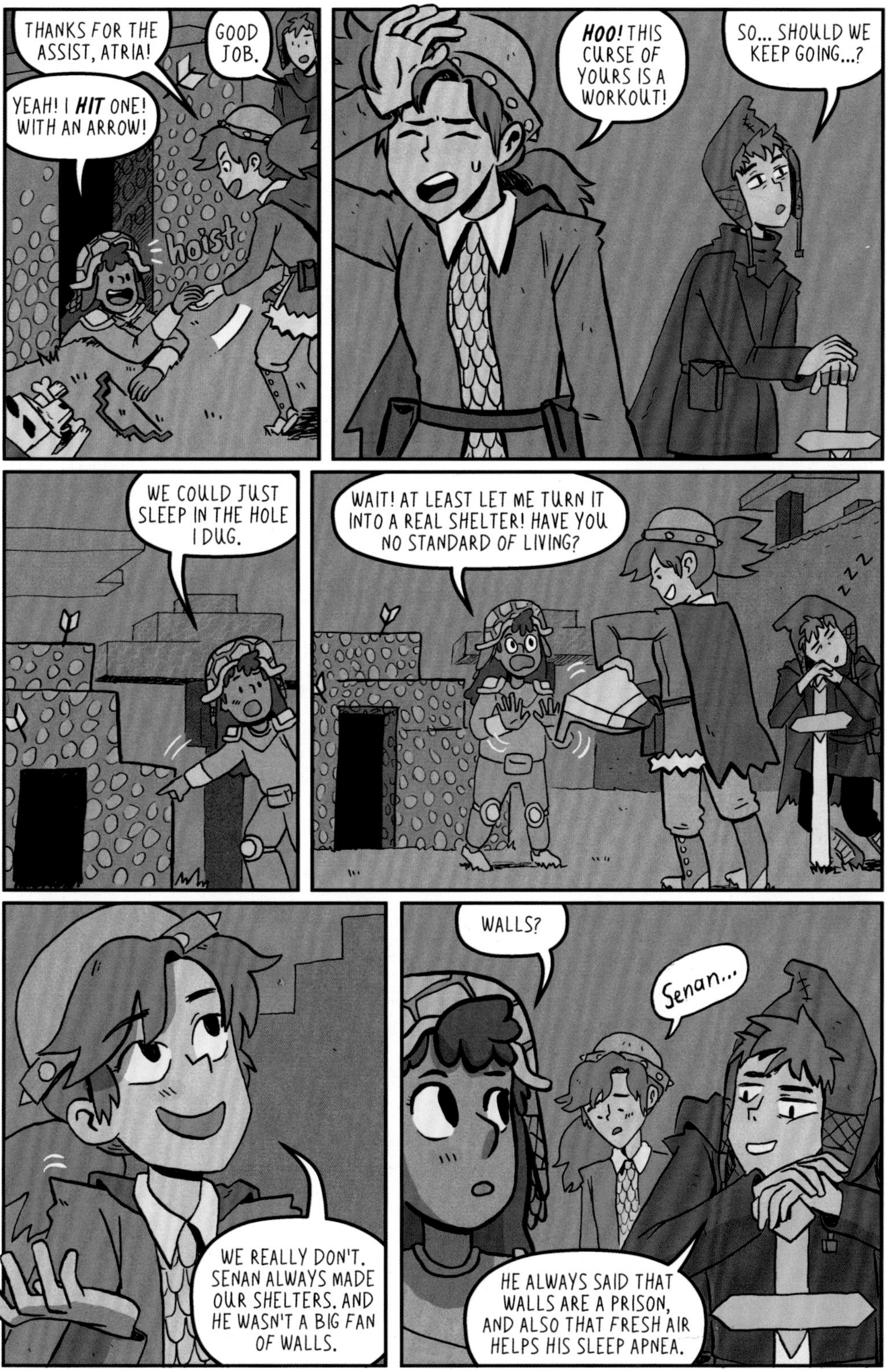
THANKS FOR THE ASSIST, ATRIA!
GOOD JOB.
YEAH! I HIT ONE! WITH AN ARROW!
hoist
HOO! THIS CURSE OF YOURS IS A WORKOUT!
SO... SHOULD WE KEEP GOING...?
WE COULD JUST SLEEP IN THE HOLE I DUG.
WAIT! AT LEAST LET ME TURN IT INTO A REAL SHELTER! HAVE YOU NO STANDARD OF LIVING?
Z Z Z
WE REALLY DON'T. SENAN ALWAYS MADE OUR SHELTERS. AND HE WASN'T A BIG FAN OF WALLS.
WALLS?
Senan...
HE ALWAYS SAID THAT WALLS ARE A PRISON, AND ALSO THAT FRESH AIR HELPS HIS SLEEP APNEA.

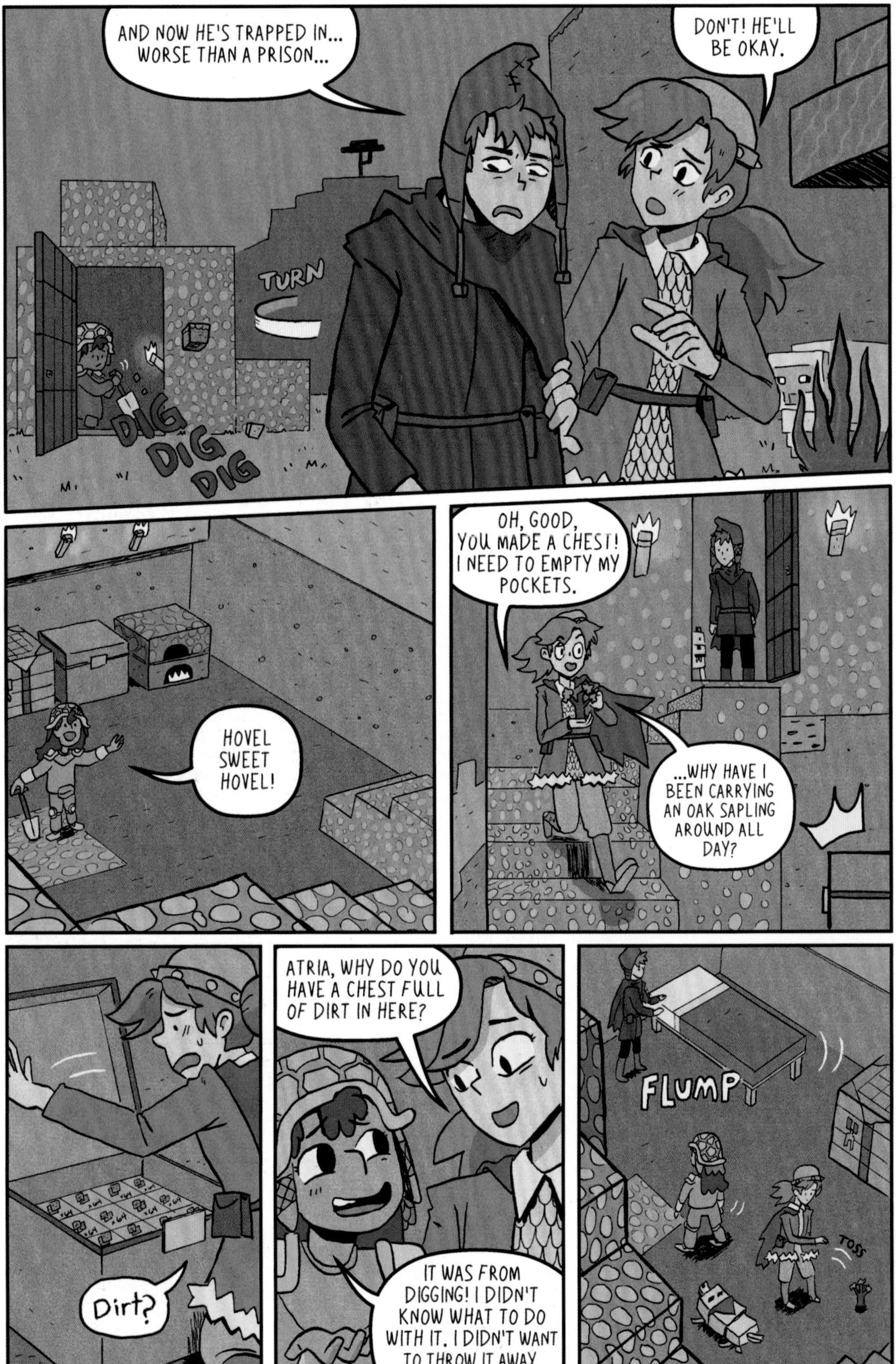
AND NOW HE'S TRAPPED IN... WORSE THAN A PRISON...
DON'T! HE'LL BE OKAY.
TURN
DIG DIG DIG
HOVEL SWEET HOVEL!
OH, GOOD, YOU MADE A CHEST! I NEED TO EMPTY MY POCKETS.
...WHY HAVE I BEEN CARRYING AN OAK SAPLING AROUND ALL DAY?
Dirt?
ATRIA, WHY DO YOU HAVE A CHEST FULL OF DIRT IN HERE?
IT WAS FROM DIGGING! I DIDN'T KNOW WHAT TO DO WITH IT. I DIDN'T WANT TO THROW IT AWAY.
FLUMP
TOSS

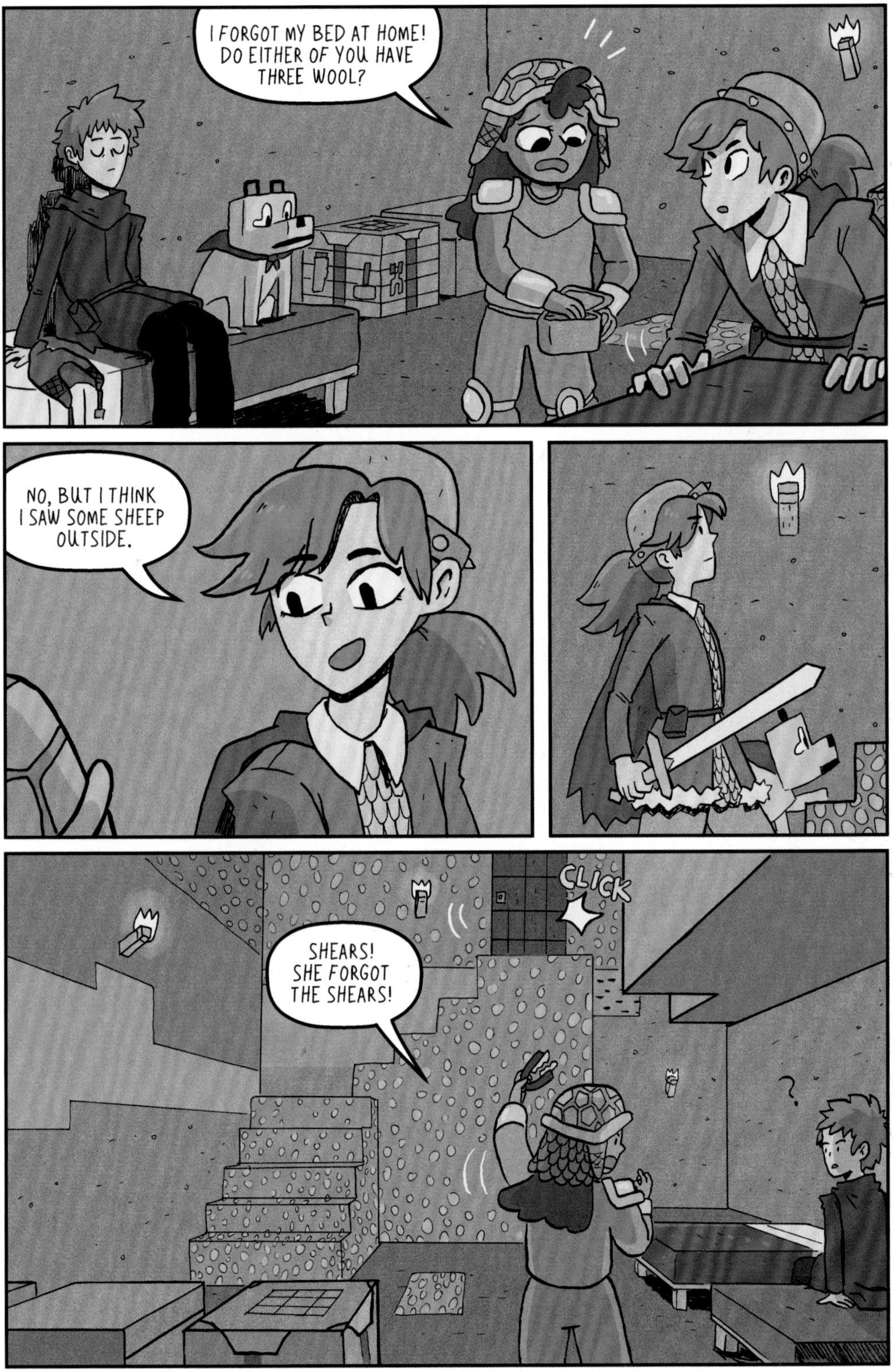
I FORGOT MY BED AT HOME! DO EITHER OF YOU HAVE THREE WOOL?
NO, BUT I THINK I SAW SOME SHEEP OUTSIDE.
CLICK
SHEARS! SHE FORGOT THE SHEARS!

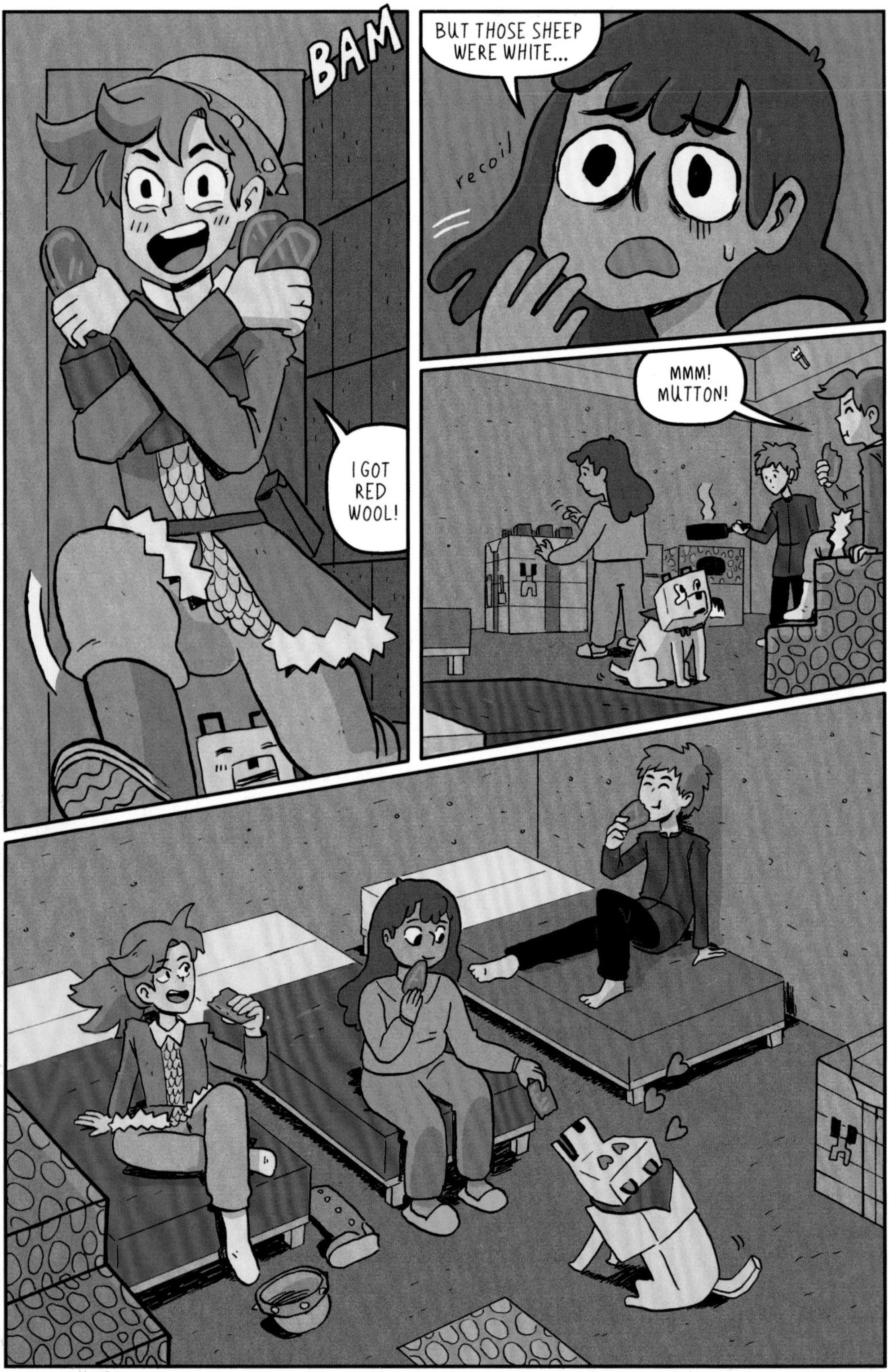
BAM
I GOT RED WOOL!
BUT THOSE SHEEP WERE WHITE...
recoil
MMM! MUTTON!

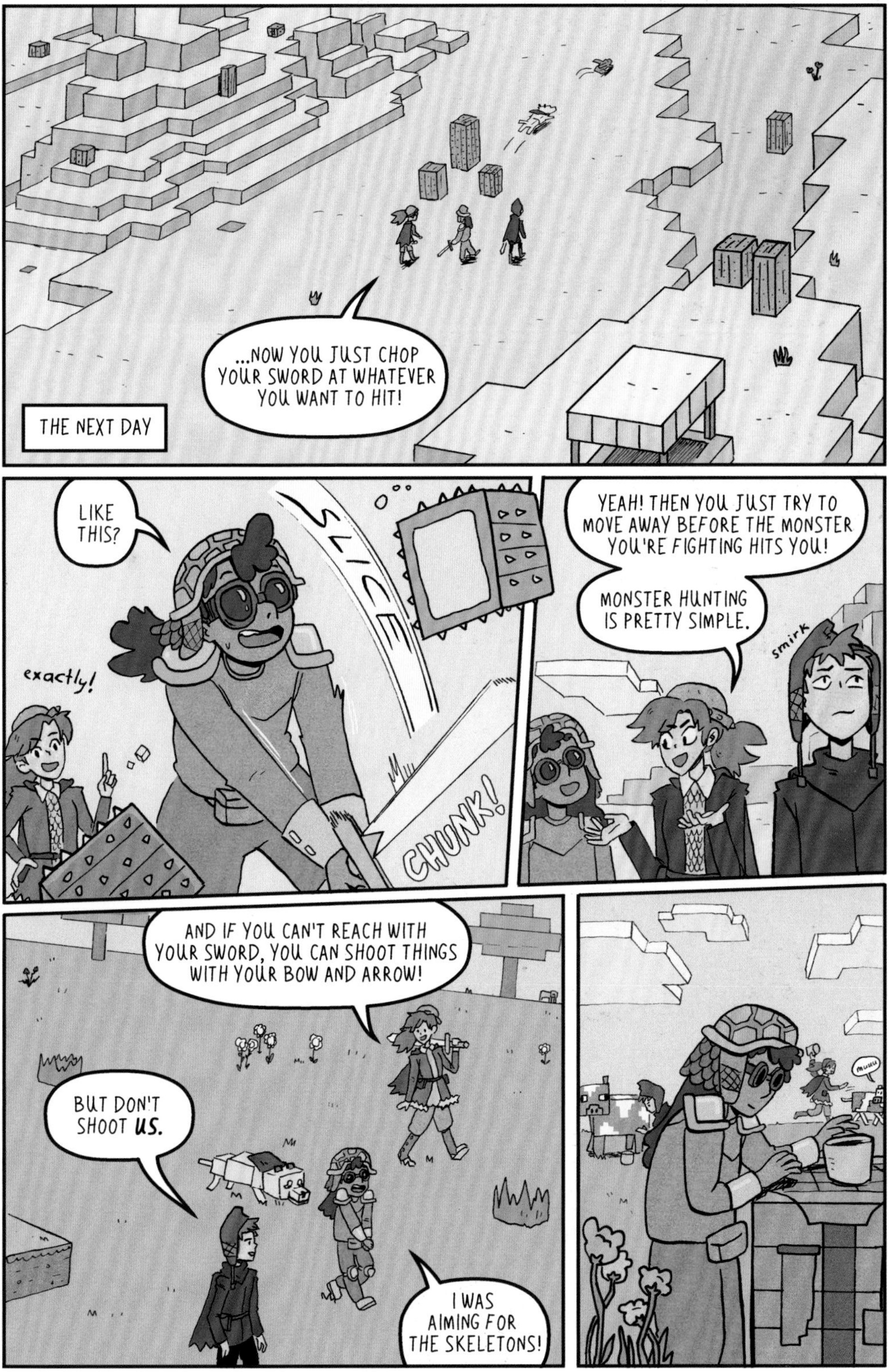
...NOW YOU JUST CHOP YOUR SWORD AT WHATEVER YOU WANT TO HIT!
THE NEXT DAY
LIKE THIS?
SLICE
CHUNK!
exactly!
YEAH! THEN YOU JUST TRY TO MOVE AWAY BEFORE THE MONSTER YOU'RE FIGHTING HITS YOU!
MONSTER HUNTING IS PRETTY SIMPLE.
smirk
AND IF YOU CAN'T REACH WITH YOUR SWORD, YOU CAN SHOOT THINGS WITH YOUR BOW AND ARROW!
BUT DON'T SHOOT US.
I WAS AIMING FOR THE SKELETONS!

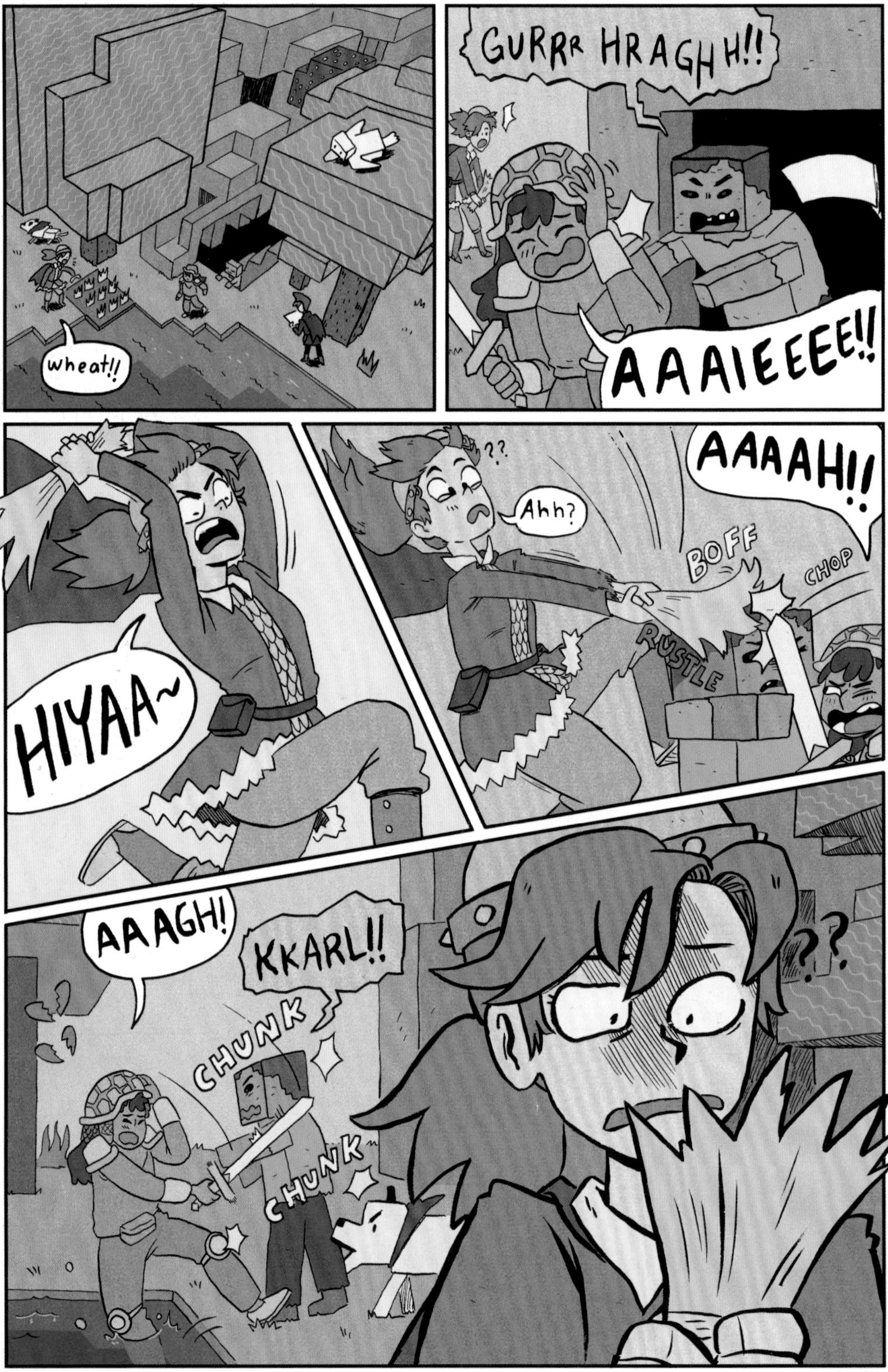
wheat!!
GURRR HRAGHH!!
AAAIEEEE!!
HIYAA~
??
Ahh?
AAAAH!!
BOFF
CHOP
RUSTLE
AAAGH!
KKARL!!
CHUNK
CHUNK
??

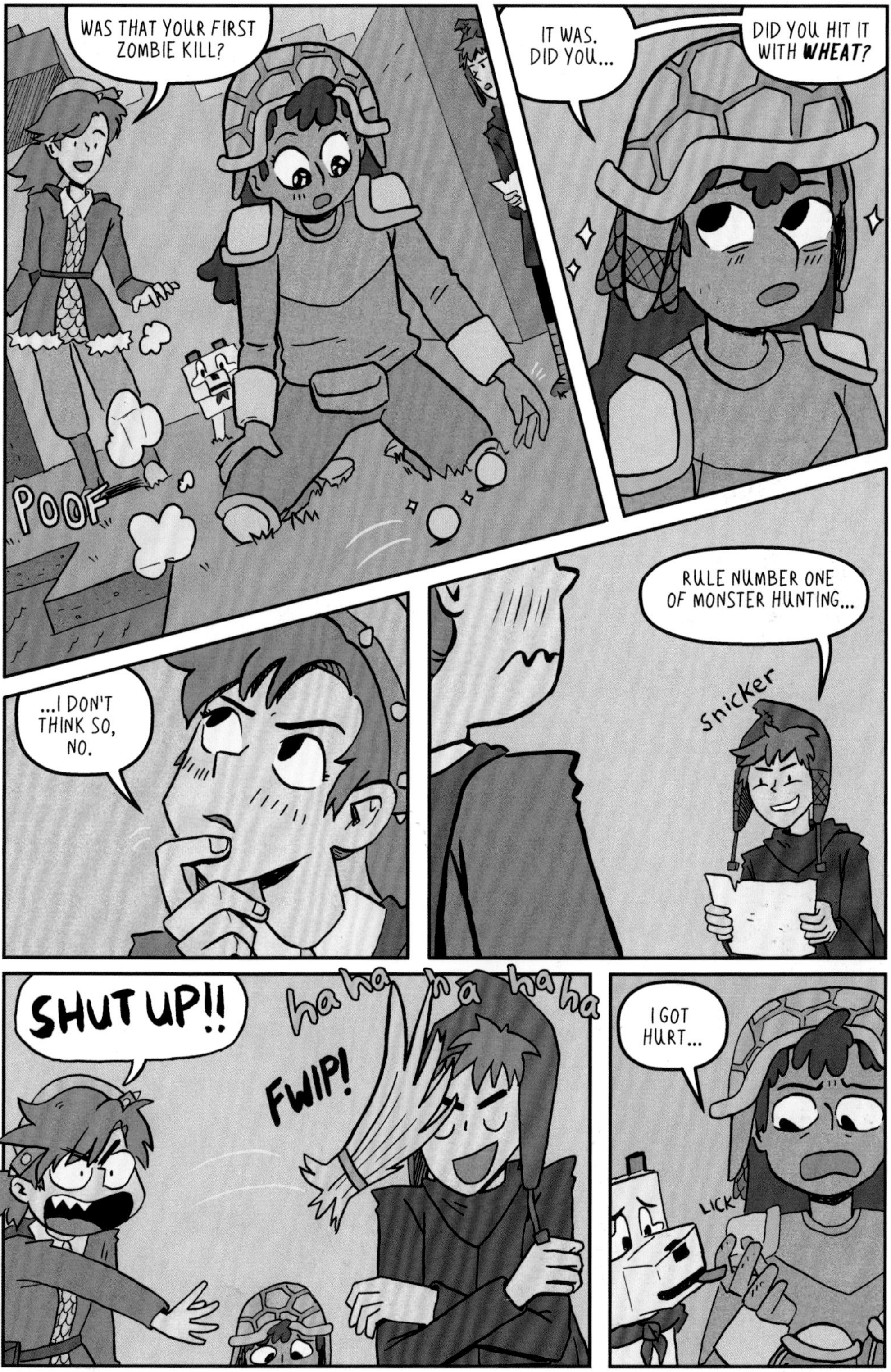
WAS THAT YOUR FIRST ZOMBIE KILL?
POOF
IT WAS. DID YOU...
DID YOU HIT IT WITH WHEAT?
...I DON'T THINK SO, NO.
RULE NUMBER ONE OF MONSTER HUNTING...
Snicker
SHUT UP!!
ha ha ha ha ha
FWIP!
I GOT HURT...
LICK

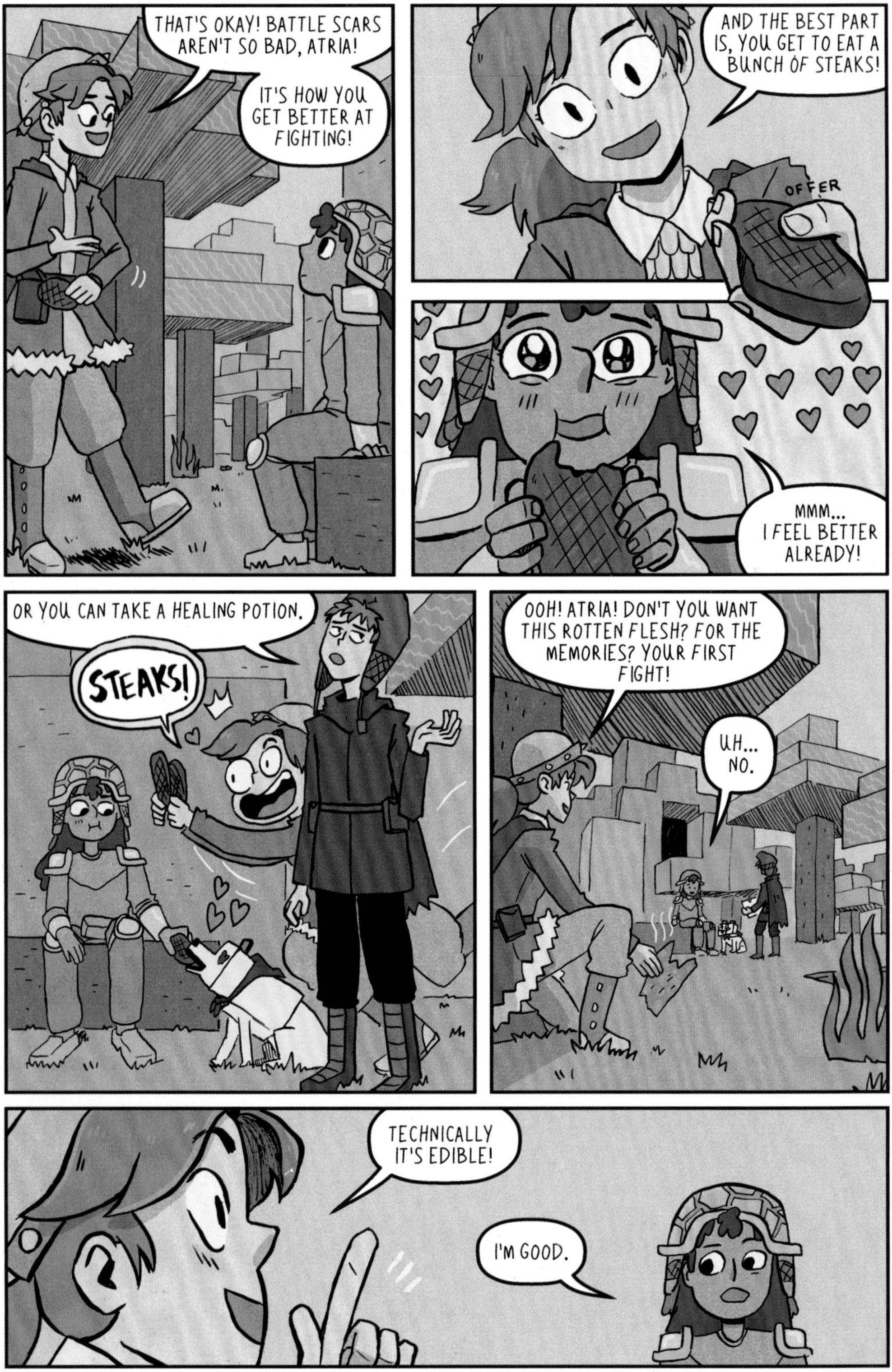
THAT'S OKAY! BATTLE SCARS AREN'T SO BAD, ATRIA!
IT'S HOW YOU GET BETTER AT FIGHTING!
AND THE BEST PART IS, YOU GET TO EAT A BUNCH OF STEAKS!
OFFER
MMM... I FEEL BETTER ALREADY!
OR YOU CAN TAKE A HEALING POTION.
STEAKS!
OOH! ATRIA! DON'T YOU WANT THIS ROTTEN FLESH? FOR THE MEMORIES? YOUR FIRST FIGHT!
UH... NO.
TECHNICALLY IT'S EDIBLE!
I'M GOOD.

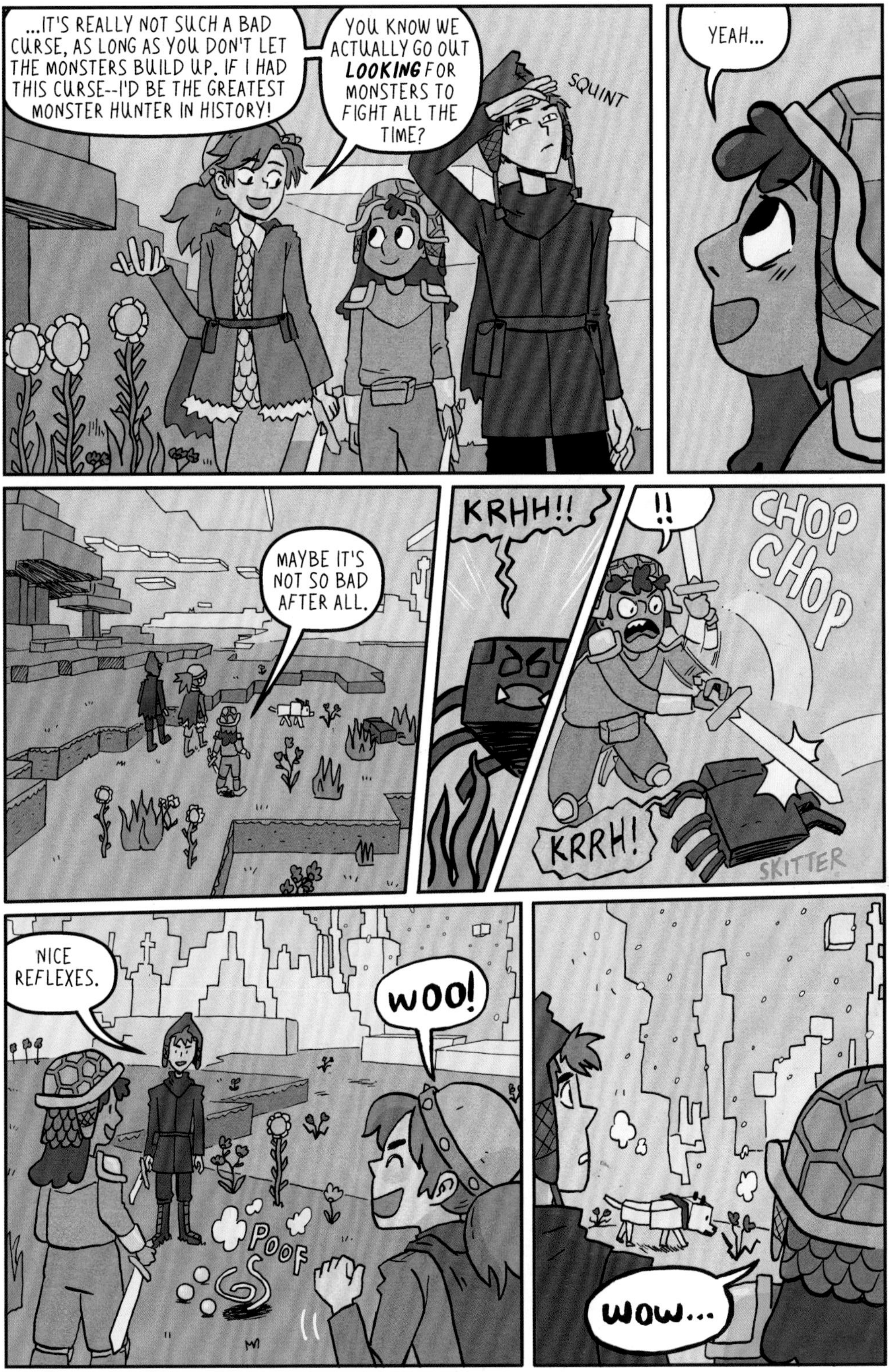
...IT'S REALLY NOT SUCH A BAD CURSE, AS LONG AS YOU DON'T LET THE MONSTERS BUILD UP. IF I HAD THIS CURSE--I'D BE THE GREATEST MONSTER HUNTER IN HISTORY!
YOU KNOW WE ACTUALLY GO OUT **LOOKING** FOR MONSTERS TO FIGHT ALL THE TIME?
SQUINT
YEAH...
MAYBE IT'S NOT SO BAD AFTER ALL.
KRHH!!
!!
CHOP CHOP
KRRH!
SKITTER
NICE REFLEXES.
WOO!
POOF
WOW...

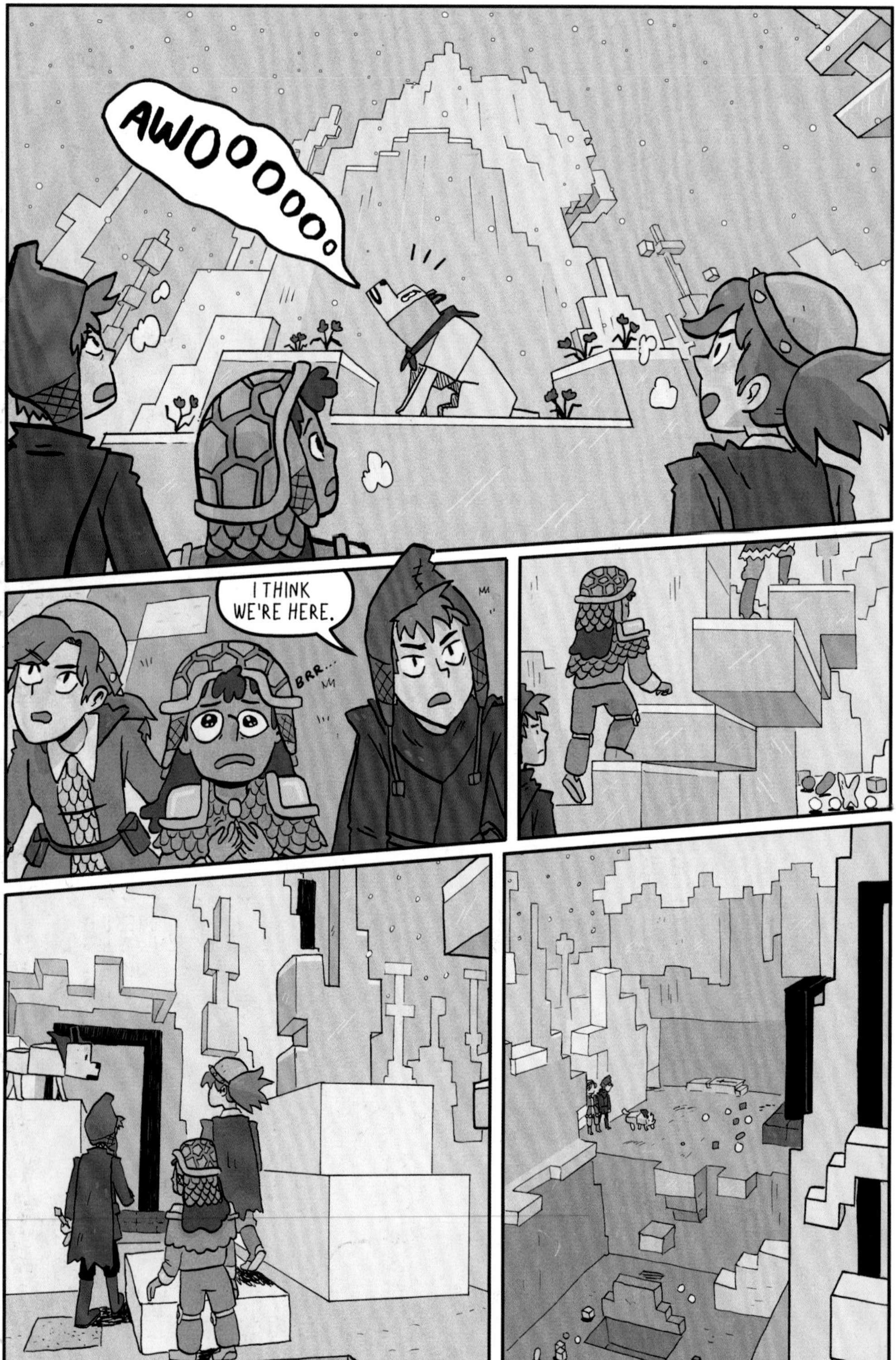
AWOOOOOO
I THINK WE'RE HERE.
BRR...

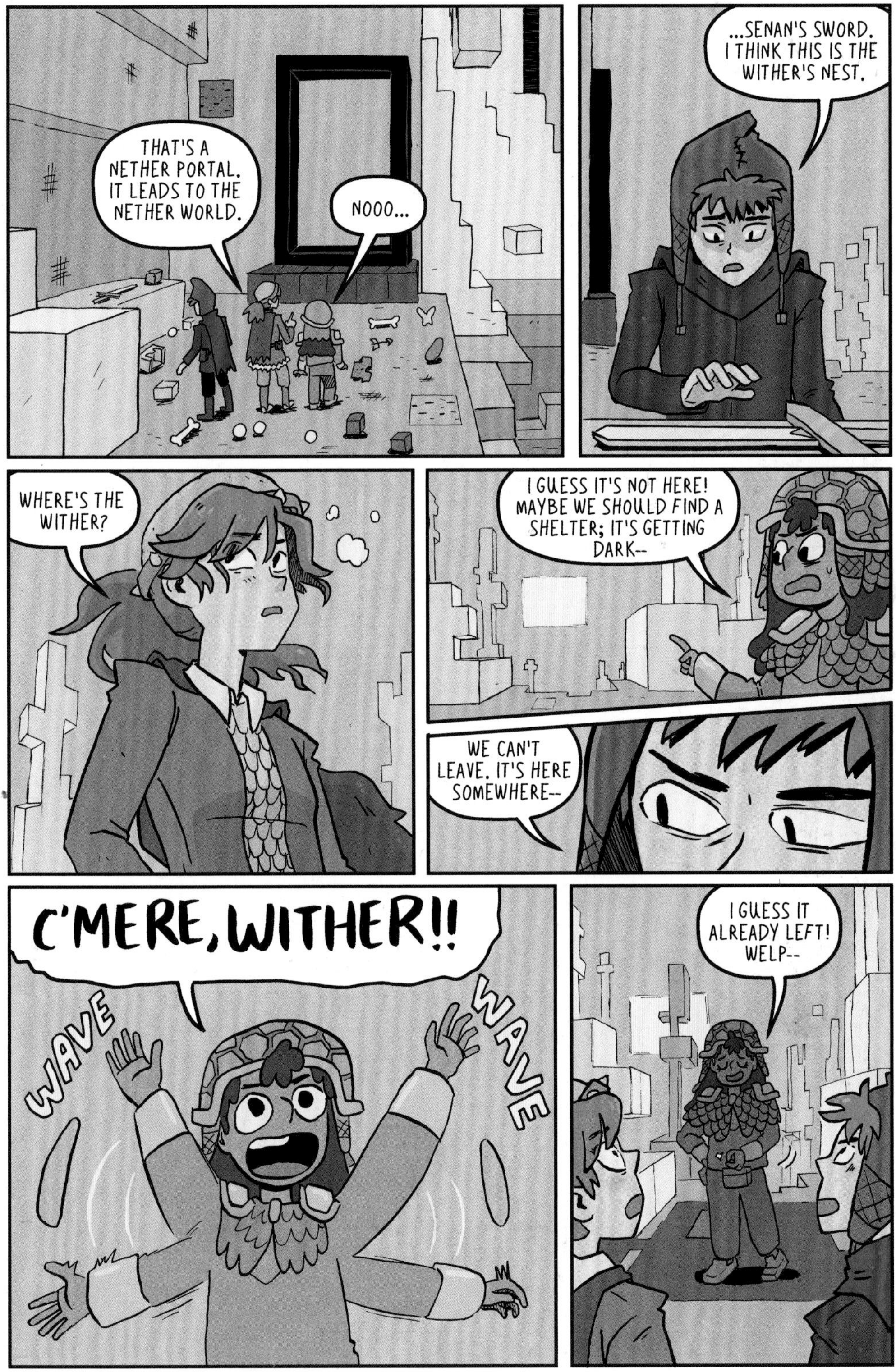
THAT'S A NETHER PORTAL. IT LEADS TO THE NETHER WORLD.
NOOO...
...SENAN'S SWORD. I THINK THIS IS THE WITHER'S NEST.
WHERE'S THE WITHER?
I GUESS IT'S NOT HERE! MAYBE WE SHOULD FIND A SHELTER; IT'S GETTING DARK--
WE CAN'T LEAVE. IT'S HERE SOMEWHERE--
C'MERE, WITHER!!
WAVE
WAVE
I GUESS IT ALREADY LEFT! WELP--

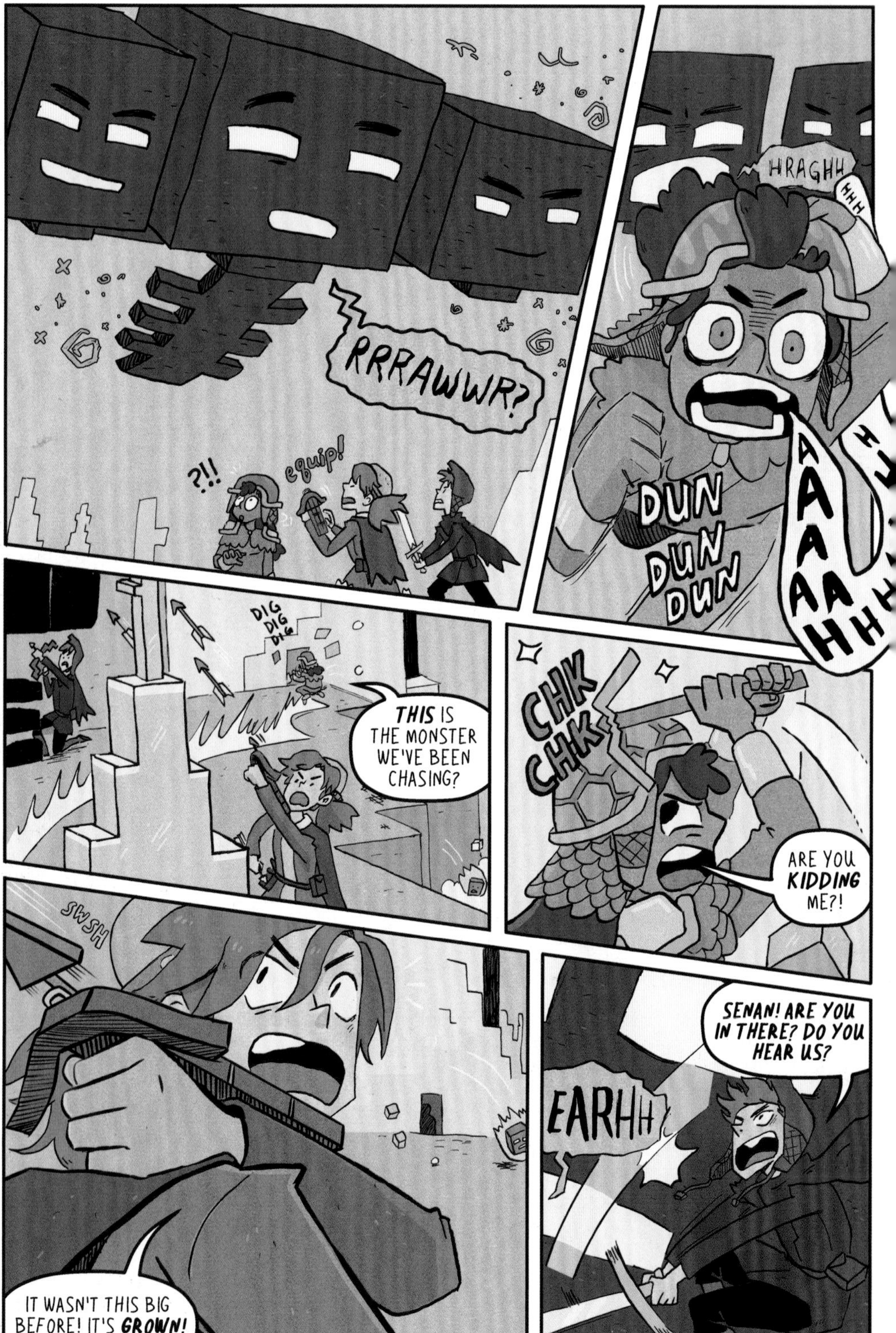
RRRAWWR?
?!!
equip!
HRAGHHHH
AAAAAHH
DUN DUN DUN
DIG DIG DIG
THIS IS THE MONSTER WE'VE BEEN CHASING?
CHK CHK
ARE YOU KIDDING ME?!
SWSH
IT WASN'T THIS BIG BEFORE! IT'S GROWN!
SENAN! ARE YOU IN THERE? DO YOU HEAR US?
EARHH

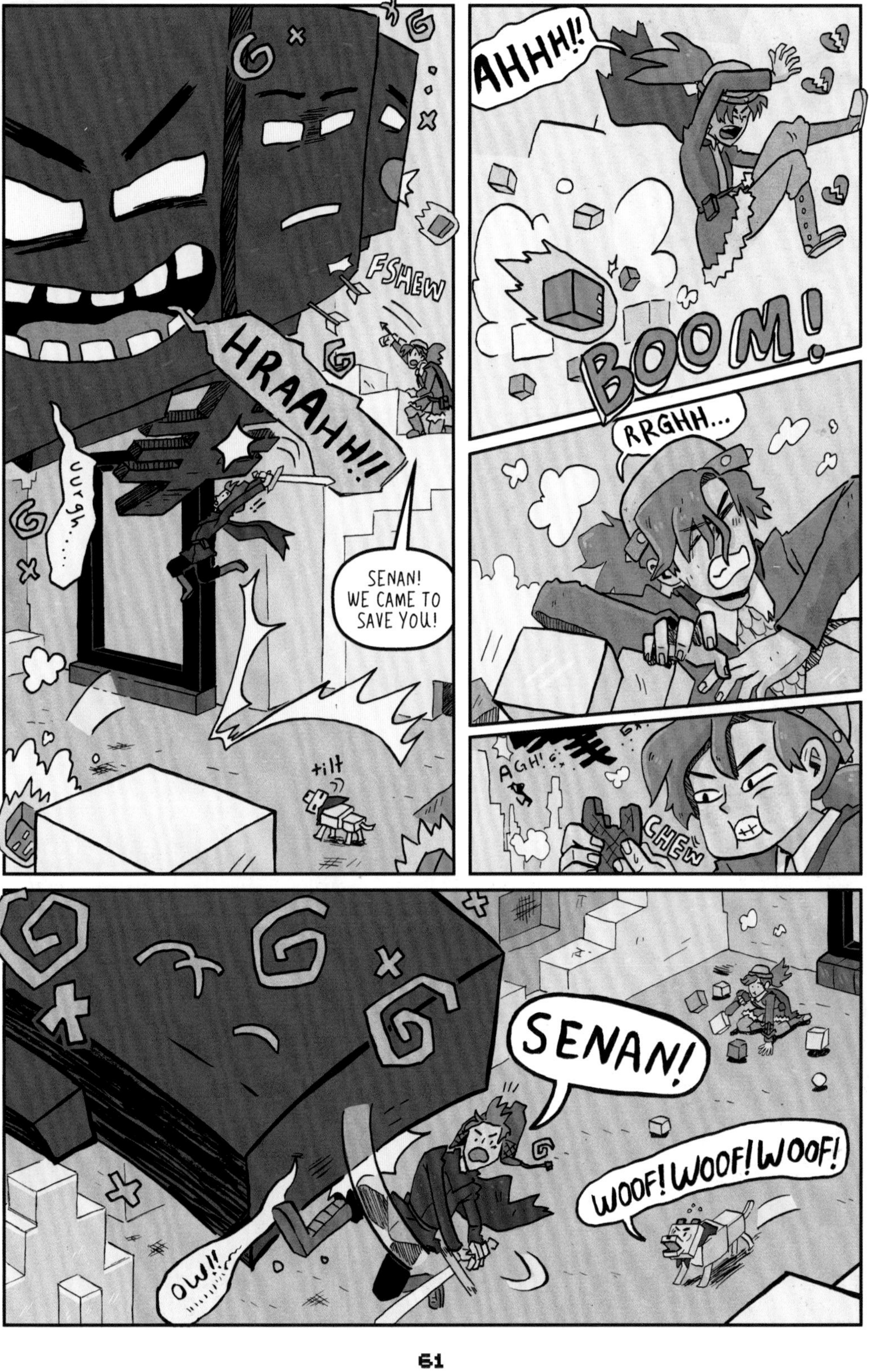
FSHEW
HRAAHH!!!
UURGH.....
SENAN! WE CAME TO SAVE YOU!
TILT
AHHH!!
BOOM!
RRGHH...
AGH!
CHEW
SENAN!
WOOF! WOOF! WOOF!
OW!!

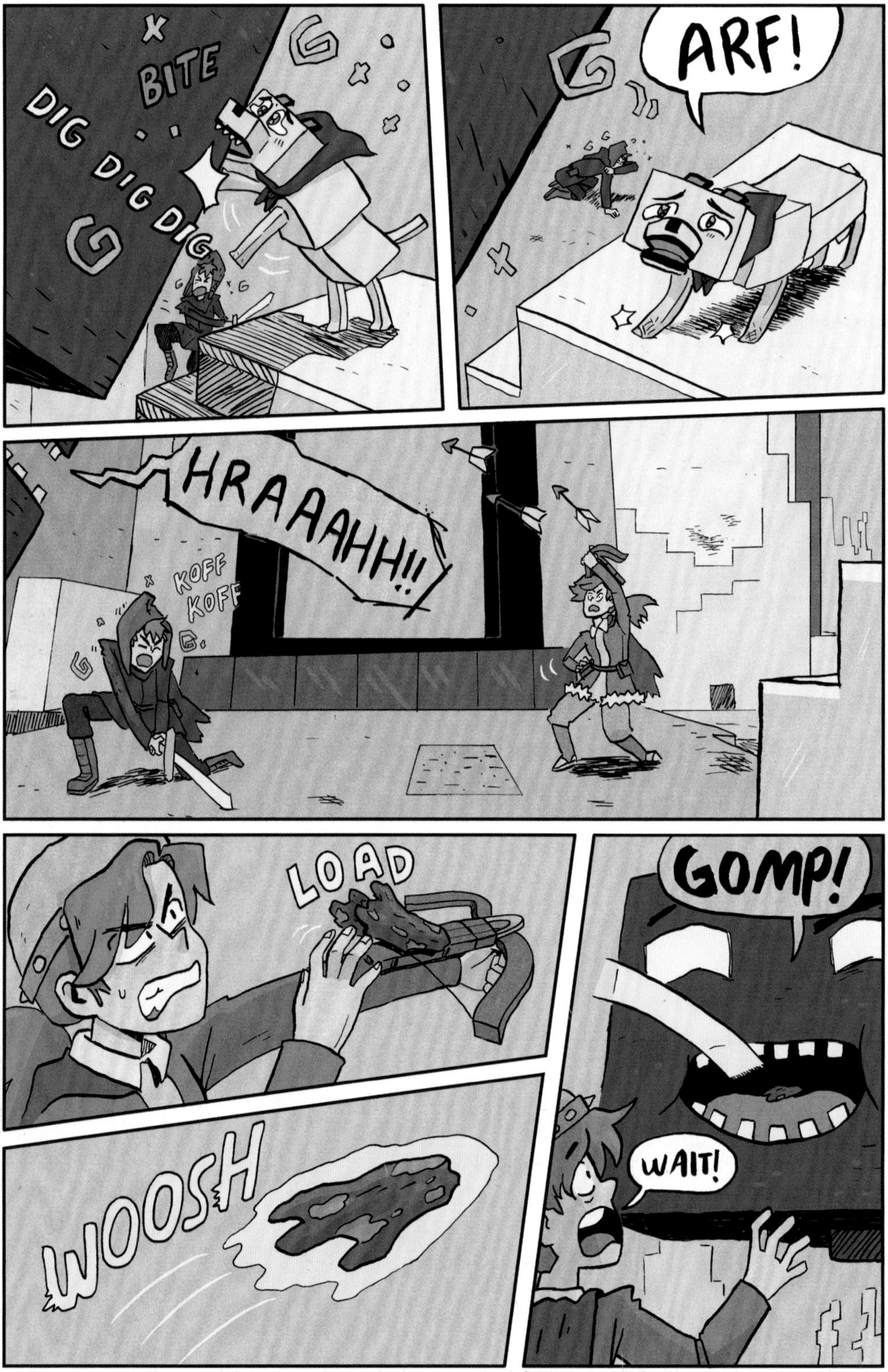
BITE
DIG DIG DIG DIG
ARF!
HRAAAHH!!
KOFF
KOFF
LOAD
WOOSH
GOMP!
WAIT!

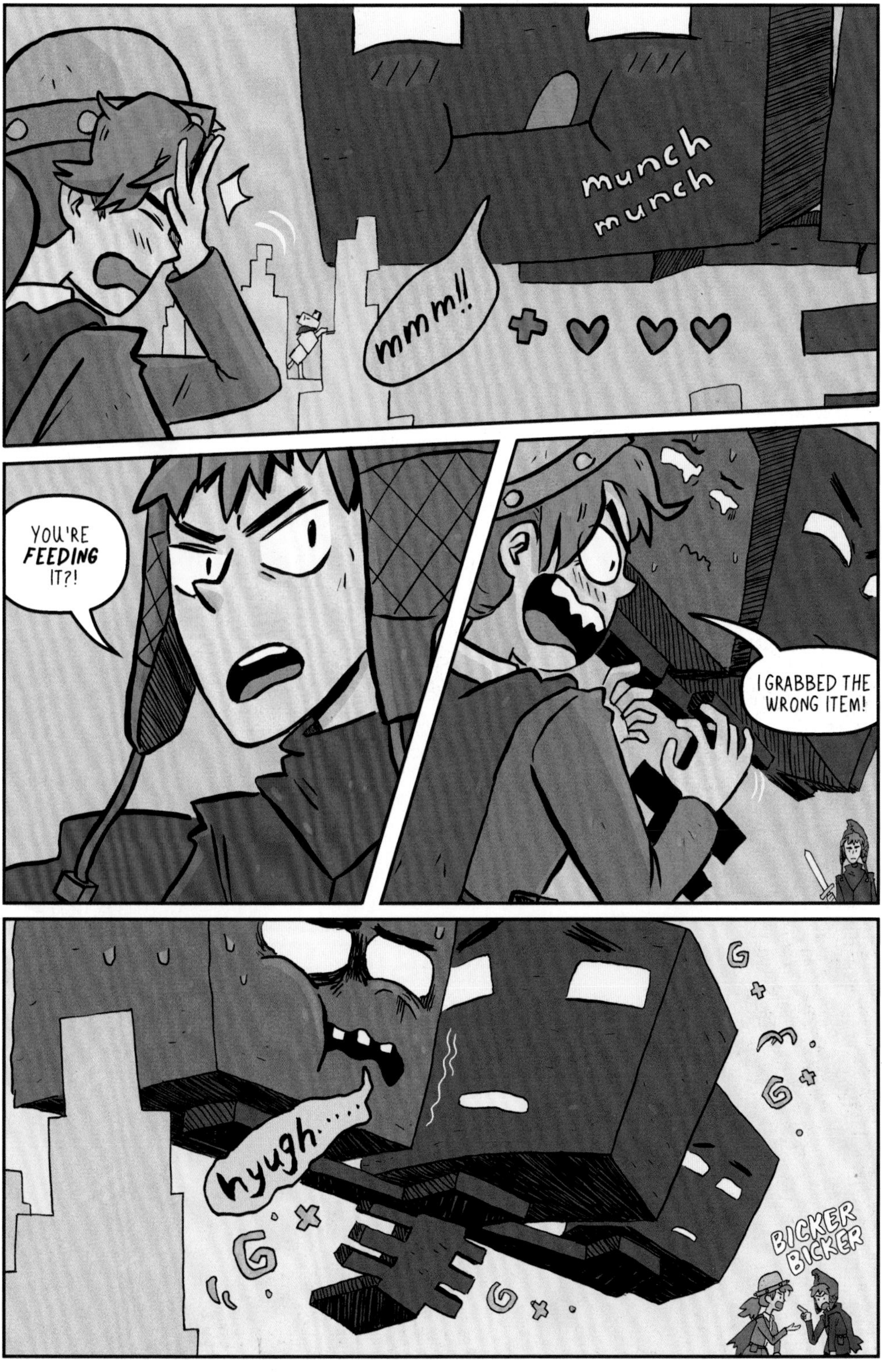
munch
munch
mmm!!
YOU'RE FEEDING IT?!
I GRABBED THE WRONG ITEM!
hyugh.....
BICKER BICKER

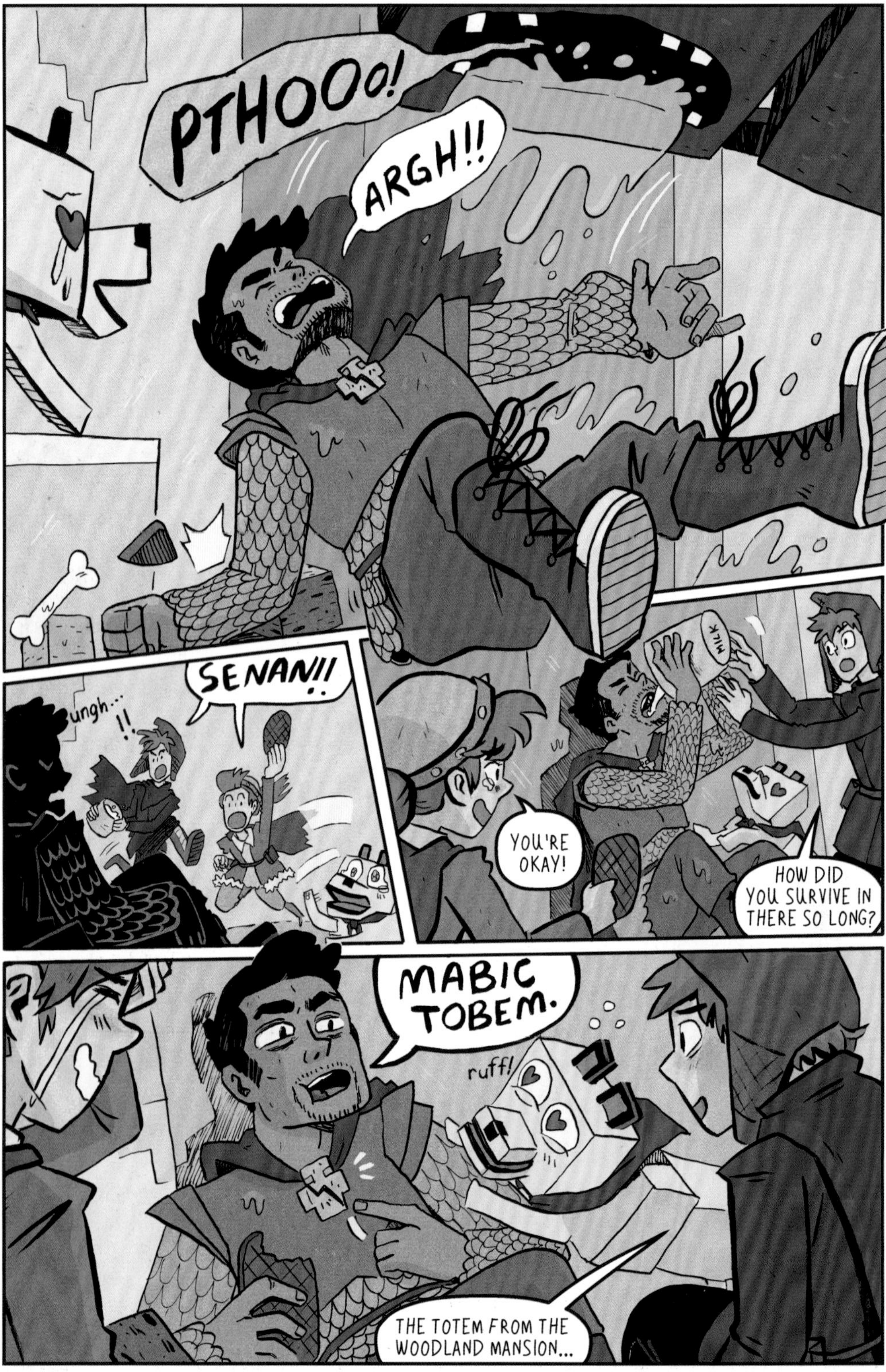
PTHOOo!
ARGH!!
SENAN!!
ungh...
!!
MILK
YOU'RE OKAY!
HOW DID YOU SURVIVE IN THERE SO LONG?
MABIC TOBEM.
ruff!
THE TOTEM FROM THE WOODLAND MANSION...

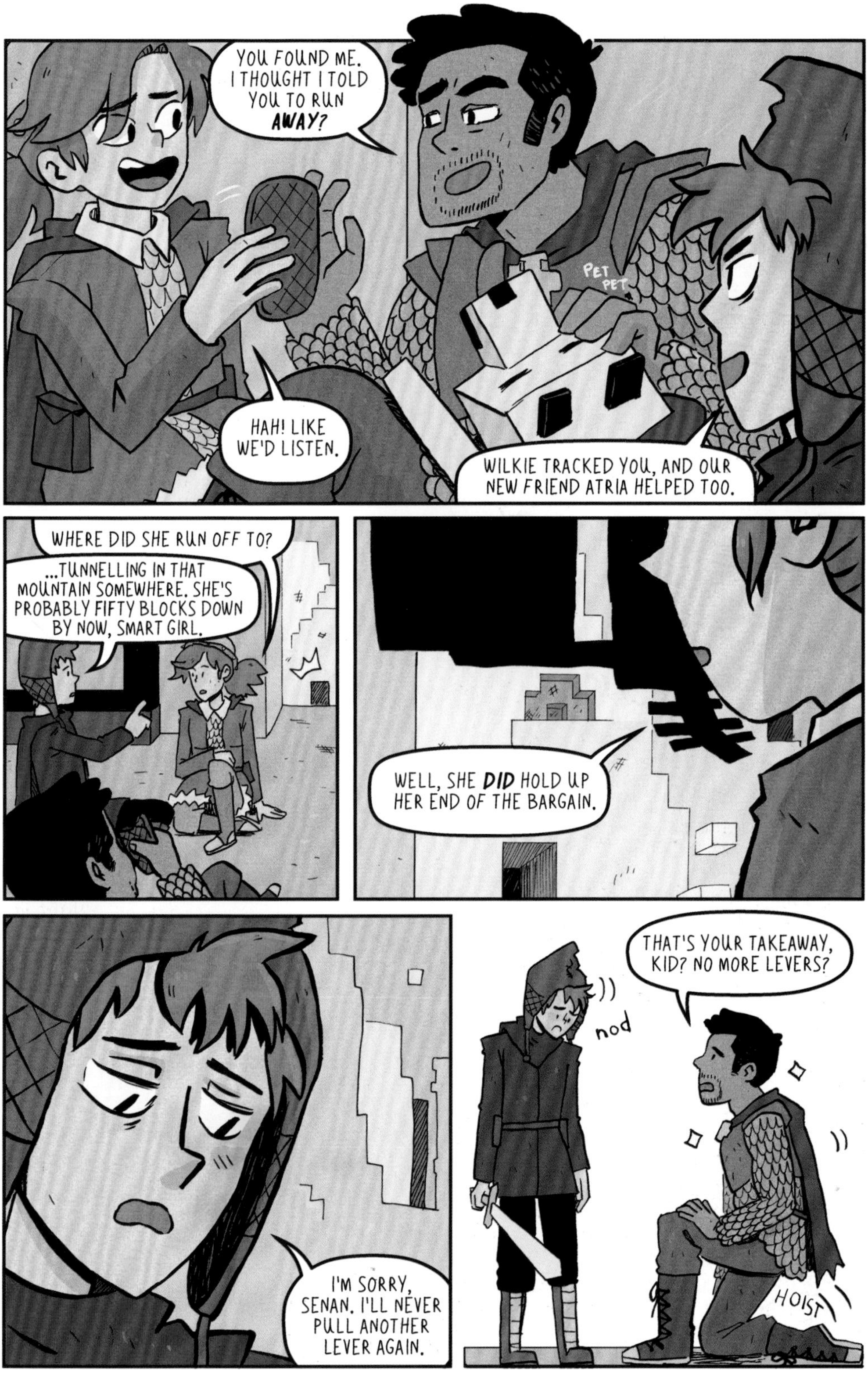
YOU FOUND ME. I THOUGHT I TOLD YOU TO RUN **AWAY**?
HAH! LIKE WE'D LISTEN.
PET PET
WILKIE TRACKED YOU, AND OUR NEW FRIEND ATRIA HELPED TOO.
WHERE DID SHE RUN OFF TO?
...TUNNELLING IN THAT MOUNTAIN SOMEWHERE. SHE'S PROBABLY FIFTY BLOCKS DOWN BY NOW, SMART GIRL.
WELL, SHE **DID** HOLD UP HER END OF THE BARGAIN.
I'M SORRY, SENAN. I'LL NEVER PULL ANOTHER LEVER AGAIN.
nod
THAT'S YOUR TAKEAWAY, KID? NO MORE LEVERS?
HOIST

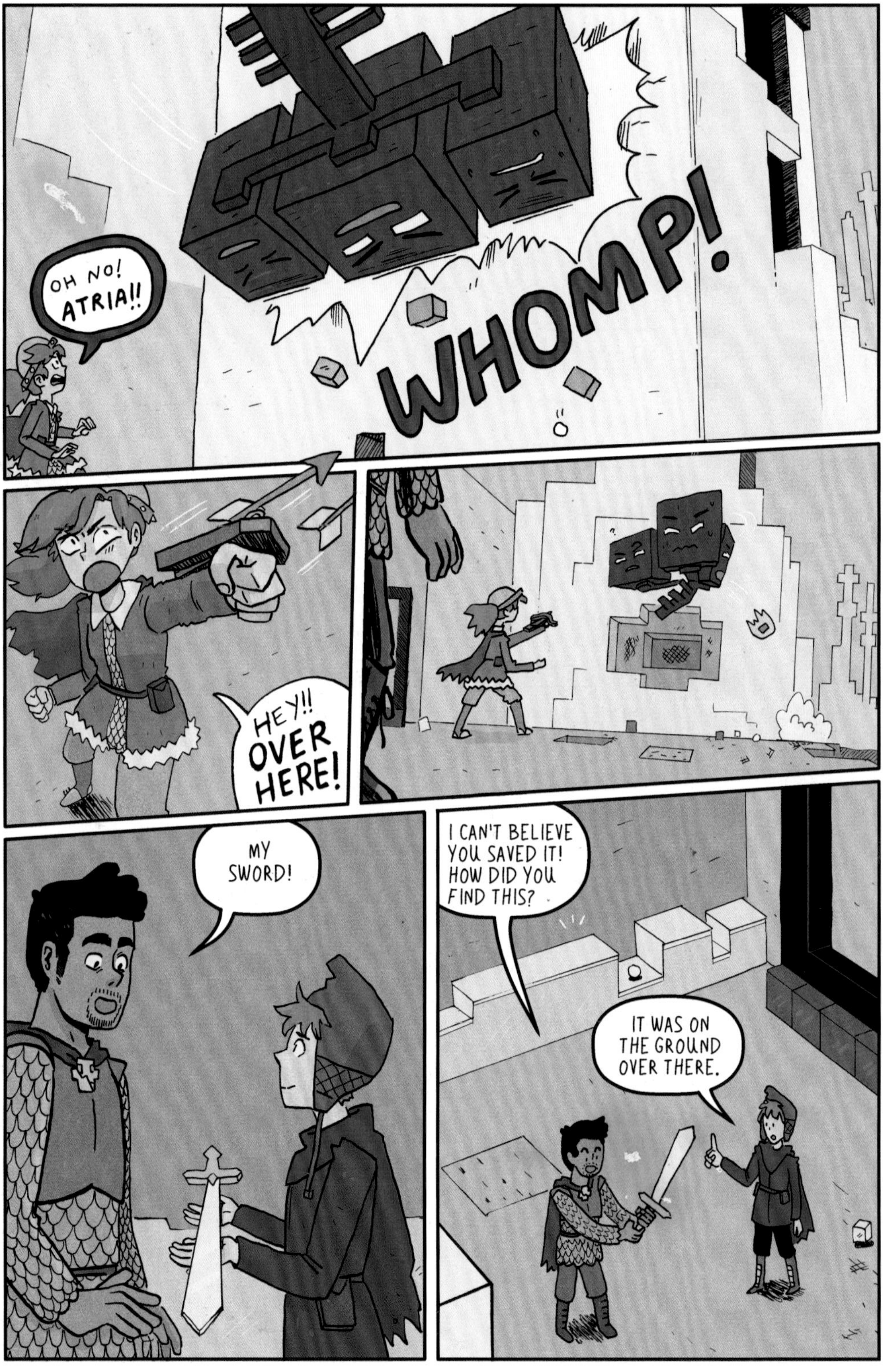
OH NO! ATRIA!!
WHOMP!
HEY!! OVER HERE!
MY SWORD!
I CAN'T BELIEVE YOU SAVED IT! HOW DID YOU FIND THIS?
IT WAS ON THE GROUND OVER THERE.

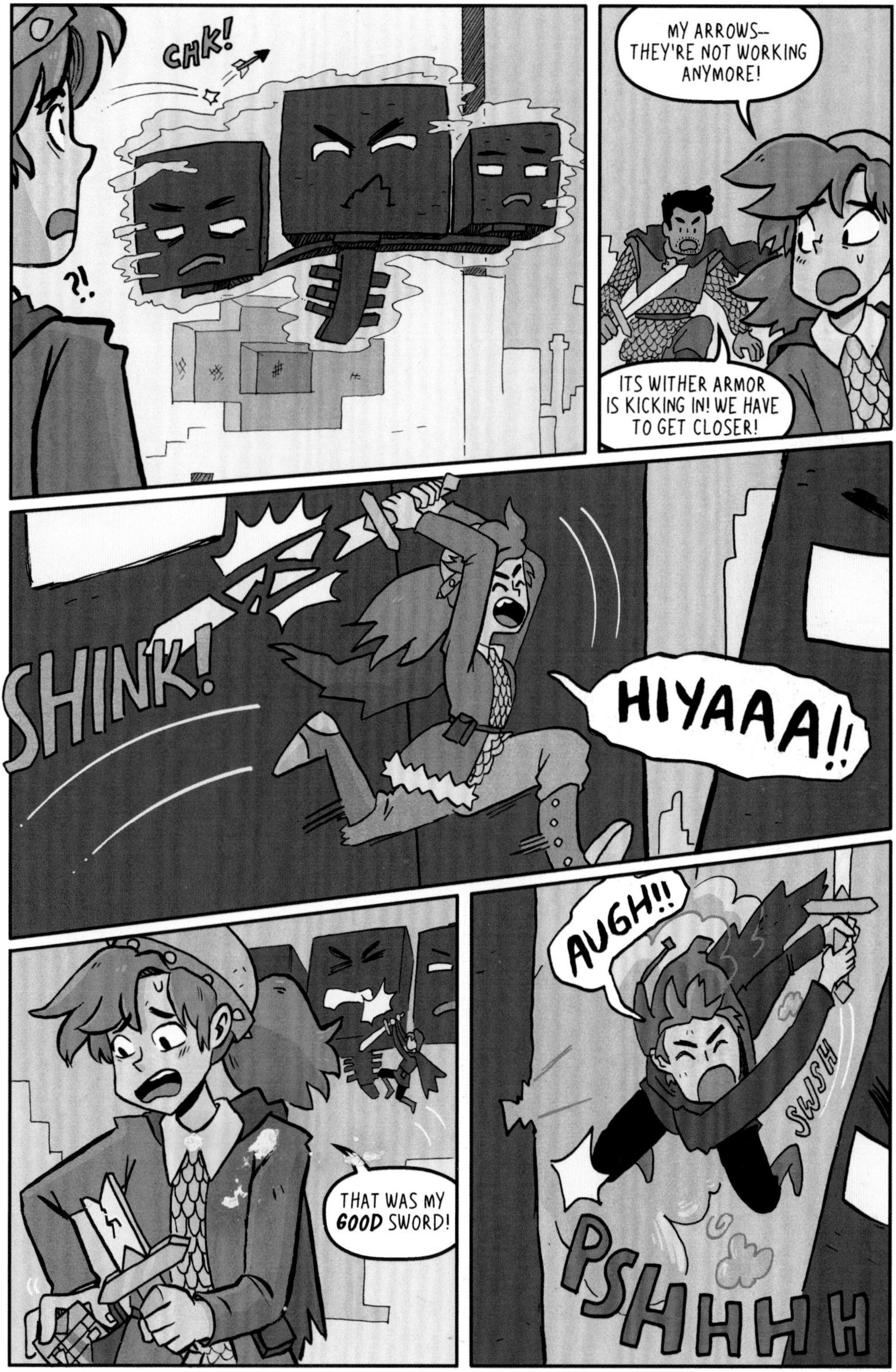
CHK!
?!
MY ARROWS-- THEY'RE NOT WORKING ANYMORE!
ITS WITHER ARMOR IS KICKING IN! WE HAVE TO GET CLOSER!
SHINK!
HIYAAA!!
THAT WAS MY GOOD SWORD!
AUGH!!
SWSH
PSHHHH

COUGH COUGH COUGH

ORION! HEAL UP!

CHUG CHUG

DO WE HAVE ANY IDEA HOW MANY MORE HEARTS THIS THING HAS?

WAG WAG

IF THIS WAS YOUR AVERAGE WITHER, WE'D HAVE DEFEATED IT BY NOW.

BUT THIS THING IS A FREAK OF NATURE. I'VE NEVER SEEN A WITHER SO HUGE.

SO WHAT DO WE DO?

WE FIGHT!

ARF!

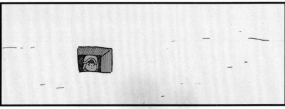

THEY DON'T LOOK LIKE THEY'RE DOING WELL...

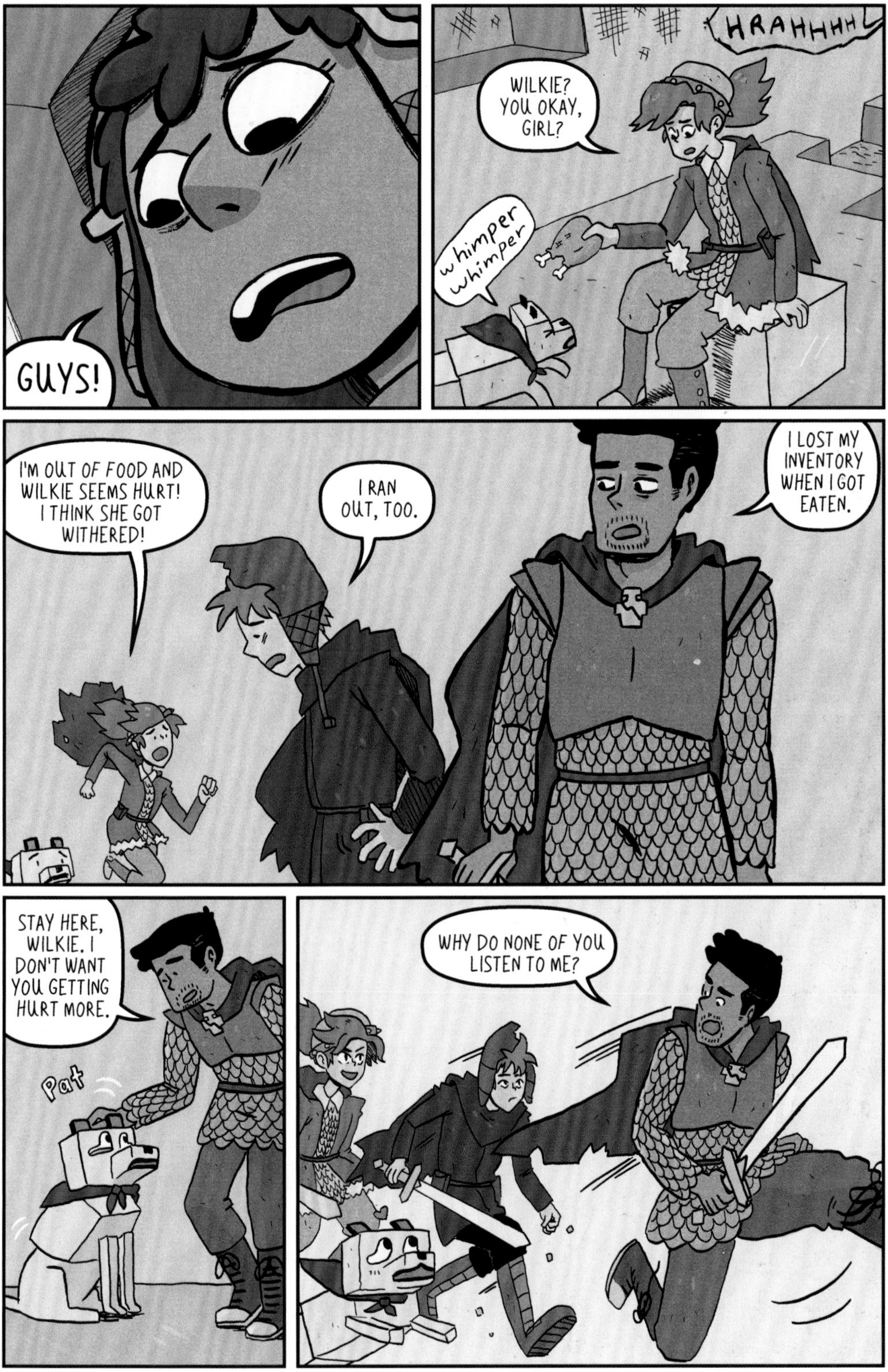
GUYS!
HRAHHHH
WILKIE? YOU OKAY, GIRL?
whimper whimper
I'M OUT OF FOOD AND WILKIE SEEMS HURT! I THINK SHE GOT WITHERED!
I RAN OUT, TOO.
I LOST MY INVENTORY WHEN I GOT EATEN.
STAY HERE, WILKIE. I DON'T WANT YOU GETTING HURT MORE.
Pat
WHY DO NONE OF YOU LISTEN TO ME?

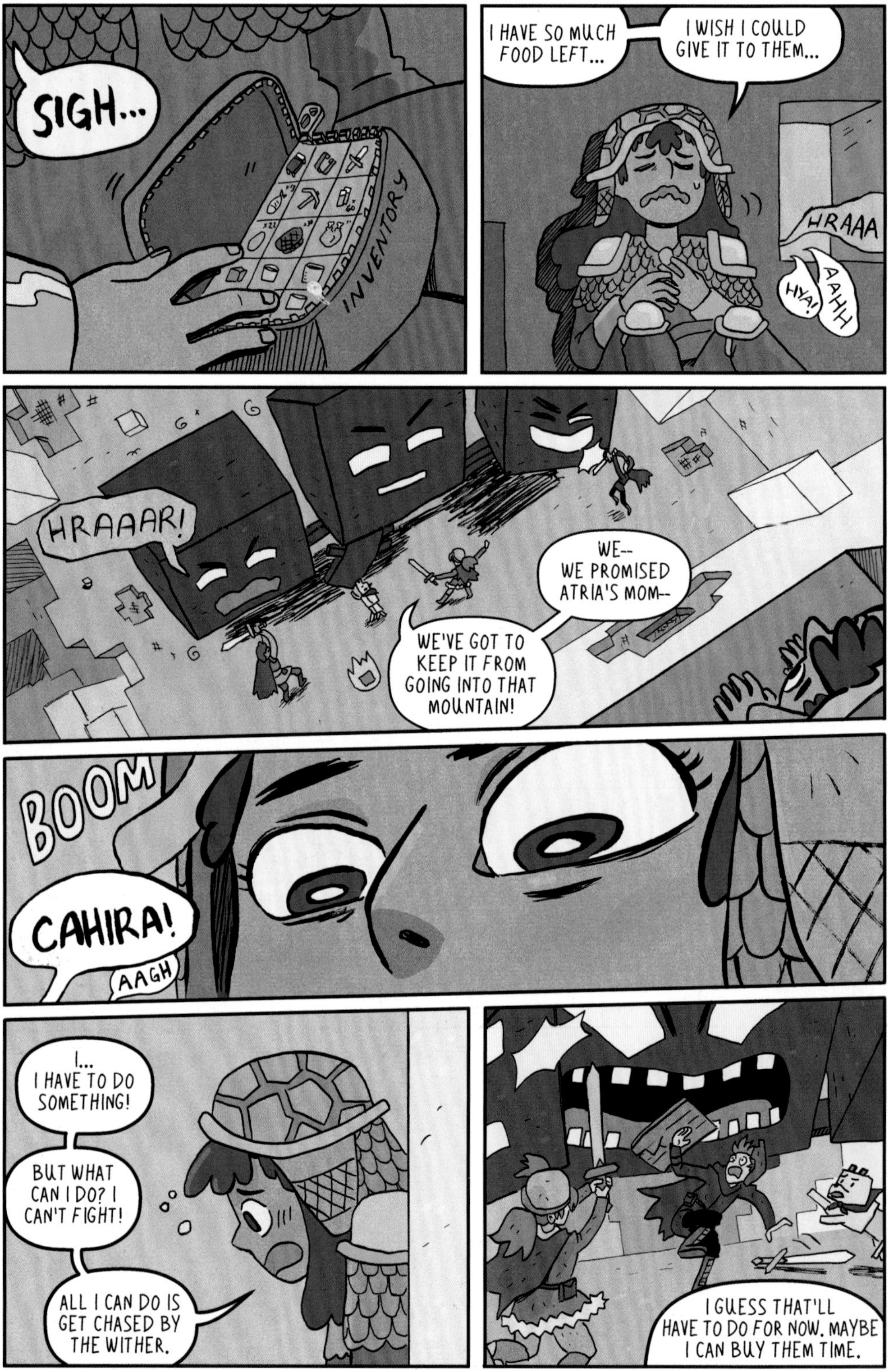
SIGH...
INVENTORY
I HAVE SO MUCH FOOD LEFT...
I WISH I COULD GIVE IT TO THEM...
HRAAA
AAHH
HYA!
HRAAAR!
WE-- WE PROMISED ATRIA'S MOM--
WE'VE GOT TO KEEP IT FROM GOING INTO THAT MOUNTAIN!
BOOM
CAHIRA!
AAGH
I... I HAVE TO DO SOMETHING!
BUT WHAT CAN I DO? I CAN'T FIGHT!
ALL I CAN DO IS GET CHASED BY THE WITHER.
I GUESS THAT'LL HAVE TO DO FOR NOW. MAYBE I CAN BUY THEM TIME.

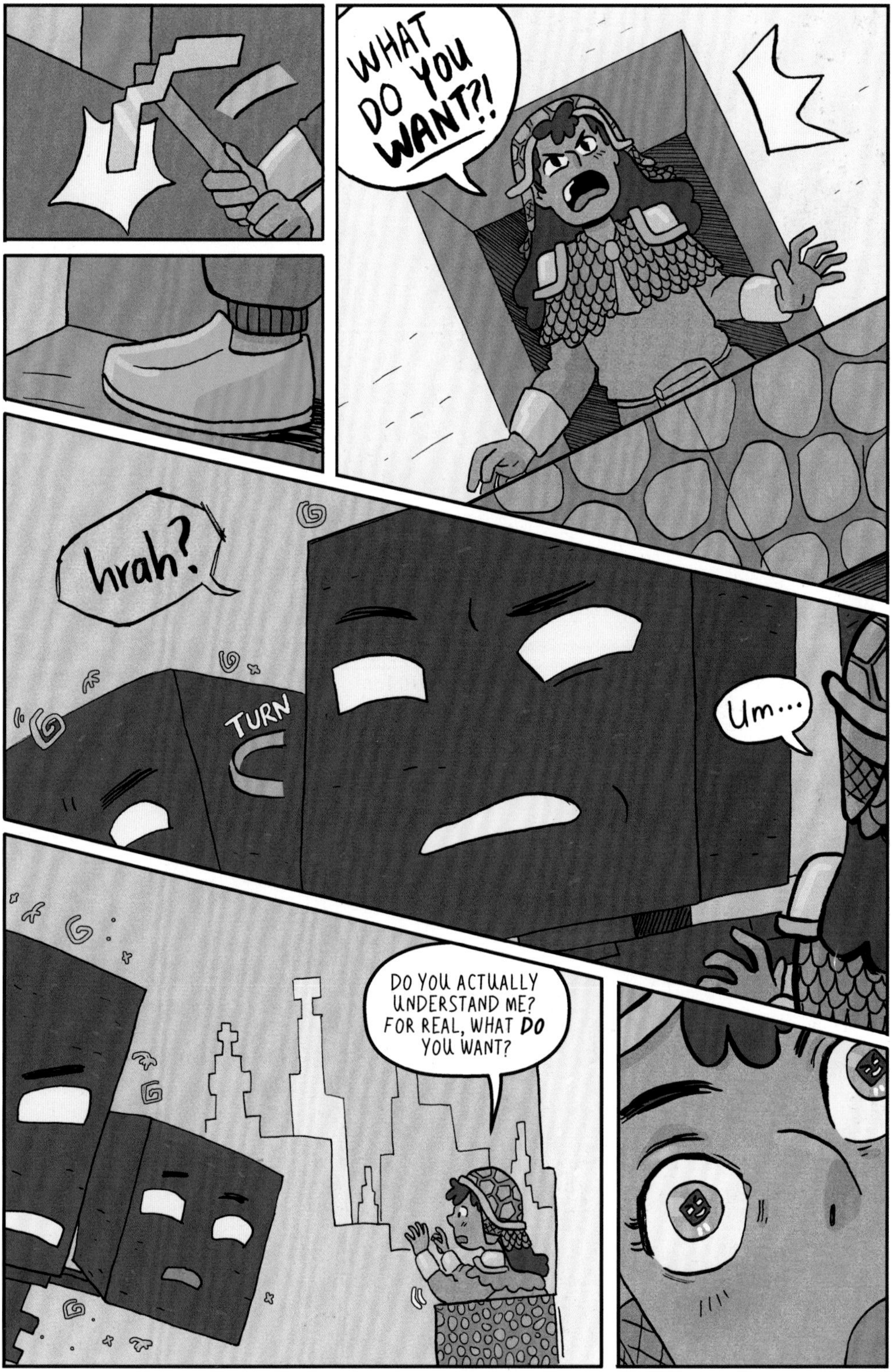
WHAT DO YOU WANT?!
hrah?
TURN
Um...
DO YOU ACTUALLY UNDERSTAND ME? FOR REAL, WHAT DO YOU WANT?

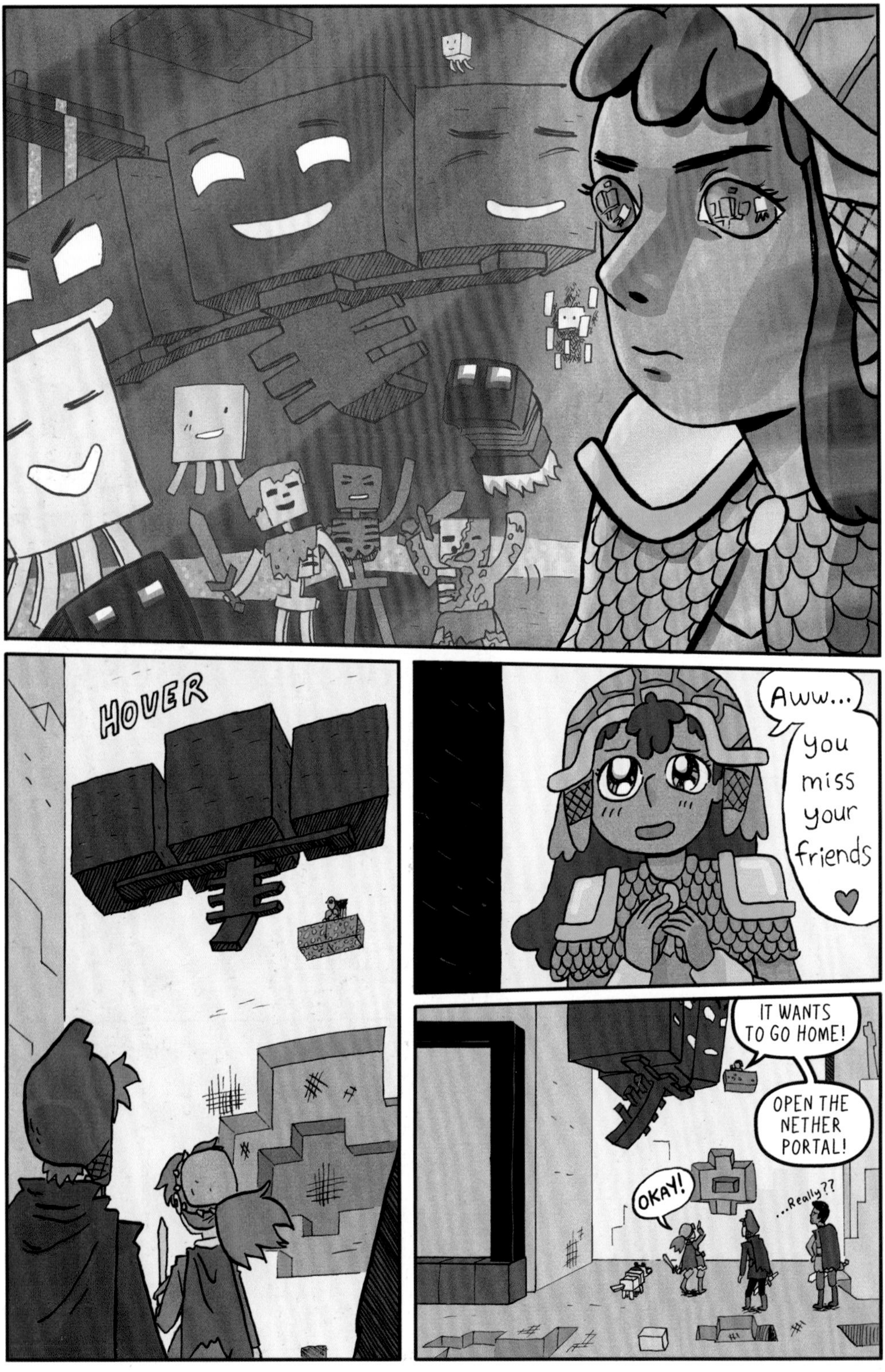
HOVER
Aww...
you miss your friends ♥
IT WANTS TO GO HOME!
OPEN THE NETHER PORTAL!
OKAY!
...Really??

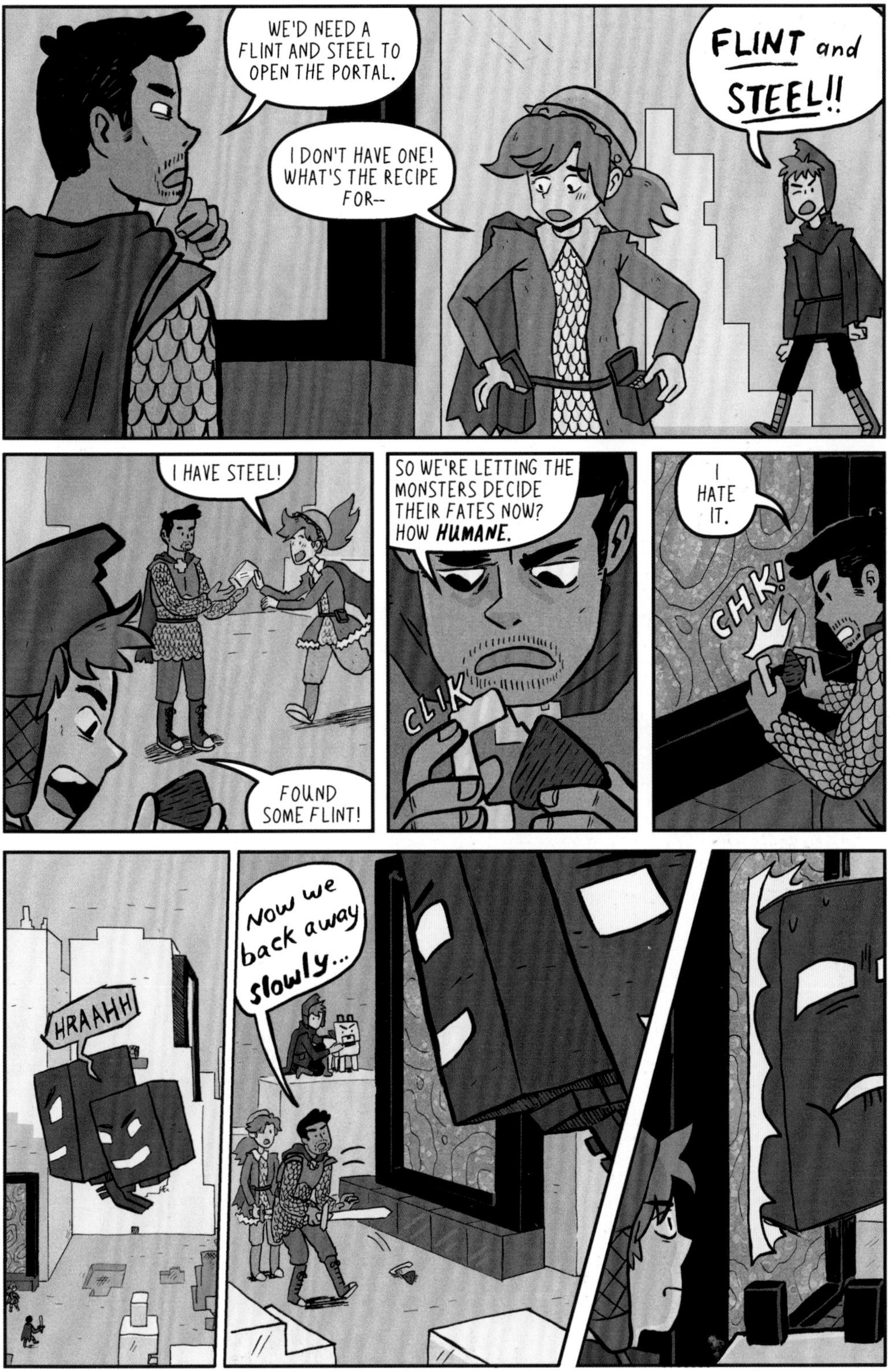
WE'D NEED A FLINT AND STEEL TO OPEN THE PORTAL.
I DON'T HAVE ONE! WHAT'S THE RECIPE FOR--
FLINT and STEEL!!
I HAVE STEEL!
FOUND SOME FLINT!
SO WE'RE LETTING THE MONSTERS DECIDE THEIR FATES NOW? HOW HUMANE.
CLIK
I HATE IT.
CHK!
HRAAHH
Now we back away slowly...

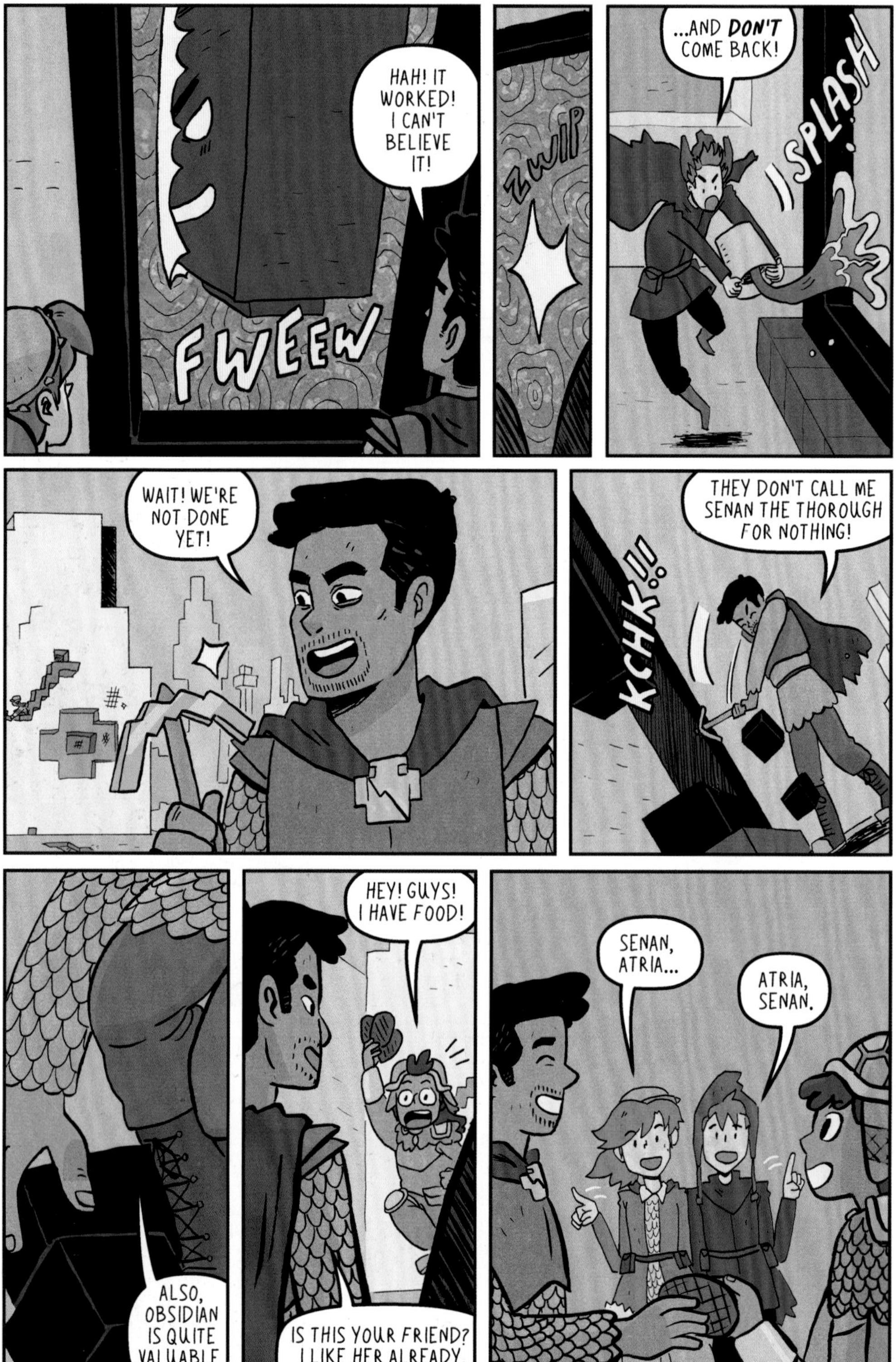
HAH! IT WORKED! I CAN'T BELIEVE IT!
FWEEW
ZWIP
...AND DON'T COME BACK!
SPLASH
WAIT! WE'RE NOT DONE YET!
THEY DON'T CALL ME SENAN THE THOROUGH FOR NOTHING!
KCHK!!
ALSO, OBSIDIAN IS QUITE VALUABLE.
HEY! GUYS! I HAVE FOOD!
IS THIS YOUR FRIEND? I LIKE HER ALREADY.
SENAN, ATRIA...
ATRIA, SENAN.

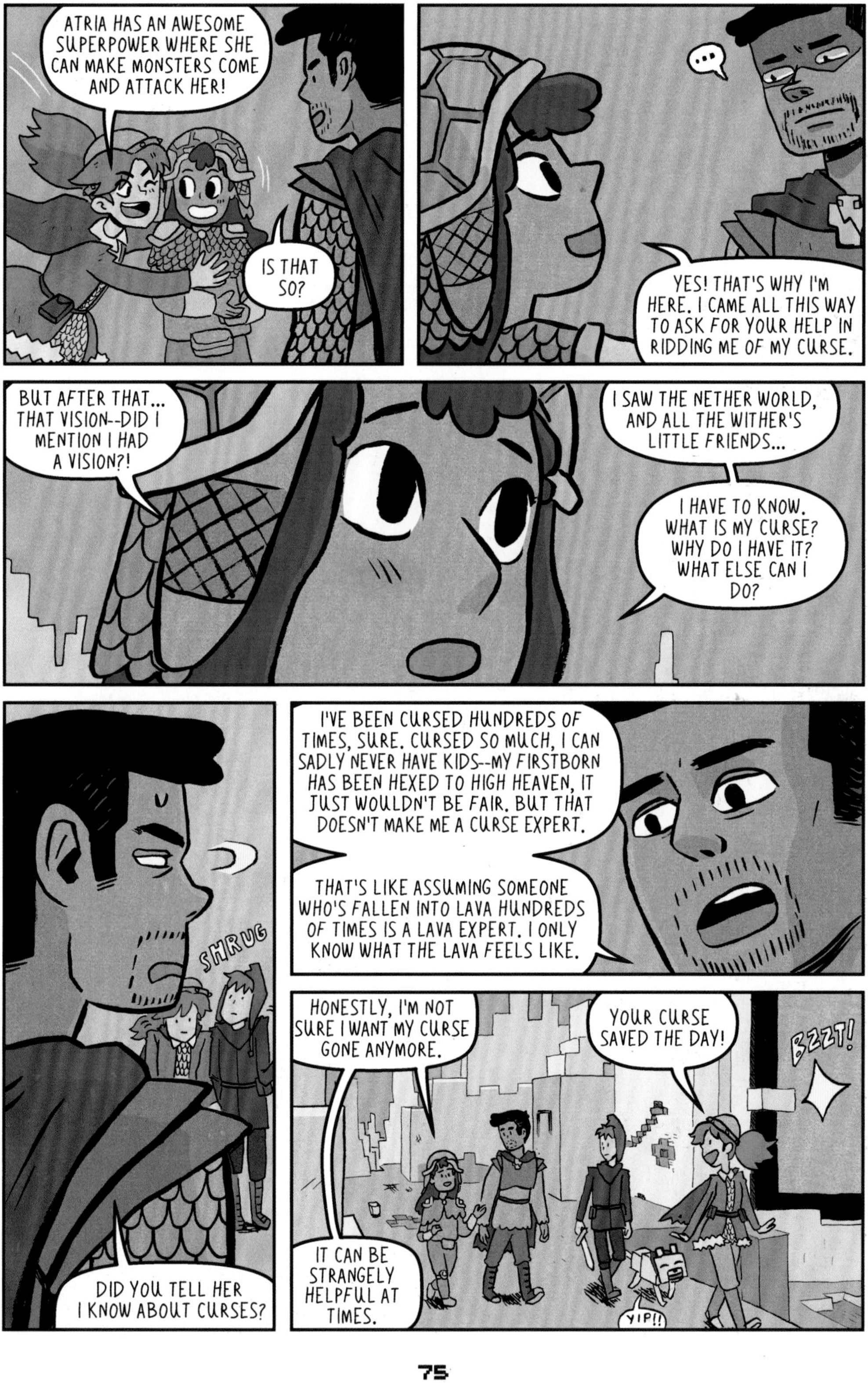
ATRIA HAS AN AWESOME SUPERPOWER WHERE SHE CAN MAKE MONSTERS COME AND ATTACK HER!
IS THAT SO?
...
YES! THAT'S WHY I'M HERE. I CAME ALL THIS WAY TO ASK FOR YOUR HELP IN RIDDING ME OF MY CURSE.
BUT AFTER THAT... THAT VISION--DID I MENTION I HAD A VISION?!
I SAW THE NETHER WORLD, AND ALL THE WITHER'S LITTLE FRIENDS...
I HAVE TO KNOW. WHAT IS MY CURSE? WHY DO I HAVE IT? WHAT ELSE CAN I DO?
SHRUG
DID YOU TELL HER I KNOW ABOUT CURSES?
I'VE BEEN CURSED HUNDREDS OF TIMES, SURE. CURSED SO MUCH, I CAN SADLY NEVER HAVE KIDS--MY FIRSTBORN HAS BEEN HEXED TO HIGH HEAVEN, IT JUST WOULDN'T BE FAIR. BUT THAT DOESN'T MAKE ME A CURSE EXPERT.
THAT'S LIKE ASSUMING SOMEONE WHO'S FALLEN INTO LAVA HUNDREDS OF TIMES IS A LAVA EXPERT. I ONLY KNOW WHAT THE LAVA FEELS LIKE.
HONESTLY, I'M NOT SURE I WANT MY CURSE GONE ANYMORE.
IT CAN BE STRANGELY HELPFUL AT TIMES.
YOUR CURSE SAVED THE DAY!
BZZT!
YIP!!

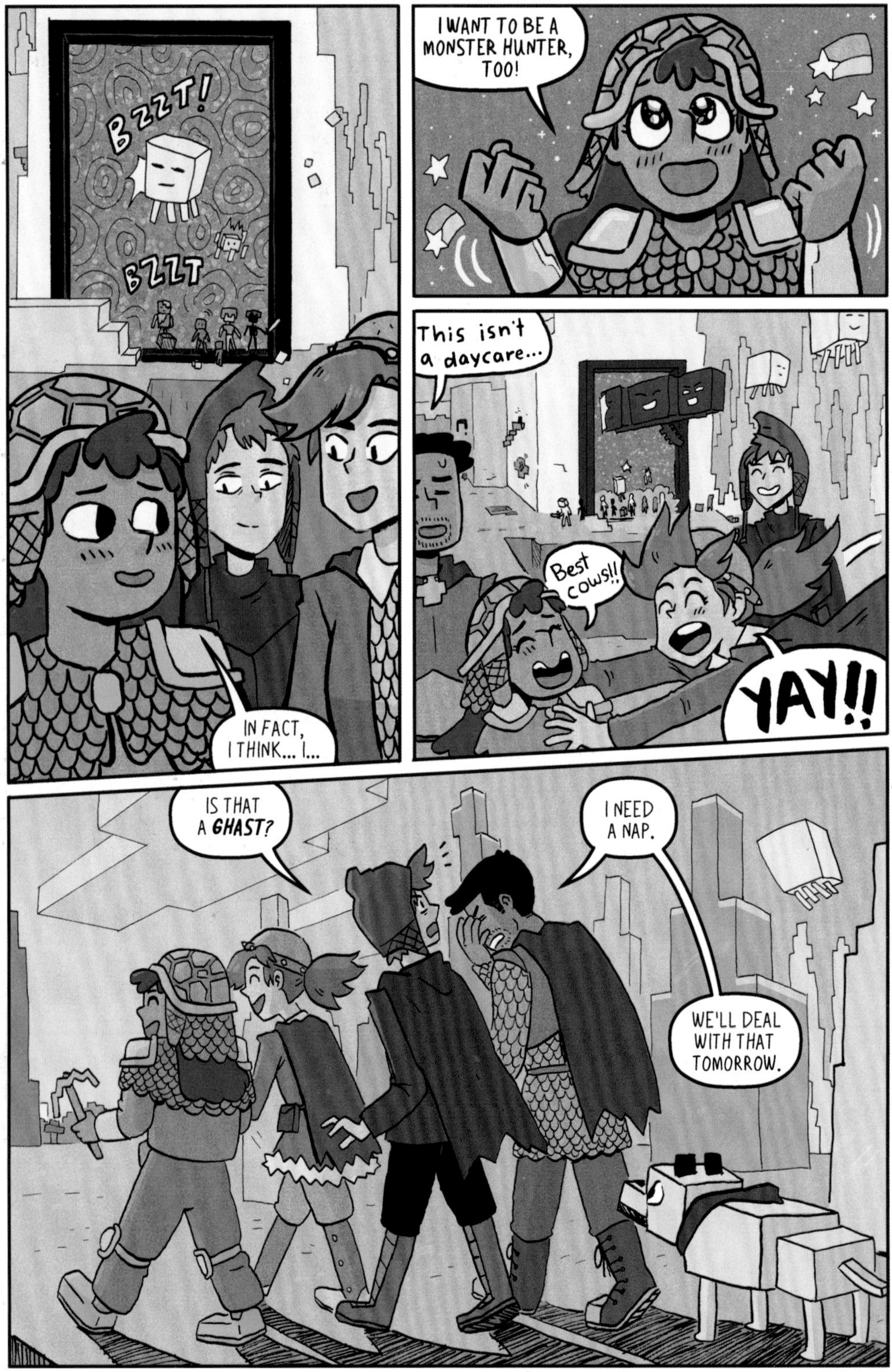

BZZT!
BZZT
I WANT TO BE A MONSTER HUNTER, TOO!
IN FACT, I THINK... I...
This isn't a daycare...
Best cows!!
YAY!!
IS THAT A GHAST?
I NEED A NAP.
WE'LL DEAL WITH THAT TOMORROW.

THE END

MINECRAFT™
SKETCHBOOK

COMMENTARY BY
KRISTEN GUDSNUK

CAHIRA. Char design?

Leather arming cap + leather vest?

CHARACTER DESIGN

When I was coming up with the designs for Cahira and Orion, I tried to make them look a little wild, and gave them lots of armor—much of it enchanted leather. I decided to give them both orange hair because I had been playing as Alex in Minecraft. I ended up changing their designs a little from this point, mostly removing extra stuff that I knew I would forget to draw. But this is more or less how they appear in the book!

I love doing character designs, because it consists of a lot of random doodling. When I'm designing characters, I usually try drawing them making different facial expressions from scenes I have planned. And I draw them from all sorts of angles so that I have a reference of what each

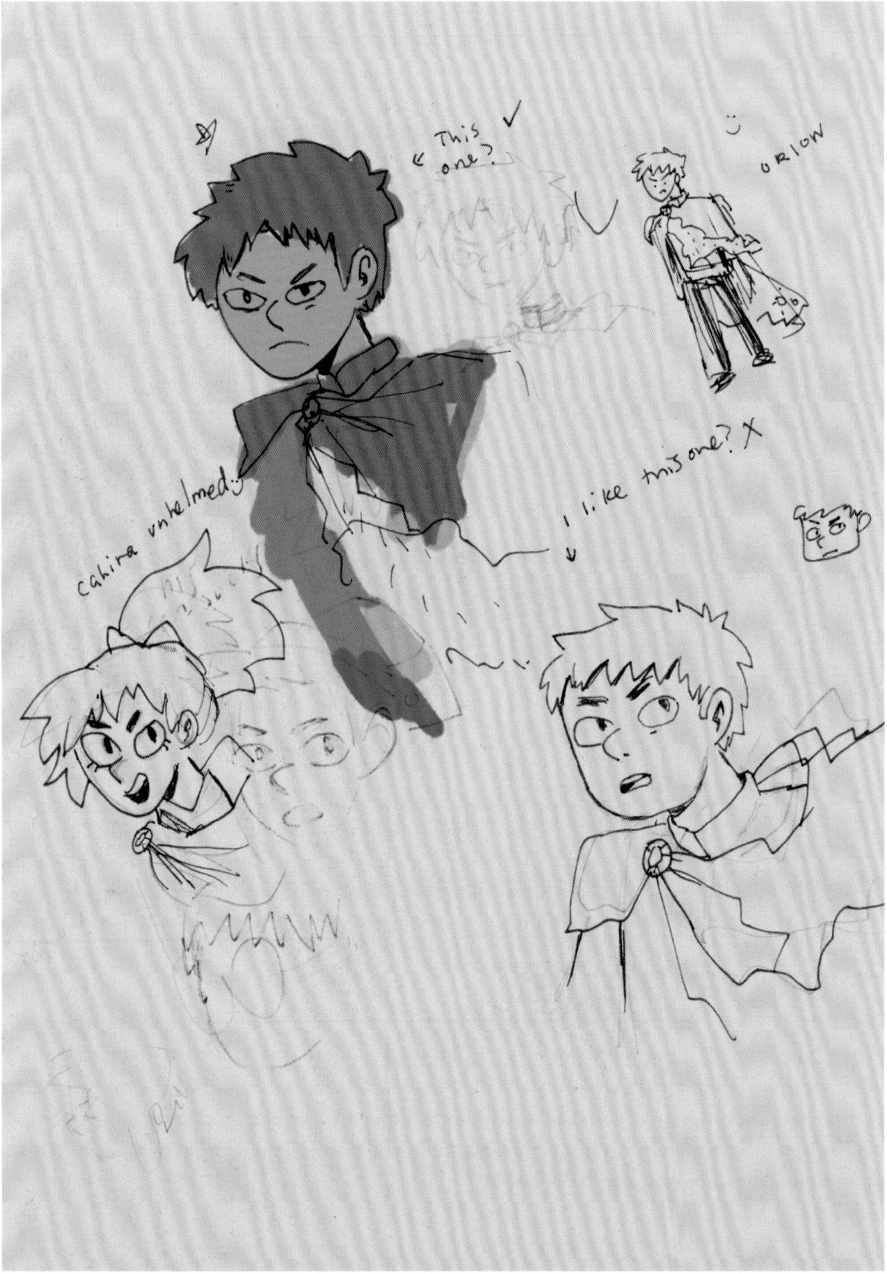

This one?
I like this one?
cahira unhelmed

character looks like from different perspectives. It helps me keep them looking more consistent. I sketched all these on random scraps of paper, then brought them into my iPad to start thinking of color schemes.

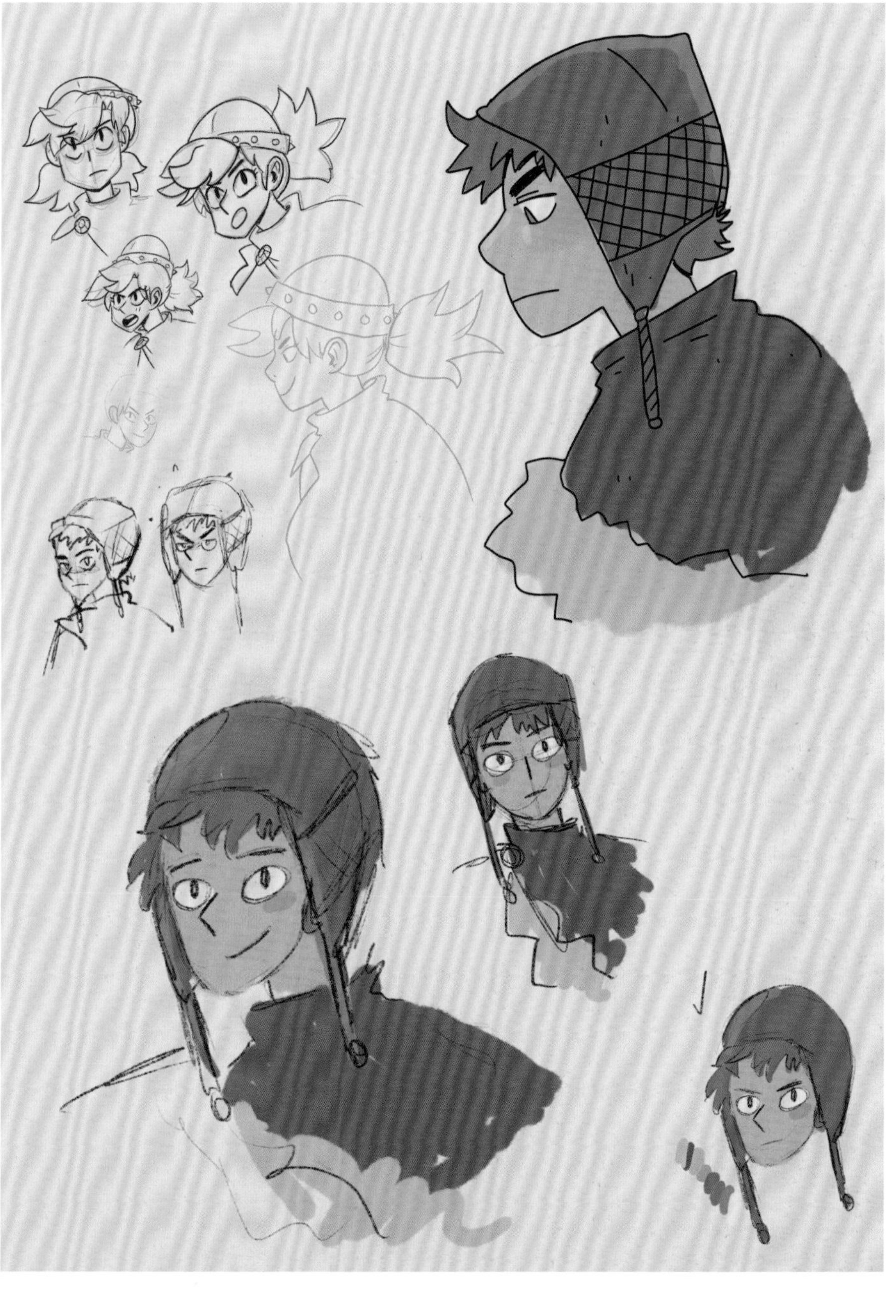

Once I decided that Atria would wear sweatpants and a sweatshirt the entire comic, I felt like I knew her as a character. Her turtle helmet and perpetual wonder at the world around her make her a really fun character to draw. Atria's mom, Ventra, is wearing an outfit based off the Cleric Villager outfit. She's like a big version of Atria, only a bit scarier. She acts tough, but she's more afraid of her daughter's curse than Atria herself is.

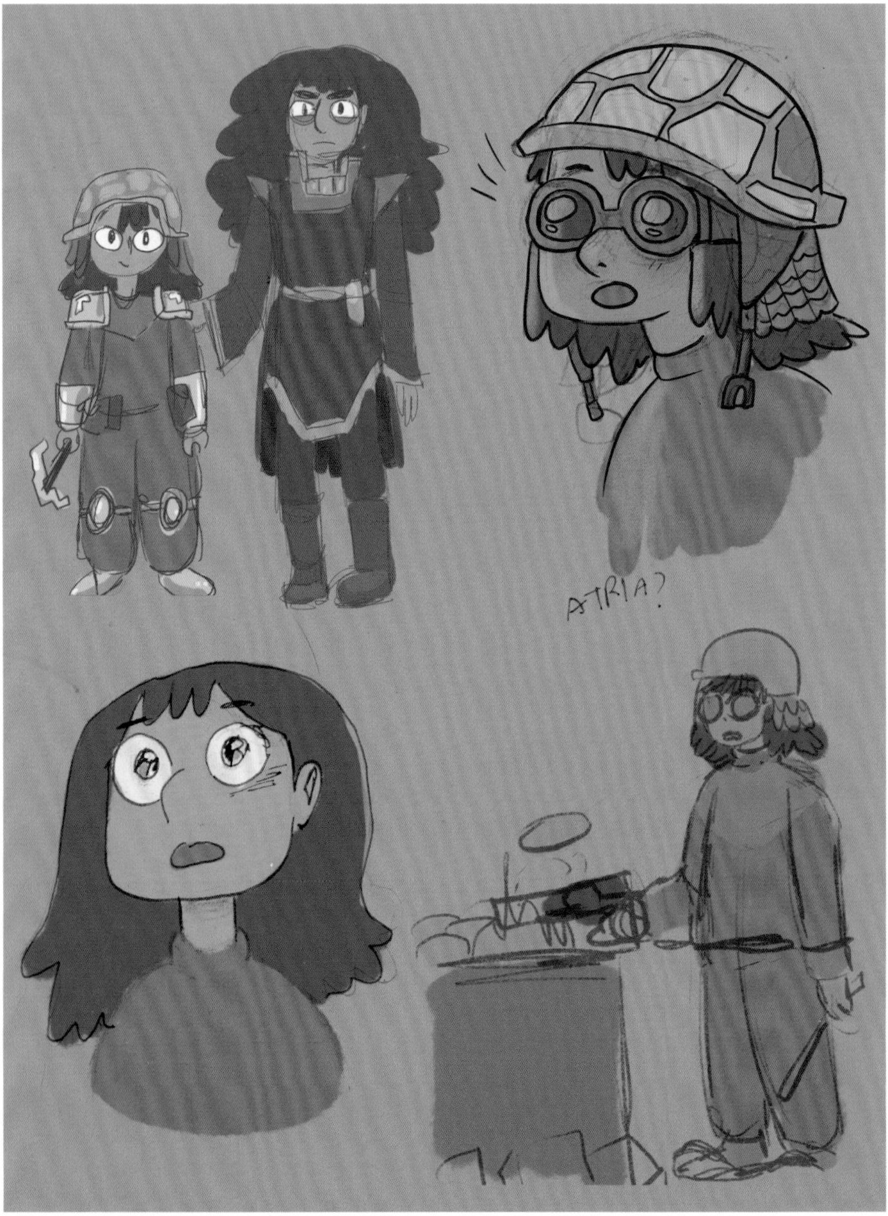
ATRIA?

One of the first times I played *Minecraft* I found a Totem of the Undying and was both intrigued and confused. It remains one of my favorite items in the game. Then it ended up turning into an important plot point here!

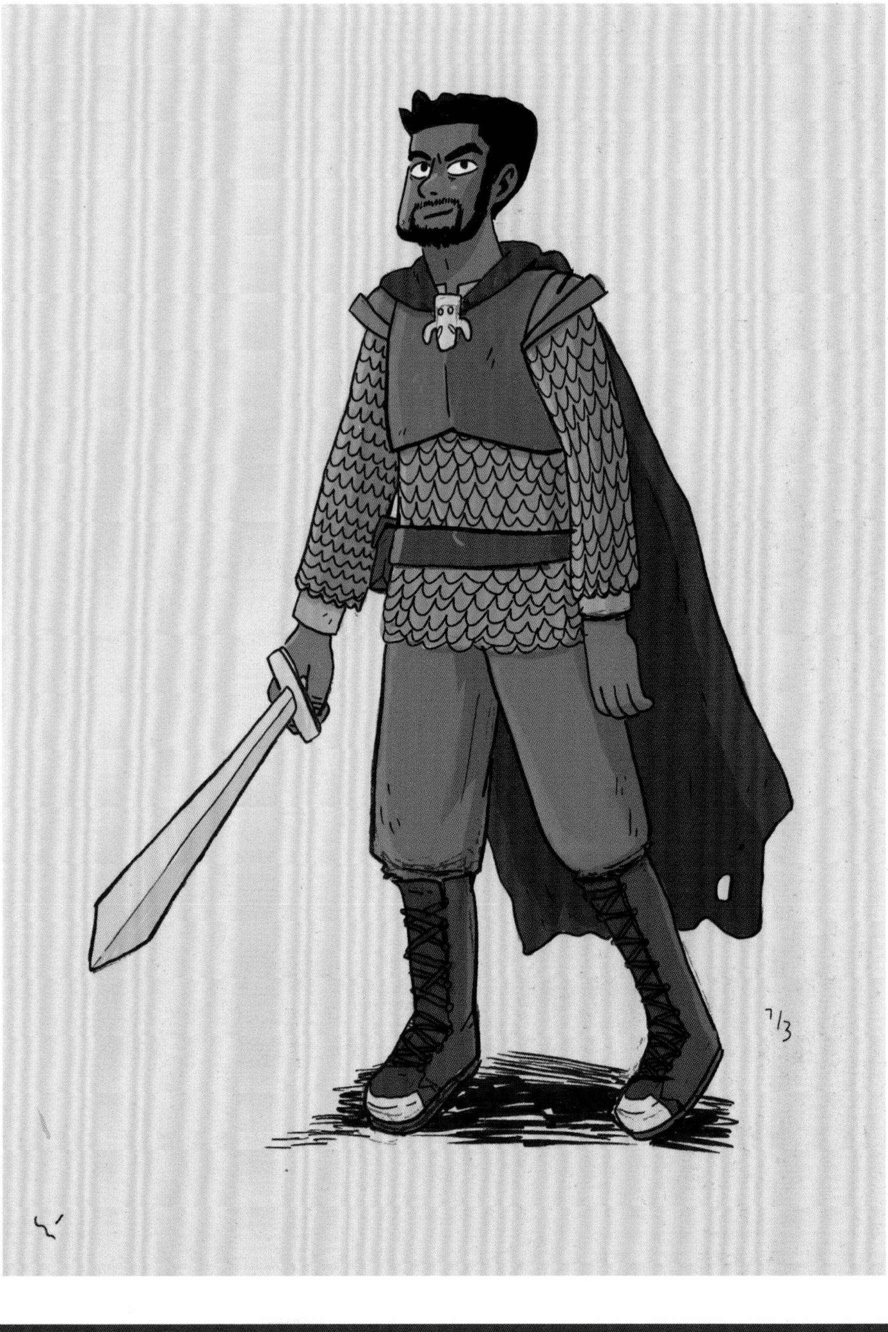

I drew layouts for this book on my tablet, and then printed it out in blue and inked it traditionally, this time with nib pens and ink.

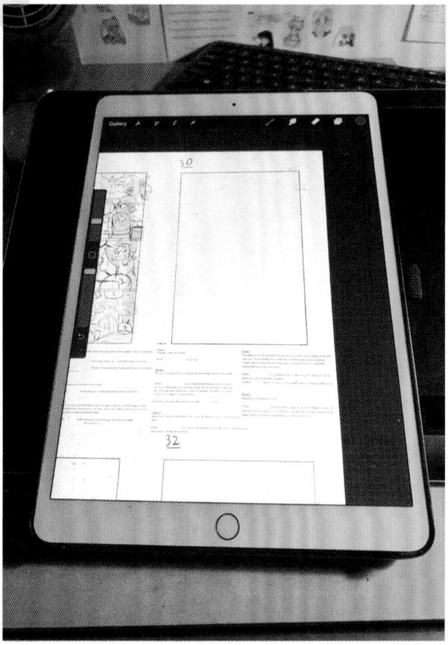

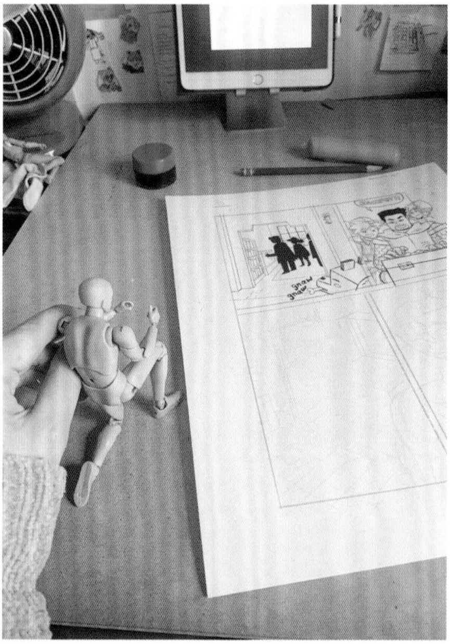

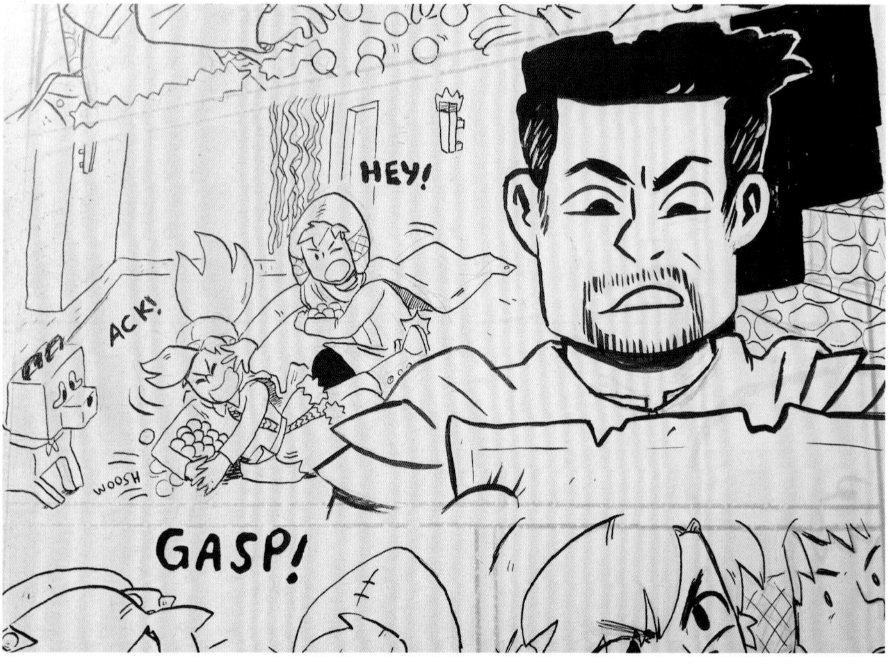
HEY!
ACK!
WOOSH
GASP!

I bought myself some *Minecraft* action figures for reference! This Wither definitely came in handy. It helped me visualize what I was drawing.

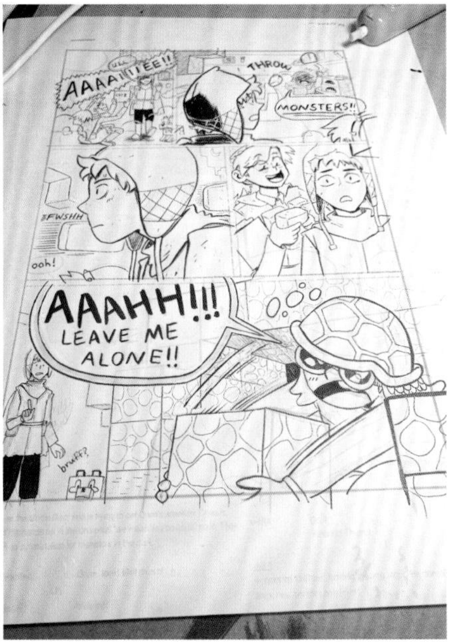
THROW
MONSTERS!!
FWSHH
ooh!
AAAHH!!!
LEAVE ME
ALONE!!

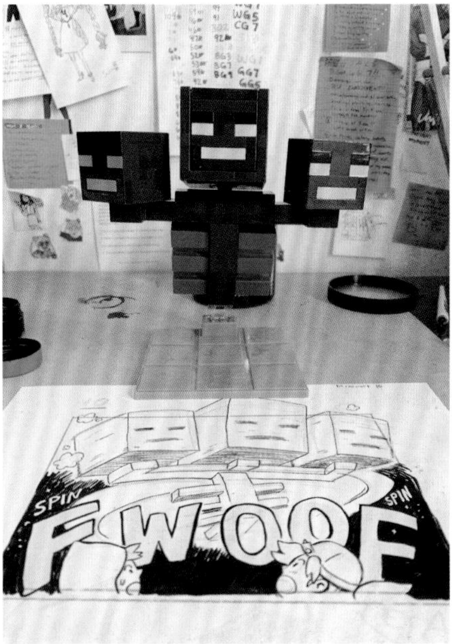
SPIN
FWOOF
SPIN

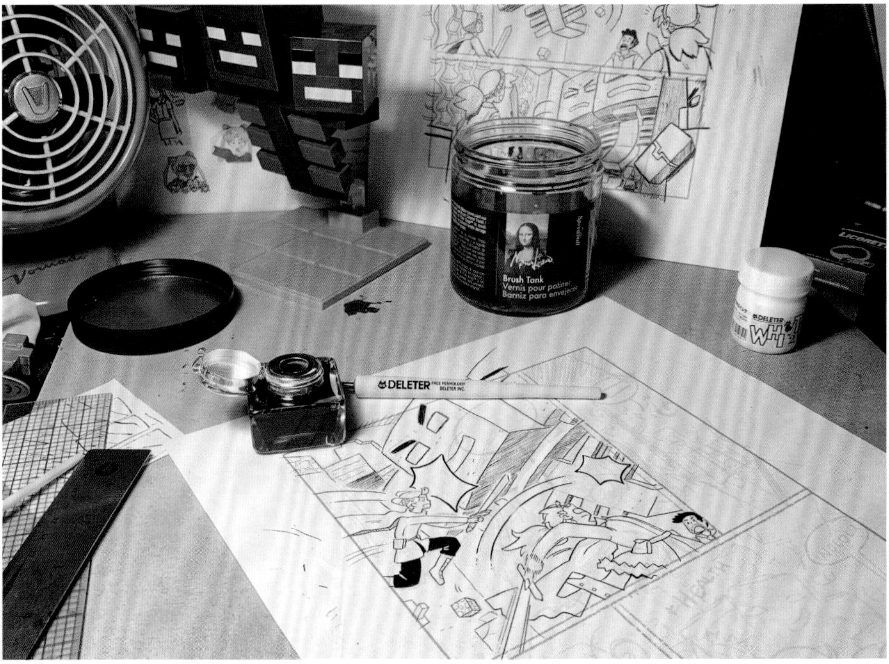
Brush Tank
Vernis pour patiner
Barniz para envejecer
DELETER
DELETER

These are the aforementioned nib pens! You dip them into ink and can get really crisp, nice lines. They can be challenging, though, and it's easy to poke yourself with one. It's a nib pen rite of passage to drop a splotch of ink onto your beautiful, time-consuming drawing. But... those lines are so crisp! It's all worth it.

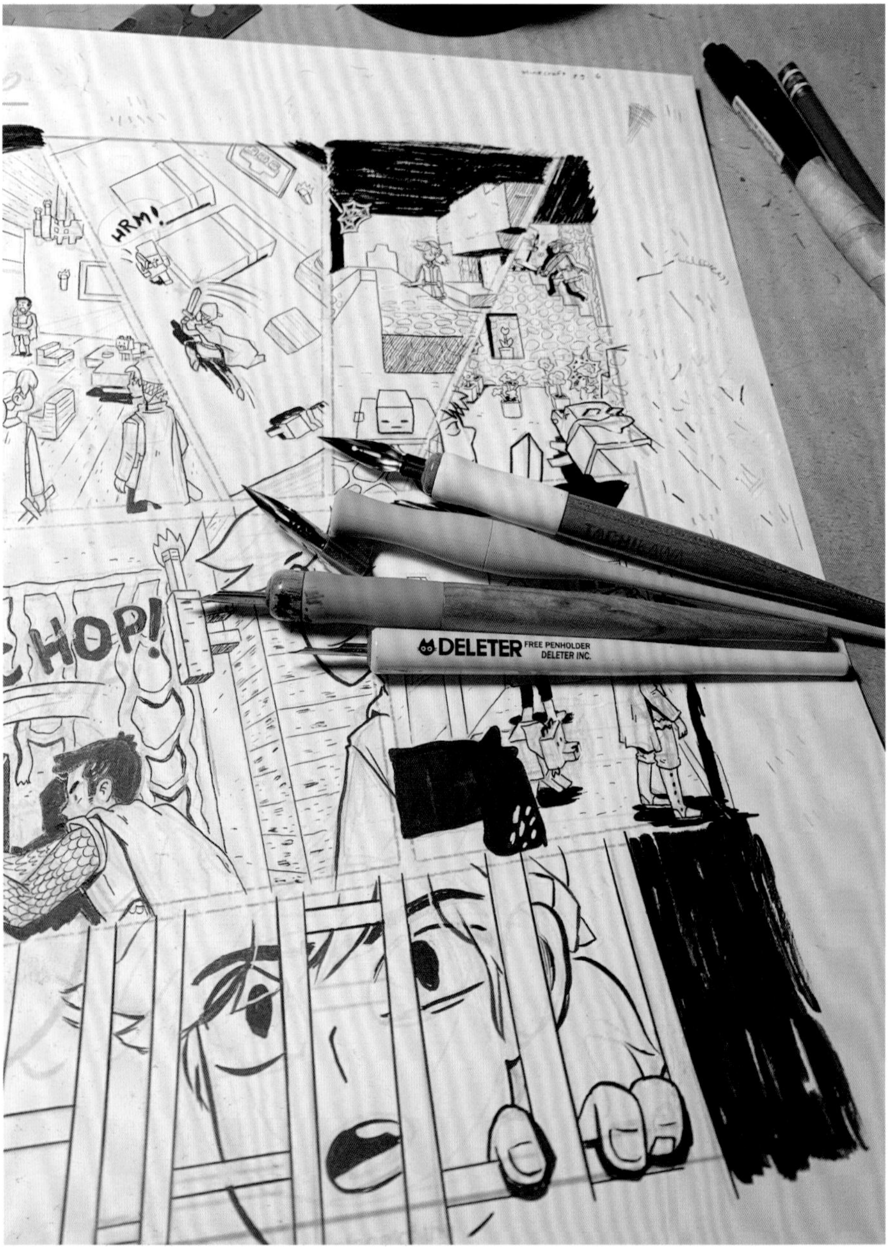
HRM!
CHOP!
DELETER FREE PENHOLDER
DELETER INC.

This is me, trying to draw this very book while my dog tenderly cuddles me. The real-life inspiration for Wilkie: Penny!!

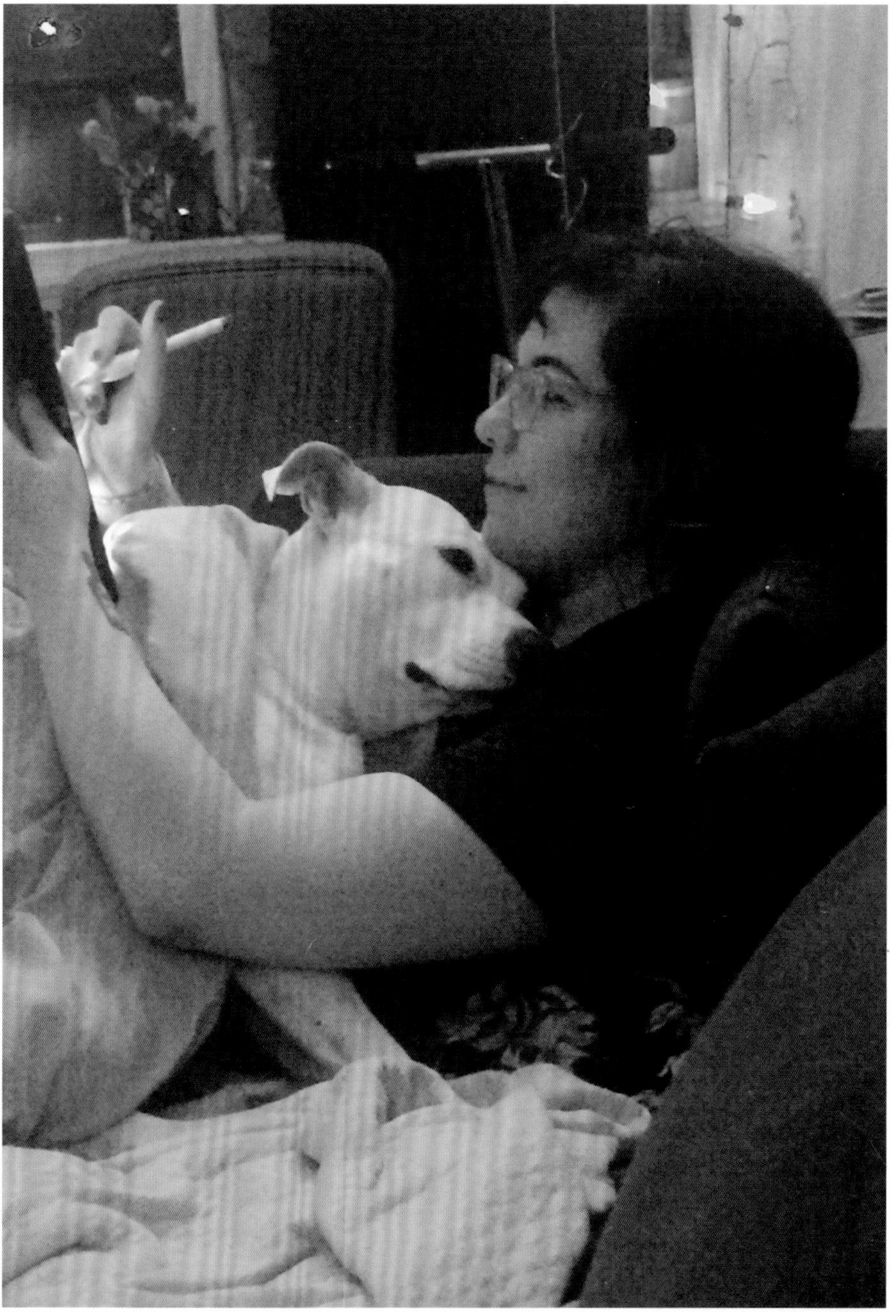

The sequel graphic novel to the hit book *Minecraft* Volume 1 from the world's best-selling videogame *Minecraft* brings new challenges for Evan when a bully chooses to target him. Evan tries to hide this from his friends, but when he and the gang find themselves in a similar situation in the EverRealm, Evan can't keep quiet anymore. As they find themselves assaulted by pirates, and then by an even bigger threat, all the players realize they must learn to rely on each other to face adversity.

MINECRAFT VOLUME 2
AVAILABLE OCTOBER 2020!

MOJANG

MINECRAFT™

AVAILABLE NOW...

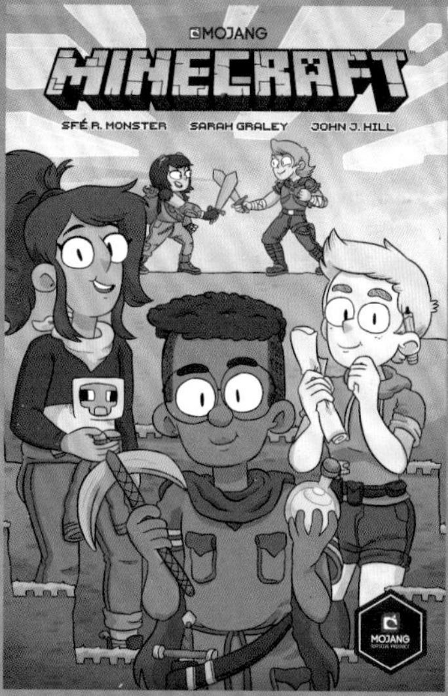
MOJANG
MINECRAFT
SFÉ R. MONSTER
SARAH GRALEY
JOHN J. HILL
MOJANG

MINECRAFT VOLUME 1
SFÉ R. MONSTER, SARAH GRALEY, JOHN J. HILL

Tyler is your everyday kid whose life is changed when his family has to move from the town he's always known. Thankfully, Tyler has a strong group of friends forever linked in the world of *Minecraft*! Tyler, along with his friends Evan, Candace, Tobi, and Grace have been going on countless adventures together across the expanses of the Overworld and are in need of a new challenge. They decide to go on the Ultimate Quest--to travel to the End and face off against the ender dragon!

ISBN 978-1-50670-834-8
$9.99

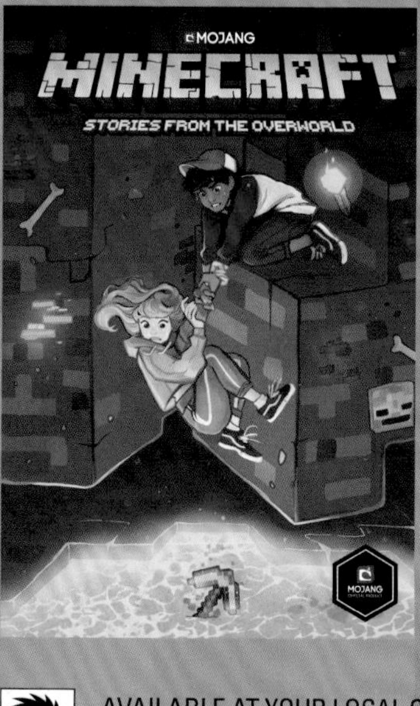
MOJANG
MINECRAFT
STORIES FROM THE OVERWORLD
MOJANG

MINECRAFT: STORIES FROM THE OVERWORLD

From blocks to panels, *Minecraft* explorations are crafted into comics in this anthology collection!

With tales of witch and pillager rivals finding common ground, a heartless griefer who bit off more than they could chew, and valiant heroes new (or not!) to the Overworld, this anthology tells tales that span the world of *Minecraft*. Featuring stories from star writers and exciting artists, this collection brings together stories from all realms, leaving no block unturned!

ISBN 978-1-50670-833-1
$14.99

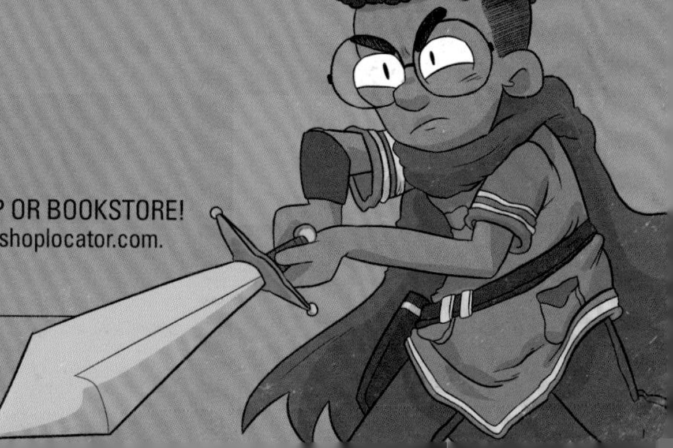

DARK HORSE BOOKS

AVAILABLE AT YOUR LOCAL COMICS SHOP OR BOOKSTORE!
To find a comics shop in your area, visit comicshoplocator.com.
For more information or to order direct visit DarkHorse.com
Prices and availability subject to change without notice.

MORE SERIES YOU MIGHT ENJOY!

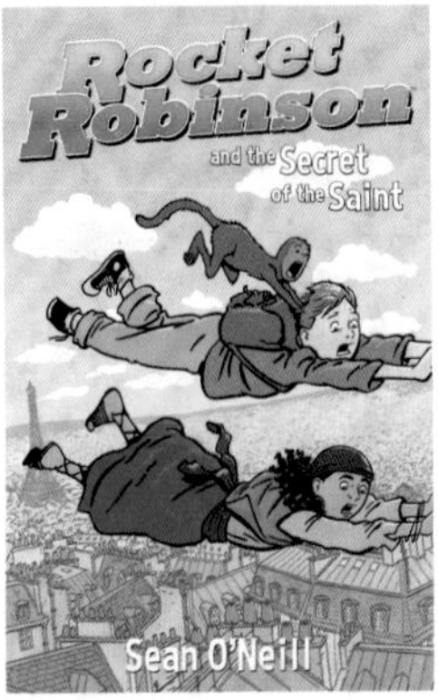
Rocket Robinson
and the Secret of the Saint
Sean O'Neill

ROCKET ROBINSON — SEAN O'NEILL

Cairo, 1933—The Egyptian capital is a buzzing hive of treasure-hunters, thrill-seekers, and adventurers, but to 12-year-old Ronald "Rocket" Robinson, it's just another sticker on his well-worn suitcase. The only son of an American diplomat, Rocket travels from city to city with his monkey, Screech, never staying in one place long enough to call it home, but when Rocket finds a strange note written in Egyptian hieroglyphs, he stumbles into an adventure more incredible than anything he's ever dreamt of.

Rocket Robinson and the Pharaoh's Fortune	ISBN 978-1-50670-618-4	$14.99
Rocket Robinson and the Secret of the Saint	ISBN 978-1-50670-679-5	$14.99

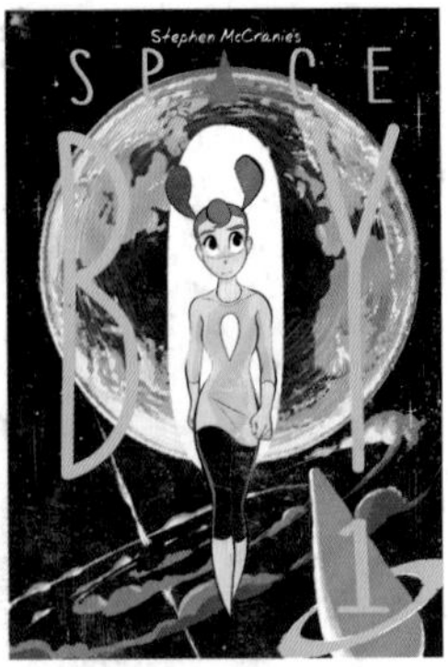
Stephen McCranie's
SPACE BOY

STEPHEN MCCRANIE'S SPACE BOY — STEPHEN MCCRANIE

Amy lives on a mining colony out in deep space, but when her dad loses his job the entire family is forced to move back to Earth. Amy says goodbye to her best friend and climbs into a cryotube where she will spend the next thirty years frozen in a state of suspended animation, hurtling in a rocket toward her new home. Her life will never be the same, but all she can think about is how when she gets to Earth, her best friend will have grown up without her.

Volume 1	ISBN 978-1-50670-648-1	$10.99
Volume 2	ISBN 978-1-50670-680-1	$10.99
Volume 3	ISBN 978-1-50670-842-3	$10.99
Volume 4	ISBN 978-1-50670-843-0	$10.99
Volume 5	ISBN 978-1-50671-399-1	$10.99
Volume 6	ISBN 978-1-50671-400-4	$10.99

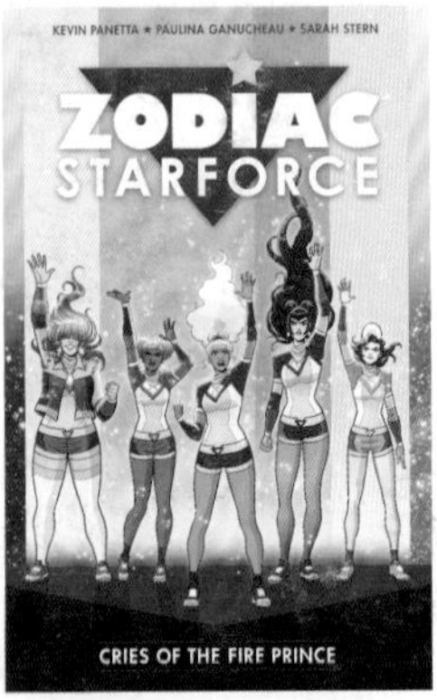
KEVIN PANETTA ★ PAULINA GANUCHEAU ★ SARAH STERN
ZODIAC STARFORCE
CRIES OF THE FIRE PRINCE

ZODIAC STARFORCE — KEVIN PANETTA, PAULINA GANUCHEAU

An elite group of teenage girls with magical powers have sworn to protect our planet against dark creatures . . . as long as they can get out of class! Known as the Zodiac Starforce, these high-school girls aren't just combating math tests. They're also battling monsters! But when an evil force infects leader Emma, she must work with her team to save herself and the world from the evil Diana and her mean-girl minions!

Volume 1: By the Power of Astra	ISBN 978-1-61655-913-7	$12.99
Volume 2: Cries of the Fire Prince	ISBN 978-1-50670-310-7	$17.99

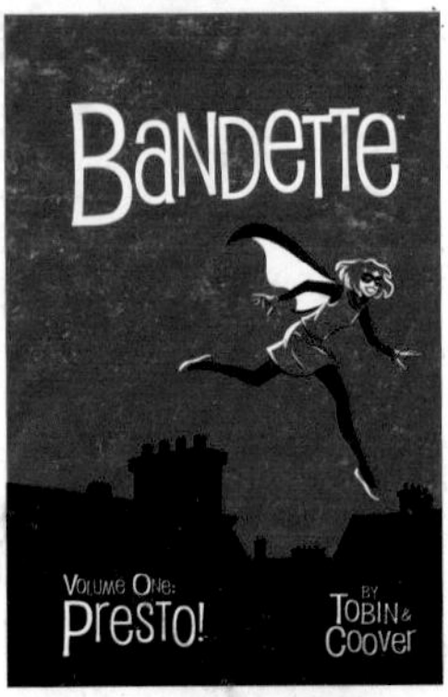
Bandette
Volume One: Presto!
By Tobin & Coover

BANDETTE — PAUL TOBIN, COLLEEN COOVER

A costumed teen burglar by the nome darte of Bandette and her group of street urchins find equal fun in both skirting and aiding the law, in Paul Tobin and Colleen Coover's enchanting, Eisner-nominated series! But can even Bandette laugh off the discovery of a criminal plot against her life?

Volume 1: Presto	ISBN 978-1-61655-279-4	$14.99
Volume 2: Stealers, Keepers!	ISBN 978-1-61655-668-6	$14.99
Volume 3: The House of the Green Mask	ISBN 978-1-50670-219-3	$14.99
